Mr. Mac and Me

Hideous Kinky

Peerless Flats

Summer at Gaglow

The Wild

The Sea House

Love Falls

Lucky Break

Mr. Mac and Me

Esther Freud

B L O O M S B U R Y

NEW YORK · LONDON · NEW DELHI · SYDNEY

Published by Bloomsbury USA, New York
Bloomsbury is a trademark of Bloomsbury Publishing Plc

All papers used by Bloomsbury USA are natural, recyclable products made
from wood grown in well-managed forests. The manufacturing processes
conform to the environmental regulations of the country of origin.

LIBRARY OF CONGRESS CATALOGING-IN-PUBLICATION DATA
HAS BEEN APPLIED FOR.

ISBN: 978-1-62040-883-4

First published in Great Britain in 2014
First U.S. Edition 2015

1 3 5 7 9 10 8 6 4 2

Typeset by Hewer Text UK Ltd, Edinburgh
Printed and bound in the U.S.A. by Thomson-Shore Inc., Dexter, Michigan

Bloomsbury books may be purchased for business or promotional use.
For information on bulk purchases please contact Macmillan Corporate
and Premium Sales Department at specialmarkets@macmillan.com.

For my daughter, Anna Kitty

Chapter 1

I was born upstairs in the small bedroom, not in the smallest room with the outshot window, where I sleep now, or the main room that is kept for guests – summer visitors who write and let us know that they are coming and how long they plan to stay. Sometimes, after a night's drinking, folk may rest there, although Mother always takes their money off them first. If she doesn't they wake up and protest they don't know how they came to be lying in that fine wide bed, say they've been apprehended and held there, in comfort against their will. But that is at harvest time, when men and boys come to wash away the wheat chaff tickling their throats, or in high summer when they've spent the day thinning out the wild oats from hay. But I was born in winter, the sea storming on the beach beyond, roaring through the night, louder than my mother, whose ninth child I was.

My father was over at Sogg's Fen searching out a rabbit, and when he came back in he brought with him news that three fishermen from Dunwich had been lost at sea. The bell was ringing in the church there, Mother swore she could hear it through the storm, and she laid me against her chest and cried so hard she nearly drowned me with her tears. 'What is it?' my sister Mary was tending her. 'Will he not feed neither?'

But Mother said she knew someone had to be taken that night, and sinful as it was, she was just so very grateful that it wasn't me.

My father gave the rabbit to Mary to skin and gut, and he climbed into bed himself, knocked sideways with the spirits he'd drunk to keep away his fright.

'We can't both be lying down,' my mother shoved him, 'or this boy will have survived for nothing.' And when he didn't rouse himself she got up and careful as she could she climbed down the ladder, and leaving me beside him, she laid a fire in the public bar in case anyone should come in for a sup.

It was Mother, more than anyone, who had the village in her blood. Born and reared up near the common where her father was a pig man. She'd never wanted to leave, never planned to, but one afternoon she was out on the street when a man pedalled by and winked his eye at her. 'Knives to grind,' he sang over his shoulder and she smiled right back at him. He was an older man, halfway to her father's age, with a ragged look as if he needed someone's caring. But he was smiling as he wheeled around, smiling as he asked her name, and soon he was offering to sharpen the family knives half price. He had his own grinder, made a fair profit if he worked all hours, and when he and Mother married he carried her away to Dunwich where he set himself up as a pork butcher. Mother said she hadn't known how much she liked the pigs till then, their bristly grey bodies, rootling and bathing in the sun, the happy way they let their babies snuffle round them, and it pained her to hear their screams rising up from the slaughterhouse beside the shop. She'd never imagined either how much she'd miss the village. She missed the washing flapping on the green, the geese that guarded it, the paths that led away towards the river and the sea. She missed the bracken unfurling in the spring, the pheasants that rose out of it, strolling glossily across the land. 'There's bracken here,' my father told her. 'Up on the heath, and pheasants too, and there's deer as well that come out of the forest.' But what he couldn't know was that they weren't the ones she recognised, they weren't the ones she'd always felt were hers.

On Sundays, in that first year, he gave in to her desire to be back home. He'd sit her on the seat of the old knife-grinding bicycle, and pedal her back across the marshes, through mud and sedge, along sheep paths less than a foot wide, screaming as they nearly tipped into the river. They had to get off to lift the bicycle over a stile at Bridge Farm and wheel it across a cattle grid at the start of Dingle Marsh, but once she was heavy with her first child, they took to walking, stretching their steps against the drawing in of evening, until the days grew too short and she too large. Then, often as not, they stayed in Dunwich where they went to the lepers' church up by the turning. She knelt by her husband's side, pressing her swollen knees into the wood, and wished herself thankful for everything she had.

Chapter 2

Father took on the lease of the Blue Anchor Inn when my sisters, Mary and Ann, were little more than babies. 'It'll bring us luck,' Mother told him, 'bless us with a boy,' although why she thought it might be lucky I don't know when the landlord before him, a Mr Frederick Easy, had fallen so far into arrears with his rent that there'd been a sale of his effects out on the street. Mother bought a tablecloth, embroidered, she was told, by his daughter Grace who'd drowned herself the year before in the water butt, and whenever she spread it out I'd think of that girl and the strength she must have had to hold herself under. What I didn't know then was how much more strength you'd need to hold yourself afloat, and the first thing I did when I remembered how I'd heard the well shaft sighing in the darkness and decided it was most likely a ghost, was I took that tablecloth and I dug a hole and buried it in the garden.

Father would have been grateful to have been buried in the earth – all his life he feared he'd end up in the sea, ever since he'd been apprenticed, aged eleven, to the captain of the *Irwell* who'd docked unexpectedly at Southwold when his cargo of rags caught fire. The last boy, it seemed, had perished in the blaze. But my father was from a family of sailors, his grandfather, father, his brother too, gone to sea before him, so when the captain came ashore my father was the first boy to be offered up. I know this although Father prefers to remain silent. His life began, it seems, when he pedalled that knife-grinding bicycle down the lane towards my mother. But I ask him sometimes when he's soft with drink what work he had to do on board, and how it felt to be sleeping in a bunk when the waves came high and rocked him nearly to the side as I'd seen in pictures in the Sailors' Reading Room. And he looks at me as if he might tell – a strange, sad look – but instead he talks about his days as a pork butcher and how he was sure he could have made a living if the shrieking of the animals and the smell of blood hadn't nearly parted my mother from her wits. 'But an innkeeper is a fine job, if you can make it pay,' he says and I catch him staring at my twisted foot, and I swear that more than once I've seen him smile as I limp away.

Chapter 3

My mother warned me early that I'd never go to sea. She'd caught me down by the harbour looking at the boats, watching and waiting for my chance to get offshore. 'That'll never do for you,' she told me. And she turned my face inland and sent me on my way.

Right from the start she'd been saving and scheming, and by the time I was eight she'd got a place for me with Mr Runnicles at his school in Wenhaston. You'll need to use your brains, she told me, and every morning I was to wait out on the road up by the Manor Farm for a lift from Mr Button who drove by in his cart. Mother herself had learnt her letters at Sunday School, with a stick and a sand tray out in the churchyard, and on weekday afternoons there was help to be had at the Wesleyan chapel on Mill Lane. 'Make the most of this chance,' she told me, fierce, and I stepped away from the flat of her hand.

Even now I'm the only boy from our village at Mr Runnicles' school. There are three boys there, older, including the son of a glazier, and two boys younger, brothers from the Lodge over at St Cross. Mostly what we have to do is copying. 'No blots, mind,' Mr Runnicles tells us, and he sits at the desk and works at his own ledger, copying his own small words into a black book, while we scratch and smudge and stare out of the window at the day going by without us.

Sometimes at Runnicles', when my copying is finished, I make sketches of the brigs moored up in the harbour. I draw them from memory with their masts and sails, but when Runnicles sees the black marks in the margin his face grows red and his eyes look ready to split open. 'Spoiled!' he says and he holds up my page as a warning to the others.

But whatever he says, and however much my mother needs me, after school I go down to the river to see if any new boat has come in. I traipse past the summer visitors with their watercolours set up in the dunes and the wooden huts some rent to store their easels and their turps. I nod to old Danky who stands on the bridge in his cord cap and his fisherman's boots and accepts payment from anyone who might like to use him in one of their paintings, the way he looks so fetching, with his white beard, and dark jacket, against the old Japanese bridge.

'Come in and keep me company,' Danky says, rattling the coins in his pocket, but I never could go into the Bell, even if nothing passed my lips, because if my father heard of it, he'd catch me by the throat and shake me till I wept. The Blue Anchor is the farmers' pub, and the Bell is for the fishermen. Once there was some kind of battle on the green, near midnight, on a warm clear night, and my father, although he was injured in the attack, still talks of it as a marvel. 'They had oars and great thick snakes of tarry rope,' he says, 'while we carried pitchforks and mallets.' My father limped home in the early hours of that morning with his shoulder shattered, and for all his talk of marvels he curses every time he has to lift the kegs, for the pain that still shoots through him.

I wait for Danky on the rise of grass outside the inn to come back out with his ale, and when he's eased his thirst he'll tell me tales of the sea, and I'll close my eyes and memorise the words he uses, the boom, the block, the bailer, the clew and cleat and daggerboard, and I wish, whatever my father says about my being a cripple and suited to some other kind of work, that I could be apprenticed like he was, and set off on a voyage that might take me up as far as Newcastle, or further, round the tip of Britain or off across the German Sea.

Chapter 4

My name is Thomas Maggs. Although I'm known as Tommy, and Tom is what I tell people if I'm asked. I'm the youngest son of William and Mary Maggs, and the only son surviving. First there was William, but he only lived a day. Then came another William who lasted long enough to see my brother James before they were both struck down by measles. I should add that my sisters started with it. But they're strong girls. Even now. And it only made them stronger. Mary is in service. Working for the master at Blyfield House. And Ann helps Mother with the inn, washes the tiles on the floor, polishes the tankards, cooks. Although sometimes at night she whispers to me how she dreams of joining Mary and wearing a white apron and eating in the big kitchen twice a day. They were born first, my sisters, before we even had the inn. But I'm forgetting. After James, there was another William, and then another James, who clung on past his first year, and a Thomas, all born before me. But I was determined from the first. Red in the face, and all over too, from the fight of being born. 'I'm not letting this one go,' my mother said as the bells tolled for the fishermen from Dunwich. 'This one's staying here with me.'

I never asked her if she said the same to those that went before. But she still says it now, reaching for me as I run past.

Not that I'm ever caught. Not even with my twisted foot. I run past her, out through the back gate, across the clover field to the river and when my leg gives out I lie down and watch the sky until it's swallowed me up and I'm flying, floating through the clouds, and I can see the moon, a white shadow against blue, and little trails of birds too busy to look down although if they did they'd laugh to see us, my mother toiling till her hands are raw, and my father, pickled with the drink, slumped in the best chair.

On Sundays before Mother goes into the church she takes a walk around the graveyard. I used to go with her, keeping to the paths, my toes itching to climb on to the graves. Now that I'm thirteen I sit on the wall and watch. Our plot is at the far end by the lane, but instead of heading straight towards it, she follows the path, looking politely at the other headstones, at the angel sitting on the Doys' family plot, at the Prettyman girl who has a grave all to herself. Our boys are in together. Their names and dates are like the letters and numbers Runnicles makes me copy, winding round each other, crossing over themselves. Sometimes my mother presses flowers into the pot that sits on their grave. Daffodils, or celandines, or if there is nothing else to be found in the garden a cloud of cow parsley from the lane, which smells of summer and everything they've missed.

Father doesn't go near the grave. He goes into the church because he must, he won't be thrown in with the likes of Buck from Dingle Farm who they say is a cannibal because he sluices out his outhouse on a Sunday. But for all his protestations Father likes the church. He likes the talking before, and the chat after, and Ann looking so pretty in her bonnet in the pew beside, and Mary who gets the afternoon off from her work up at the big house. He likes the folk complaining about the weather, one old girl who looks up at the sky, whatever it's like, and says when she was a child the warm days lasted all of six months and now, if it wasn't for the leaves on the trees, you wouldn't know it was even summer. And it makes me happy to see him there because it's the one day of the week he doesn't have a drink, not so much as a thimbleful till after lunch.

Danky comes by with his sister – a smart God-fearing woman who keeps an eye on him – and he tells Father, when he asks, that his own mother may be doing well for ninety, but all day she sits by the fire as miserable as a cat.

The church lies inside the ruins of a larger church that was made from stones brought up from the beach. Sometimes I meet Ellen there – her father is the blacksmith – and we play coppen ball among the ruins. We let the ball land on the graves, and when we find it we read out the names of the people who lie under. Albert Crisp and his devoted wife Ermentruda. That makes us laugh. Robert English. His daughter Florence, sadly taken from us. We're always hoping for something funny, so we're careful when we play never to let the ball fly down to the far end of the churchyard, so we don't have to read the names on the short grey stone beneath my mother's flowers.

Chapter 5

The summer I turned twelve I got myself a job. I'd heard the rope-maker George Allard needed a boy to turn the wheel. And I saw him one morning as I was shifting about down by the harbour, watching old Danky standing on the bridge in his fisherman's hat and rolled-over boots while two lady painters made a likeness of him in oils. Danky stands there half the day when he isn't on his boat, and even when he should be on it – the fish aren't going to catch themselves – and then he takes the money he makes from 'modelling', as he calls it, straight into the Bell and drinks it down in beer. If only he'd come into the Blue Anchor, just once in a while to keep my father company, but the fishermen stick to their pub and the farmers to theirs and the truth is there's not really need in the village for both. 'You can start next week,' George Allard told me when I asked after the job. And he promised to pay me a shilling at the end of every month.

These last long years George Allard's been working for a rope-maker at Lavenham, but now he's home again and set up on his own – Allard's Rope, Twine and Norsel Works – using his garden as his walk and, if need be, the path that runs outside the gate and down across the fields to the marsh. My job is to turn the wheel while he teases out the hemp, walking backwards, easing it out slowly from the strick around his waist. 'Keep your wits about you and you can learn a trade,' he tells me as he goes, 'you don't want to be following your father into the licensing business. No good comes of that. Feeding the devil, that's the truth.' And as I turn the wheel he tells me about London and how if there's a war, we'll have to stay here on the coast and defend it from the enemy.

'A war, with who?' I ask. I'm sleepy from our early start, and he tells me the story of the Battle of Sole Bay, how in the first hours of the morning of the 28th May, a French frigate sailed into Southwold and roused the town with news that a Dutch fleet were little more than two hours away. The town was full of sailors resting while their ships were fitted up, and their commander, the Earl of Sandwich, was in an upstairs room at Sutherland House, too distracted by the charms of a young chambermaid to notice at first the seriousness of the threat. But by dawn, despite the chambermaid, every vessel at anchor on the lee shore had put out to sea and between them, the French and English had seventy-one ships, each with forty guns.

'On the 28th May?' My eyes are wide. It is only the middle of June now. But Allard shakes his head. 'Don't they teach you anything at that fancy school of yours?'

He gathers up his twine and comes back to where I'm sitting at the wheel. 'This battle was fought two hundred and fifty years ago.' He stops, and I stop turning. 'But that's not to say it couldn't happen today. Ships were set on fire, men were thrown into the sea, and the thunder of the guns brought people hurrying from all the villages around to stand in a crowd along the cliff. But as the day went on the news for our side was not good. Not after the French disappeared over the horizon, by accident or design we'll never know, and soon we heard that the Duke of York's two ships were destroyed and that Lord Sandwich was last seen leaping into the waves.' George Allard turns his stormy eyes on me as if he'd been there himself. 'An order went out that no person was to leave the town. And so they stood all day, the men, women and children of this region, stones in their hands ready to defend the land. But the Dutch never did come ashore. At sunset the battle ended. The Dutch sailed away. And both sides declared victory. But over the weeks that followed, close to two thousand bodies were washed up along the coast. Even Lord Sandwich could only be known by the Star and Garter stitched into his clothes, and to this day if you go into Sutherland House and stand quite still and quiet, you'll hear the weeping of the little chambermaid who haunts the upstairs rooms.'

George Allard takes a long step back. 'So keep a watch, my boy, as I have done. Keep your eyes on the horizon and your ear to the ground. It's our job now. If the enemy is to land anywhere, this is where they'll land.' He teases out more hemp and backs towards the gate, and at a nod I start up the wheel, keeping it smooth and regular even as my thoughts are spinning fast. I picture an army docking at the pier. They'll come across from Holland with felt waistcoats and wooden shoes and as the men and women stream out to defend Southwold, I'll make a drawing of their boats. My drawings will be needed. Evidence. I may even hand them in to Runnicles, and let him record my findings in his black ledger of facts. And he'll see that I am useful after all. My name will be there for ever in his diary. Thomas Maggs.

Chapter 6

There are two seals who've made their home downriver of the ferry. I watch them with their rubbery heads, their small bald eyes blinking, and I think that if I slide into the mudflats by the jetty and slip and roll and flap my arms, surely I'll soon learn to swim. I ask my sister Ann but she says she has no time for swimming and I daren't ask Father anything about the sea. He hasn't set foot on the beach, he says, for twenty years, and if it was up to him he never would again. He says it as if he's under threat of being forced down there regular to do chores, but it's Mother and me that goes poltering when the tide is out, catching up the coal to place into a sack, although he's happy as the rest of them to sit by the smoulders of the fire.

Danky can swim. He didn't know he could, but one dark morning a storm blew up from nowhere and he was thrown from his fishing boat and tipped into the wash. Dinks and Benny both went down, lost in the waves for ever, but before he knew it Danky was paddling like a dog. In with the tide he came, flapping and heaving up on to the shore, and crawled into the Bell where they pulled off his boots, tipped the water out, and poured warm brandy down his throat until he started raving and they knew he'd be all right.

'So why did you never learn?' I ask when I find him on his bench, and he looks at me sideways and mutters, 'Bad luck to learn. Best to hope you'll never need to know.' And when I keep on about the seals he turns to me. 'Have nothing to do with it,' he says. 'If God had wanted us to swim he'd have given us fins. Keep to the spinning, that's the way.' And he winks at me and starts in on a song, so low and gravelly I have to bend my ear towards him.

'In the merry month of June, when all the flowers were in
    bloom
I took a stroll around my father's farm.
And I met a pretty miss, and I asked her for a kiss
And to wind up . . . her little ball of yarn.'

Danky grins, and although I'm blushing, I keep my ear bent for more.

'Oh no, kind sir, says she, you're a stranger unto me
Perhaps you have some other little charm?
Oh no, my turtle dove, you're the only one I love
Let me roll up . . . your little ball of yarn.'

Two men come out of the pub. Gory, from Lowestoft, moved into the village not more than five years since. And Tibbles, who mends boats.

'Sure I took this fair young maid, just to dwell beneath the
    shade . . .'

'You coming, Danky?' they say to him, and he heaves his body up and stamps away with them towards the sea.

Chapter 7

In the cellar where the beer is kept there's a trapdoor. I come across it one evening when father is too unsteady to go down, and a splash of light from the lamp I'm carrying falls across the hinge. I kneel on the cool stone and try to inch it open. But it doesn't budge so I take the shovel and I ease it up. Inside there are steps. 'Mam,' I scream, 'Mam,' and she hurries down, her face white, her hands bunched into fists, and when she sees me, standing there, grinning, she cuffs me – once for giving her a fright, and again for sneaking where I shouldn't.

But it's too late. I've seen them. There are steps leading down from the trapdoor, dug into the earth, and my mother has to tell me, when she has the trapdoor firmly down, how years ago, before the lighthouse, smugglers would watch out for the wrecks and bring the cargo in to land. Smugglers' tunnels. I'd heard stories, but we have one right under our house. And now I watch from my window for ships, lost and struggling, listing to the side. At night I scour the waves, the silvery tips, hoping for small black vessels heading out to relieve them of their bounty. But all I ever see is the beam from the lighthouse at Southwold, built for the new century, a year before I was born, flashing out over the sea. It's saved a hundred lives a year, my mother says, but only last winter a Norwegian three-master came ashore at the foot of Gun Hill, and her crew had to be rescued, every last one of them, by breeches-buoy, and the ship broken up where she lay.

All winter I watch, but the boats have charts and navigators now to steer them round the sand banks, whichever way they shift, and although I give thanks for each one that sails away to safety, I keep a special lookout for shadows on the shore and smugglers rowing across the waves to see what they can find.

Chapter 8

If I could swim then I could get across the river myself and not wait for the chain ferry that's always on the other bank when I arrive. Instead I join the people standing in a queue and squeeze myself in beside the wagons, and the cows and sheep. There's no other way to get to Southwold unless you care to walk the three miles up to Blythburgh where the road crosses the estuary as it narrows, and trek from there around the spit of land, past Bulcamp, where the madhouse is, and on along the road for half the day. There's no short-cut to be taken without wading through marsh and bog, and I remember Runnicles teaching us how Southwold, long ago, was no more than an island, hemmed in on all sides by river and sea. If only someone had thought to build a bridge, one for people and not just for trains, although there are some who are brave enough to risk the railway line that runs across the Blyth above the harbour. I tried it once. It nearly finished me, for the slats are placed so far apart that you must stretch your body like a crab from one to the next, and if a train is to come, there is no way to save yourself except by leaping over the railing into the water below. I was nearly at the far side when I heard the rumble of the engine, and my arse in the air, my bent foot singing with the pain, I forced myself on, faster than I thought was possible, tears burning in my eyes, only to find as I lay shaking on the other side that the noise was nothing but my own heart beating. I lay on the ground and laughed. And then the train did come, breaking open the day, and I imagined myself beneath it, pressed flat, the breath torn out of me, my foot sliced off. When it had passed I stood and shook myself, and I struggled on to Southwold, where I sat all afternoon in the Sailors' Reading Room, looking at the models of the ships, copying down the details of the sails, the square sails and mizzen sails, the stay sails and the foretop-gallant sails, until I was calm.

Chapter 9

Mr Runnicles is losing patience with me. When he looks through my book he says I must copy out my work at home, with no sketches and no blots. Neat and tidy, that's what he wants from me, without a single picture of a boat. There's a table in the public bar set against the wall, just big enough for my ledger, and I like to sit there on a Saturday morning when Father is away over at the brewery ordering the ale. But this Saturday a man comes in, not anyone I've seen before, and he stands at the bar talking to Mother. He's got a gruff voice, low and hard to understand, with rolling Rs and sudden lifts and burrs, and if I close my eyes I can hear the chimes and rises in it just like the girls who come down from the Highlands every year to gut and pack the herring. But those girls are mostly red and pink and jolly, whereas this man is dark, with a stern, pale face, and eyes as black as bark. Glasgow, he tells Mother, is where he's from. Scotland's first city. A great bustling place. The best there is. Although he's ready, just for now, to be leaving it behind. He coughs then and a shudder runs through him, even though it is July, and warm. He orders a pint of beer, and a half of stout to take back to his wife who's preparing a picnic at Millside, and he hands over two stoppered flasks to be filled. Millside. I cease my copying and I listen hard to see if he says anything about the Millside ghost. I want to ask him if he's ever heard the sound of apples falling. A woman had been buried there, a tall woman – they found her remains when they put a new mill shaft in, and the sound of apples falling, heavy as a cart tipped up, is the sound that's been heard just before they see her gazing in at them through an upstairs window.

Before I have a chance the man is standing at my table looking down. 'Very nice,' he says to me, and I feel myself heat up as I try to push the mess of my first copying out of the way. 'No,' he bends closer. And asking if he can, he lifts the paper with the smudges and inspects my margin full of boats. There are yawls and wherries, barges, smacks, and one long yacht with a cabin and a galley.

'Do you make these sketches from memory?' he asks, and I have to look up at him to catch the oddness of his speech.

'Yes,' I say, because I don't want Mother knowing how often I sit beside the river and copy the boats that are moored there, or how many hours I spend staring into the glass cabinets of the Sailors' Reading Room where models of all the greatest ships are on display. Schooners and frigates, warships and cruisers, and one big old fishing boat Danky made one winter when there was no fishing to be done. There's a painting too of the Battle of Sole Bay with the fireships blazing and the cannons crashing into the wooden hulls of the frigates, as alive to me now as when George Allard first told me the story.

'Very nice indeed.' The Scotsman hands back my book and he pays Mother her money and goes out with his flasks.

It is only a day or two before I see the Scotsman again, walking along beside the river. Mac, he is called, at least that's what they call him when they whisper his business in the bar. And now I see why he is making so much talk. He looks for all the world like a detective. He's wearing a great black cape and a hat of felted wool, and he is puffing on a pipe as if he's Sherlock Holmes. He has a bad foot, I hadn't noticed that before, his shoe is all stacked up, although it doesn't stop him walking fast with his stick hitting the ground so that I have to hurry after, with my own twisted foot, to keep him in my sights.

He crosses the bridge and I keep down behind the dunes as he heads for the beach. Every few minutes he halts and looks back, as if he suspects he might be being followed. But it can't be me he sees. I know the land too well.

It's getting dark. There is a big moon, pale as cloud, hanging over the sea and for a long time he walks along the tideline. I keep to the high land, dipping down into the marram grass whenever he looks round, but then it seems that he accepts he is alone because he stops and stares out at the waves. He must be searching for clues of some kind. Just like Mr Holmes. And he's looking so hard he doesn't seem to notice how the water is washing in around his boots. I leave him to it, and go back to the harbour to see if any of the night fishermen have come to untie their boats, but all is quiet so I sit there on the wall, wondering what Mother will say now that I've missed my chores, and wishing I hadn't seen that look on Father's face which means it is a drinking day and there's nothing I can do. I'll wait, I think, until he's too unsteady to lash out, and then there he is, Mac, standing right in front of me, the pipe puffing white into the night. 'Enjoy your walk?' he asks, and without even the flicker of a smile he limps away up the street and over the green so that for a long while, even though I'm half starved for having missed my supper, I'm too frightened to follow.

Chapter 10

The strange thing about Mac is that you don't see him all day and then just as it starts getting dark there he is, in that great cape, striding out on his walk. But he isn't a detective, I soon discover that. He's an artist, and he has a wife who is an artist too, with thick red hair piled on top of her head and fastened with a pin. They've taken a studio, a hut it is, although you'd never know it now they've made it their own. They've cleared it out and painted the wood white and they have tea parties in there, sometimes just the two of them. That's when I first saw her, Mrs Mac, sitting outside on a crate, painting a row of poppies and below it a row of babies, fat and laughing on a scroll. I stop to have a look. And through the half-open door I see tea laid out with white fluted cups and a jug with a black stripe and everything so beautiful even though underneath I can still see it is a hut, Bob Thorogood's it is, with the coils of rope hung on the wall, and a hank and an eye splice left behind.

'You're the boy from the Blue Anchor,' Mrs Mac catches me looking. 'My husband says you've made some fine drawings of boats.'

Blood gushes to my face. I want to run, but if there's one thing that Mother's proud of, it's the manners she's cuffed into me. I stare at my boots.

'Will you have something to eat?' she asks me, and I flush again because it's not as if I haven't noticed there are sandwiches on the table beside the pot of flowers, the finest wild ones you could find that won't last till nightfall. I say I will because I don't want to give offence, and I take my sandwich on its petalled plate and I eat the little triangle of bread, so fast that I have to search myself for what is in it. Honey. There's a string of it on my lip.

'I'll be off now, thank you.' And I take my leave of Mrs Mac and keep walking till I'm at the mouth of the river where it meets the sea.

Father's on the run again. That's what Mother calls it. When he starts in on the ale at lunch and drinks till there's a fight. I go to Mother in the scullery where she's busying herself with the scrubbing of a pan, and I would have stayed there to defend her, if I'd not seen the rolling pin she had to hand. 'You go on up to bed now, Tommy,' she says quiet, and we listen to him, from the empty bar, roaring out commands.

It's too early for bed. Instead I slip into the evening and, keeping to the shadows, I run down to the sea. The tide is out, and green webs of seaweed trail across the blackened harbour wall. Don't ever climb there, Mother has warned me, but I'm tired of her warnings and her endless fears, so I catch hold of the rough stone and pushing with my one good foot, I force my way up. Towards the top there is a ridge of wall. I've seen boys up there, babbing for fish, although I'm never asked to join them, but even so, I know it can be done. I strain and pull, my fingers scraping against the smashed-up shells, and the higher I get the louder I can hear the sea, surging below me through the gulley between groynes. And then I'm up. I swing my legs over and find the wall is narrower than it looked, the water below dark and deep, the tide about to turn. I edge myself around to face the comfort of the dunes and that's when I see him, Mac, walking away from me along the beach. I sit quite still, but he is trudging over the shingle, his gait uneven as he sinks into the stones, his black-caped back towards me. What is he looking for? I wonder as Mac turns to the tideline and stares out at the sea, and as he lifts a pair of binoculars, I imagine his eyes straining all the way to Holland and on to Germany to see if what they say about a war is true.

Chapter 11

School is finished for the summer and George Allard has me turning the handle long hours for his rope. 'This strong twine'll be in demand,' he tells me, 'when the trouble comes. Horses and string, barley and grain. That's what we'll need. Not beer. Folks'll turn their backs on beer. They'll see it was the ale that distracted them, misted up their eyes, and they'll spit it out and curse it for the bad luck that it's brought.'

I take his money but I don't say a word. And I don't pass every penny on to Mother either as I usually do. Instead I keep a thruppence in a knot under the mattress, and the following month I do the same. Now, when I find myself alone, I lift the mattress and I count my coins. There will always be people who need a drink, I tell myself, to see them through the day, you don't grow up around an inn without learning that, but even so, if times are pressed and guests are short they might just stop at the Bell and not come on to us, and so I keep counting, and count again, for it eases me to think there is something small laid by.

The next time I pass the huts down on the river, Mac himself is sitting outside with a board across his knees. He has a jug before him stuck with a few sticks and he is using a tin paint-box like a child's. I stand and watch him. He's drawn the outlines first in pencil and now he's using the tip of his brush, spreading colour, filling the dry wood of the twigs from inside. I squat down beside him. He has a stem of larkspur, must have picked it from the Millside garden, and he squashes the brush into the powder, stirs and flattens it until the pink is mixed, and then he lets it spread out inside the pencilled lines so that the edges catch it like a dam. He uses blue, the crushed blue of canvas, and yellow and red for spots and creases that I don't see are there, overlapping each other and ballooning into buds, so that they seem to be growing right there before us, the stalks silvery, the leaves grey.

I sit there for an hour, my breath still, myself forgotten, until Mac looks up and asks if I need tea. I say I don't, but my stomach growls in contradiction, and Mac goes into the hut. 'How're the boats?' he calls, his voice like a song, and I look around to check that we're not overheard.

'Coming on,' I lie, thinking of the ink scratches and the scribbles of my vessels, and I search his larkspur with my eyes to see how it is done.

The bread, in four triangles, is arranged on a china plate, with one coloured petal set into its design. There is cheese inside, and a sprinkling of cress. I look into the hut for Mrs Mac but she's not there. 'Thank you,' I say again. And I turn away so he won't see how hungrily I force it in.

Chapter 12

Mother is out, and Father is upstairs sleeping off his lunchtime ale, when an old woman pulls open the door of the inn. Her face is scored with lines and a thick white whisker stands out on either side of her chin. I've never seen a witch before but even so I know she is one. 'Spare me a sixpence,' she says and her voice is an inland voice with no trace of the sea. Ann, who is sitting at the table sewing, says we haven't a sixpence to spare, and even if we had we wouldn't part with it. But the old woman looks at me as if she can see the knot of money tucked under my bed, and she waits. I wait too, so long that Ann puts down her sewing and comes to stand beside me.

'If you cross my palm with silver,' the witch-woman tries again, 'I'll tell you the man you're going to marry.'

'What if I don't want you to?' Ann flushes. 'For it may not be the one I've chosen.'

'Whether it's the one you've chosen or not,' the woman smiles, 'it's the one you're going to hev. He's on a ship right now, standing there with a knife in his hand, splicing roope and thinking on you.'

The blood drains from Ann's face. And I know, because I've heard her mention it to Mother, that she's set her heart on Jimmy Kerridge who left Southwold on the *Flying Horse* and hasn't come back for more than a year. 'So I'll be marrying a sailor?' Her voice rises to a gasp.

'He'll be back,' the old woman nods, 'to claim you for his own. Sure as this boy here has two moles above his elbow, a half an inch apart.'

'I do not!' I say. 'I'd knowed if I had.' But later, once Ann has given the woman red herring and a dish of tatters, and she's sat inside and had a rest, I climb the ladder and creep through the room where Father is snoring on his back. I duck down through the low door to where I share the bed with Ann, and I strip off my shirt. See, I hiss, there's nothing there. But when I squeeze the skin around and twist my chin over my shoulder, there are two brown bumps, soft as velvet, on the side of my arm.

I lie down on the bed and wish I'd thought to ask what the future holds for me. Not whether I am getting married, I don't care anything for that, but whether I'll get aboard a vessel and sail away like Jimmy Kerridge out over the horizon to where I've never been.

Chapter 13

It's Mary who hears it first, borrows a bicycle from the gardener up at the big house and races here so fast her cheeks are red and her hair hangs loose out of her cap. But she still has her white apron on, and her boots are gleaming with the polishing she gives them last thing at night. 'It's the war,' she says as she flies in, 'we had it on the radio at Blyfield House. Someone's been shot. Not just the King of Greece. An Archduke of somewhere.' She's panting fit to burst. 'It'll come to me. But that's what's started it, and now Germany's declared war and the master says there's no avoiding it. He's sent his two oldest boys to Southwold, to offer their services at the town hall. He says he'll be proud if they're the first to be called up.'

It is a Saturday and there are three men in the bar. Old Tilson and his brother Fred. And Mac, who'd come in an hour before and is drinking one drink slowly, in that way I know, which means it has to last. The Tilson men look up. 'You don't say,' their mouths are open. They lost a cousin in the Boer War, and before news could travel back his wife had named their child Pretoria May because the phrase was always on her lips: Pretoria May win.

'We'll best be off,' the brothers say, and as they push open the door we hear the church bells ringing, loud and urgent enough for anyone at all to stop and wonder at them. Father pours himself a glass of Scotch, and when Mac looks up, he pours him one too.

'Good Lord,' Mother is by the open door. 'They're not wasting any time.' And I go and stand beside her, and there, coming up the street, is a wagon loaded up with luggage, and on the box beside the driver, in a hat garlanded with flowers, sits Mrs Tilbury who spends her summers at the low house by the ferry. Three of her children sit behind with their nurse-maid, and a wiry, white dog called Madam, and they wave at us cheerily as they pass by.

'Where are they going?' I ask, and Mother crosses her arms and shrugs.

'Away from the coast.' Father joins us, the smell of whisky hot on him. 'Where they think it's safer.'

Mac drains his glass. 'I'll be away then too.' Pulling his cape about him, he steps out into the street.

'Wait,' I call when I see he's turned towards the sea, 'I'm coming with you.' And although Mother clutches at my shoulder, I slip out of the door.

I've never walked with Mac before, only followed him, and I wince as our two crippled feet snag on the same uneven ground. We pass the Bell, empty of its men, and climb down into the scrub of land below the dunes. What will we see? I wonder as we climb through slipping sand, and as we come up over the ridge of the beach I expect to find warships already massing out to sea. But there's nothing there. Just the *Belle* steamer gliding towards Southwold, and Danky in his corded cap and wading boots, throwing out a line.

Mac walks down to the edge of the water and stares out to the horizon. 'We were thinking of travelling on from here,' he says quietly, 'to Paris, and Vienna, but now . . .' he shields his eyes, 'I'm not so sure.'

We walk on, following the line of the beach until it curves, treading in single file over the hard sand below the shingle, and then, as if it had been agreed, we climb the wall of stones and cross the top, and skelter down the other side towards the wooden bridge that crosses the flat river. Two swans live on this river, their reflections stretching white and deep, and here they are today, leading their young brown family in single file. Mac stops when we come to the top of the marsh and snaps off a twig of hawthorn. He examines its crinkled leaves and the swivel of its thorns and slides it into the pocket of his cape. He stops again when we reach Hoist Wood. There are old trees here, ghost trees I think of them, so long have their trunks been stranded from the sun, but their tops are green where they stretch them, and some leaves grow in shafts of light.

'If you're still here in spring,' I tell him, 'I'll bring you to this wood at daybreak, that's when you hear the nightingale. At dusk too, if you're lucky.'

'I'd like that.' He is gruff. But we both know he won't still be here by spring. The summer visitors pack up every year at the first curled leaf of autumn and they don't come back until the following July.

As Mac and I cut back across the common, stopping now and then while he examines a flower, we see a stream of people moving along the path that runs down from the church. They have trunks, and bundles piled on to prams, small children running alongside, and one old lady in a black bonnet, sitting on a cart. As we join them, I see the two Miss Bishops, who've rented our big room each August every year since I was small, hurrying along. Father is behind, red in the face and sweating, carrying their bags.

'Where are you going?' I ask them, quiet, so as not to rile Father who looks ready to spit blood. And they look at me, eyes wide with fear. 'Home,' they say. 'To Wanstead. We have to get to safety.' And they explain how they owe it to themselves and their one remaining family member, a niece who is not entirely well.

As they are talking we hear the train roar over the bridge, and all along the path people pick up speed. 'Give us a hand, boy,' Father says, his shoulder sagging, and so I take one of the bags from him and let him fall behind while I hurry on with the Miss Bishops to the station. 'Thank you,' the older of the sisters says. 'I'd give you something for your trouble but we need every last penny for our fare.'

'Honestly,' the other shakes her head. 'Declaring war on a Saturday when the banks are closed. We had to borrow money from Mrs Lusher at the shop. Poor woman, and we weren't the only ones asking for a loan.' She digs into her pocket then and brings out a packet of peppermints, and dipping her fingers into the bag she presents me with a round chipped sweet.

I slip it into my mouth. 'Thank you.' And I'm surprised to find how much I mind seeing their tweed-skirted figures climbing on to the train.

'We hope to be back next summer,' one tells me when Father has lumbered up with the last bag. 'Indeed,' the other one agrees, and she takes hold of my hand. 'Thomas,' she whispers, 'I left a little sketch drying on the window ledge of our room. Keep it for me, will you? It's just a sad old thing of geese on the green. Nothing much, but I'd be glad to look at it again.'

I nod. I know their ways. How they cluck and sigh over their efforts, cheering each other on when each piece is done. The younger Miss Bishop likes to paint animals – rabbits and horses and, more often than not, our hens – while her sister is only interested in the sea. Whatever the weather she sets up her easel in the dunes and catches the waves, using up her palette of colours on their browns and greens and blues.

The train hoots, doors slam, and with a wrench it steams out of the station, packed to bursting, faces pressed against the windows, regretful, excited, glad to have their holidays broken into if it means they are included in the goings-on of the world. I stand and wait till the train is out of sight, until I can no longer hear the clack of its wheels as it steams on its way to Blythburgh. I turn, but Father has slunk away, so I walk back across the common, past the place where Mac was last seen inspecting a wall of gorse. He'll be gone soon too. Even now Mrs Mac will most likely be packing up their things and I think how I've never had a chance to ask him if he's seen the Millside ghost. I want to tell him how I saw it, Mother and I, although Mother will never admit to such a thing. And I promise myself that if I meet Mac again I'll tell him how we were walking to the top of the village just as the light was turning grey – going to visit Mrs Horrod whose husband had taken ill – when I looked left into the mill yard and there she was, looming out of the shadows, half as tall as a barn. Mother reached for my hand and began to run. I turned my head for another glimpse, but Mother was rushing me along too fast and she didn't pause or slow her step until we were outside Mrs Horrod's door. 'Why did you pull me along so?' I asked her then, I could hardly get my breath, and she rapped hard on the wood and said she didn't like to keep nobody waiting. 'Or was it because you saw that lady in the yard?' And she scowled at me and tightened her grip so that my fingers squashed and mashed up inside hers.

Chapter 14

Mr Allard is wrong, men do need beer, more than ever now that we're at war, and I spend my days running back and forth between his rope-making and the Blue Anchor to help with chores. Each night that first week regulars from the village crowd into the inn to talk, and Father keeps his place at the top of the cellar steps drinking with the best of them, ready and waiting to go down and bring them more. Men who've been in the Boer War, they are there, nodding and muttering, and young recruits with more to say than you'd think possible, about the type of man who doesn't volunteer to fight. With each new voice Father drowns another pint and soon, as he crashes down the ladder, he's sighing and staggering with the pain in his shoulder where he fought all those years ago on the village green.

'Will these waters be safe to fish?' someone wants to know, and there's a hush as we imagine the men in the Bell weighing up their future.

'Folks'll always need to eat,' an old man mutters, and I wonder if the Highland girls will come down for the season now to gut and pack the herring into barrels.

'Thing is,' Father raises a glass, 'this is where the enemy'll land, there's nowhere nearer. We'll need to keep a lookout night and day.' And I glance over at his bleary face, the beer swimming in his eyes, and hope we're not all to rely on him.

For a day or two I don't see Mac, or Mrs Mac, and I fear they've gone back up to Glasgow. But one evening as I'm shutting up the hens, I catch sight of Mac's black cloak, swishing along the track behind our land. I seize up the last chicken, a fat white bird that's stopped on the ladder as if it's had a thought. 'Come on now, old girl.' It always surprises me, the hot feel of a hen's body below the cool feathers of its wings, and I hold her still a moment, her eyes spinning, her head cocked. 'In you go then,' I force her through the door, and as soon as her tail feathers are safely inside I slam the coop shut and race to catch up with Mac. But Mac must have stepped off the path, for when I come out into the field there's no sight of him. I follow the track all the same, slip through the arch of blackthorn at the corner, and push my way along a tunnel of sedge, so high it closes above my head. My feet slip as I tread the narrow boards, threatening to squelch into the water lying still on either side, and I remember how I lost a boot in there one winter when I slid into the mire and Mother cried over the loss of it and beat me. But today I go slow, leaving Mac to fight his way through before me, and I breathe in the dry smell of the reeds, still warm with that day's sun.

I find him on the other side, at the top of the dune, his back to me. 'Mac,' I call as I scramble up the shingle, but by the time I reach the top he's dropped down to the other side. 'Hey, it's me,' I try again, but he's standing on the shore now, and the sea is in his ears.

I lie on my back and slide down the slipping stones of the bank, puffing up a cloud of dust as I go, and as I fall I think of my father and what's he's missing when he avoids the sea. If the *Irwell* docked today, and George Farthing was looking to offer an apprenticeship, I'd tell him the story of *Treasure Island*

– Runnicles read it to us, four pages a day – and the pirate Long John Silver who only had one leg. 'Story it is,' my father laughed at me when I told him. 'You need two good legs to be taken on board a ship. That's the truth.' And he laughed again and shook his head as if I'd invented the whole thing.

I get up and dust myself down and walk along the tideline, the water lapping in against my feet. Slowly, very slowly, I gain on Mac as he follows the curve of the beach, his feet like mine on the wet sand, his eyes never leaving the sea. The evening is still, with hardly a ripple; the sun, as it sets inland, striping the sky pink.

'Listen,' he calls over his shoulder, without ever looking round. I stumble to catch up with him, and when I do he hands me his binoculars, and as I raise them to my eyes, I hear the guns thundering across the sea from Flanders.

Chapter 15

The next Sunday, after church, I go across on the ferry with Mother to Southwold. The town is half empty, the beach with its bathing machines and goat-cart rides deserted. We stand on the promenade where last week families strolled with dogs and picnic baskets, and stare at the pier, the longest in Britain, and the pride of the town, until today, when its wooden legs, creeping into the sea, look like they may be running out to greet the enemy. But we haven't come to wonder at the empty town, we've come to read the declaration pinned to the wall of the town hall. And we're not the only ones. We hover behind a crowd, subdued and whispering, and then, slowly, although we've heard the worst of it by now, we shuffle forward to see the words ourselves. Defence of the Realm Act. We read it together. 8th August, 1914. *His Majesty in council has power during the continuance of the present war to issue regulation for securing the public safety and the defence of the realm.* It seems these words are too important to read silently, and I listen to my own voice and the voice of my mother as we stumble from one phrase to the next. *Power. Duty. Admiralty. Safety. His Majesty's forces . . . Regulations . . . Court martial . . . Punishment.*

The act, I read this to myself, one word ahead of the rest of the crowd, *is designed to prevent persons communicating with the enemy, or obtaining information for that purpose. Or any purpose calculated to jeopardise the success of the operations of any of His Majesty's forces, or the forces of his allies.*

I have to stop and breathe, and when I do I find my mother has fallen silent too. We wait there for a while, listening to others around us, counting up everything that, for the sake of the nation, is no longer allowed. But it is only as we walk home along the towpath that we speak the worst of it into the day.

Opening hours of all public houses will be from this moment on reduced.

Alcohol may only be sold from 12.30 to 3 and then from 6.30 to 9.30.

All beer must be watered down.

Neither of us say anything, but I feel my mother's heart, like mine, jittery with alarm. How will we manage when we hardly make enough to get by now? And the inn open from five in the morning until midnight if customers desire. The worst of it is that no man may buy another man a drink. *To buy a round of drinks is from henceforth prohibited.* I see Father's face turn black with fury when we tell him the news.

My feet drag. Perhaps we can give him the other end of the list first. Show him it's not only us who must suffer. Night fishing is banned. And the ringing of church bells is now illegal. As is the feeding of bread to chickens, and the buying of binoculars. I wonder if, like Mac, you already own binoculars, whether you must hand them in and if so to who? But there is one rule that is the most important rule of all. It is written many times, backwards and forwards and all round every way. And it is important Father knows it: no person must do anything that helps the enemy. No discussing of military business, or spreading gossip about the war, no signalling – with bonfires or fireworks, or even the strike of a match at night. And if this rule is broken it is punishable by death.

As we reach the harbour and push on to the ferry, I'm seized with fear that even now we are not being careful enough. What if there's a spy among us, a German in disguise lying hidden in a skiff beside the jetty? But scour the river as I do, I only see Danky sitting outside his shed puffing at his tobacco. And one of the Mollett boys on his stomach fishing with a length of twine.

Chapter 16

I have more time now that the Blue Anchor must close its doors for long stretches of the day and night and I use my extra hours to make an inspection of the coast. I creep down there at first light, to check nothing, or no one, suspicious has washed in, and when that is done I'm away over to George Allard to inform him we're still safe. 'Good lad,' he tells me and we set to threading the machine, attaching the yarn to the three pegs so that when I crank the handle they twist together like a plait. 'Got it?' he looks at me, eyes lowered as if he's giving me the gift of life, and I nod, serious, even though I know it's not what I plan to do with mine. For whatever they tell me, and however it is done, I'm determined to get out to sea.

Mr Allard's son, Abb, is joining up. He's seen the posters, just as I have, one pinned up outside Mrs Lusher's on the village green.

> Young men of Southwold and District.
> Your King and Country need you.
> Another 100,00 thousand men wanted.

George Allard tells me that we already have the greatest army in the world and the most powerful navy. Our very own Suffolk

Regiment has been in India, one thousand strong, crack shots the lot of them, and with hardly a casualty these last twenty years. But now there will be a chance for new men to join up. New men like Abb who lives next door with his wife and two small boys and works as a mechanic over at Rendlesham, mending the farm machines that have put so many men out of work.

Allard walks backwards through the wet grass, talking all the while, his voice growing louder as the sun strengthens above us and he approaches the gate. 'I'd go myself if I wasn't so damn old. But if they need me . . . I'll have it be known I'm willing to give it a go.' Often he's still talking when he backs out into the fields, and I have to strain my ears for his words as I keep turning.

On my way home I make sure to walk past the Bell to check the landlord is sticking to the government's new rules. It's noon, and I'm half starved for my lunch, but I stop there all the same and try the door. It's locked, that's certain, but as I press my face against the windows, double-paned as they are with bottled glass, I swear I can hear voices coming from inside.

'Bell's all locked up,' I tell Father, hoping to steady his mood, but I needn't have put myself to so much trouble, because it's clear he's been drinking since early, his face heavy, his eyes greased. Sometimes I think Father's only good for one thing when he's on the run, and that's avoiding. He sits in the small bar, supping on his own, and I daren't ask, although I want to, whether he's watered down his beer.

Mother sets lunch on the table, a pot of soup with vegetables from the garden, and a loaf of bread that's still warm from the oven. We sit and bow our heads, even though it smells so good I have to stop my hands from reaching for my spoon, and we wait, but Father stays where he is. Maybe the drink has filled him up, it seems he doesn't need to eat when the ale gets hold of him. 'For what we are about to receive,'

Mother's head stays low, 'make us truly thankful.' And I notice she has a bruise along her cheek, a bloom of purple, spreading up towards her eye.

I daren't look at Father. My breath is coming fast, and I'm fearful I'll run full tilt at him and knock him from his chair. I tried it once. When I was younger. And I'm still smarting with the memory of how he tripped me up and sent me to the floor. I look to Ann instead, but she's not noticed. She's fidgety and restless, and her lips move with Mother's as if to hurry along the grace. 'Jimmy Kerridge's ship has docked,' she whispers then, 'so if anyone can spare me I'll go across this afternoon to see how he has fared.'

'Has he sent any kind of message?' Mother frowns, but even though Ann has to admit that he has not, she darts her eyes across at me, and I hold her gaze and feel with my hand for the moles at the top of my arm to show I've not forgot.

'What's this I'm hearing?' Father barks from his seat. 'You're wanting to be off chasing after sailors?'

Mother sits up straight. 'He's right, Ann,' she says. 'There's no comfort to be found there, and anyway, we may not manage here without you this afternoon.'

Ann's whole body is still. But when the bowls are cleared and she unbolts the door, there's no crowd of customers pushing to come in.

We wait till Father has slumped over in a doze, and then I walk with Ann as far as the ferry. I hope the witch-woman is right and she does marry Jimmy Kerridge because then when he next sets off on a voyage, he can put a word in for me with the captain, vouch for the fact that despite my addled leg, I'm quick as a bird. I watch until Ann reaches the other side and steps off on to dry land, her white cap dancing, her face as bright as butter when she waves.

I walk along the river, eyes peeled for invaders, past Danky's hut, and Mac's, but both are locked, without a sign of life, so I keep walking until I'm at the railway bridge. I can see the church spire, but not the time on the clock, and I turn inland and take the track that winds across the common. The gorse smells strong today, sweet and heavy enough to eat, and I remember old Danky's teasing: *When the gorse is in flower tis the season for courting.* And I hear the sound of his laughing, for the bright yellow gorse blooms most of the year. I walk as far as the churchyard and lean on the back gate, and even from here I see that Mother has placed a bunch of sweet william on my brothers' grave. When did she pass by? A rise of envy leaps up in me, and I lift the latch and step through.

Almost immediately I'm calmed. There's a different air in here, still and quiet, as if the hedgerows and the pebbled walls seal in their own time. I kneel by the grave and prod the pale-purple centres of the flowers. Fresh and breathing. They can't have been picked more than a few hours since. I close my eyes and trace the shapes of my brothers' names. William. William. James. William. James. And that other, earlier Thomas.

What would they have looked like? I wonder. Fair and blue-eyed like my sisters? Or nut-brown like me? But one thing I do know is that they would be standing straight and tall, all six of them, without my twisted limb. I asked Mother once and she said yes, they were all born perfect – just unlucky and called away too soon. I try to imagine them as they'd be now, standing in a row, the eldest in uniform and Father, proud as an army captain, with no need to be drowning his despair in drink.

William, William, James, William, James, Thomas. I whisper their names, adding my own as I lie down beside them, my back pressed into the grass. I look up at the church tower. The big hand of the clock is quivering towards the hour and I tense my body for it even though I know the bells won't chime. Without the bells it is the starlings that I hear, a flock of young ones, racketing and chattering, fighting each other for a worm. I turn and watch them, brown-feathered, bandy-legged, and I laugh as the smallest one nips in and takes it. Indignant, the others raise their voices, sharp and wheezy, no sign of a song, and I sit up slowly. Hello, I say, counting. My heart squeezes so hard it hurts. I know who you are. And even though it is God who must have sent them, it is my brothers who have shown themselves to me. My brothers who have come. William, William, James, William, James, I name them, and there, that scruffy one, the one that took the worm, that's Thomas.

I lie and watch them for another hour. Smiling. Feathered with softness. And even as I lie there in the grass I'm thinking of the next day when I'll be back. And the day after if I can get away, and I wonder whether there will be school after the harvest, or maybe Runnicles will volunteer himself in some learned capacity. But surely he is too old for the war, and it seems to me that everyone I know is too old, or too young, and then I remember Jimmy Kerridge. Of course he won't be able to take me with him when he next sets sail. He'll be needed in the navy, he'll be sent out to destroy enemy ships, sink submarines, and as I lie there in the churchyard, the clock striking silently above me, I curse the war, although I do it secretly under my breath because I know if anyone were to hear me it would be punishable by death.

Chapter 17

Mother's bruise is yellow, with a frilly edge of purple fading round the eye, but it doesn't stop her coming into Southwold to wave goodbye to the recruits. There is a crowd in the market square, with our volunteers, the life nearly squashed out of them, pressed against the Swan Hotel. Mrs Horrod's boy, Vic, is there, and Ron Sutton, the Spence brothers and Peter Girling who will have to take his nickname, Girl, with him to foreign shores. They aren't in uniform, I'm disappointed to see that, but in their best suits, flat caps, shirts, waistcoats and ties, black boots re-soled and polished to a shine.

We follow them on to Gun Hill, to get a last glimpse of the sea, before we head to the station. There must be a hundred of them or more, and each with their own flock of women coming along behind, feathers fluffed up like a pack of geese, while the men stand back and watch them, arms crossed, faces cracked with pride.

I climb on to the station-house roof to get a better view and I see Mr Allard, stiff and awkward, and his wife, fighting back her tears. Their son Abb has his small boys gathered in his arms, while his wife looks on, a handkerchief pressed against her nose. Runnicles is there too, nodding and counting, and I imagine his fingers itching to set it all down in his book. There's

47

my sister Ann, standing beside Jimmy Kerridge, dark and neat, not much taller than she is, who is to be off a week on Friday with a group of navy reserves. He's promised her that they'll be married as soon as he returns. A winter wedding is what they hope for. Not that they've told Father. Instead they've been using every afternoon they have to walk along the lanes that lead into Hoist Wood, taking the narrowest paths that force them to wind their arms around each other and squeeze in tight so they won't be snagged by brambles. At night in bed Ann twists and turns, the blood in her veins too hot for rest, and in the mornings, exhausted by the battle of her dreams, she drags herself up and sits by the cold fire.

'Can I not move to the big bedroom?' I hear her ask Mother. 'Now that the Miss Bishops are gone?' But Mother shushes her. That room is the one nice thing she has and she'd prefer it if no one ever stepped in there again. 'Someone might want it,' she says. 'And Lord knows we need the rent.' And she leaves the window open and a jug of flowers on the ledge, and the quilt she made before she even met my father, folded over the bed.

Three days after we say goodbye to our recruits a regiment of soldiers arrive. They are on their way to Belgium but they stop with us first to prepare themselves for war. The Bedfordshires, they are. And for the most part they are billeted at Henham Hall, although a dozen or so are sent on up to Blyfield House where Mary tells us they have them sleeping on camp-beds in the ballroom.

The Bedfordshires have been with us less than a week, when the Royal Warwickshires, and then the Hampshires arrive. Some of them move on fast, but there are always more. Soon the hotels and the guesthouses are full again, and at Blyfield House Mary must share her bed with the scullery maid, so that soldiers from the Royal Fusiliers can be billeted in the attic. She comes over to us on Sunday, full of news. How Cook has threatened to leave if she has to skivvy for sixty extra men *and* share a bed with Violet who snores. Father laughs, although he has been uneasy all week, not saying a word to anyone but customers. And Mother takes Mary upstairs to inspect the good room which she has made ready for two soldiers from the Welsh Fusiliers who will be arriving on Wednesday. Mother wishes they were from the Royals – Mrs Horrod has been boasting she has royalty in her house – but you have to accept who you are given, and not say a word about it.

Southwold is full to bursting and our village too, but they keep on arriving. George Allard is right, we must have the biggest army in the world, because soon they are sleeping in the village hall, in tents up on the scrub, or out in the open, hard up against the new barbed wire that has been spun along the tops of the low cliffs.

Every morning I check the beach. Check the inlets and the gulleys, the river that lies behind the dunes. For these men, however smart their uniforms, will never know the land like me. In the afternoon, if I can get away, I look in on my starlings. They chirp and scrap and chatter for me, and when I've had my fill, I find my way across the river and climb up on to the station roof to see the soldiers coming in. I watch them, scrubbed and ready for action, their kitbags on their shoulders, and I scan their faces for signs that they are eager as I would be to set off into the unknown.

George Allard isn't happy about these new rolls of wire, wrapped round with spikes, and made by some infernal machine. They have it in great loose coils along the cliff path beyond Dunwich and already it's patched with white flags of wool torn from the coats of sheep that stray too near. Mother and Ann go up there and pull it free and they have a pillowcase full already which Mother plans to card and spin and knit into a jumper for me to wear next winter.

'They're already ordering in their strong rope from elsewhere,' Mr Allard frets as he teases out the flax, 'and soon they won't be needing any kind of rope at all. Nor wooden fencing, or brick walls.' And he shakes his head and curses the inventions of man that only bring misery to the lives of others. 'What kind of a land will it be then, full of wire fences, with no cover for the animals or the birds?' And he trudges backwards, plaiting as he goes, for once, in silence.

I don't tell Mr Allard about the wool in case he thinks it's stealing, and I warn Mother to keep her knitting away from our two Welsh Fusiliers. It may be against Dora, as everyone calls the Defence of the Realm Act now, to take wool that isn't yours. But there's no time for our soldiers to notice or not notice the lumpy beginnings of my jumper, because no sooner have they settled in than they are gone. They are needed at the Battle of Belgium, and they set off on their ship while Mother, Ann and I stand at the water's edge and wave. Two weeks they were with us. That was all. And in all that time Father didn't have a drink. Now he goes down to the cellar to check supplies and comes up with a cupful of ale for no one but himself. It's not long before he's down for another. 'Ahhh,' he sighs and a smile flips across his face. 'That's better.' His eyes have brightened, there is colour in his face, and if I didn't know what is likely to come after I'd think it was for the better too.

Instead I sit at the table, head down, and work on my boats. I'm drawing a clipper with three masts and a mizzen sail that's sliced across sideways like a set of sheets. There are square sails too, and a jib sail to catch the wind from behind. I've drawn the ship in pencil, and now I must go over it in ink. But the ink smudges against the knuckle of my finger and I'm so disappointed I want to take the nib of the pen and stab it into my arm. But I daren't draw attention to myself. Not to even give a quick jab at the table. And so I bite my lip hard and I turn my paper over and I start again.

When Father comes up with his third pint he tips his head back even as he climbs and I feel it in my stomach, the dread knowledge of his thirst. It's as if he's lost on a plain, the sap sucked out of him, and now, however much he drinks, he can never get enough. He's not always bad like this, when he's on the run, but the first night after he's been on the water wagon, that's when it's best to look out. And true enough, after the fifth pint the raging starts. The few customers we have slip out through the door, but I daren't move from my seat. I lean low over my paper and let the pen run over the faint lines. This is what it must feel like to be a rabbit, waiting in the corn for a man to club you on the head, and I imagine dropping to the floor, crawling across the tiles and streaking to safety up the ladder. But Father has an imaginary foe. An army of them. He's conjured them before, although when sober he will never be drawn on who they are. He snarls at them and curses and when he knocks a tankard to the floor, Mother comes out of the kitchen, her sleeves rolled up, her hands dripping. 'William Maggs!' She takes his arm as if she has nothing to fear, and Ann, who's been hovering behind her, flits round and seizing hold of me rushes us both out of the room.

'Is this the way to run an inn?' Mother scolds, and he storms back, 'I'll have no petticoat government, don't you know!' And he says it again, louder, as we scuttle up the ladder to bed.

Mother laughs, because sometimes laughing is the thing that works. But she's not laughing for long.

I'm cold tonight, for all that it's still August, and I lie against

Ann's back and pray for Mother whose clear voice I can hear in the room below battling against his wild one. There's a crash, it may be a table going over, and I fear for my boat, half finished, the ink still wet. The back door slams, and I hear Mother's steps rush out into the night. I want to get up and go to her, but our room opens into theirs, and I daren't come face to face with Father at the top of the ladder. I tussle with him in my thoughts. Kicking at his face, twisting away as his hand grabs at my ankle. I free myself and stamp on his fingers, so that he slips one rung and I give a cheer.

Ann elbows me and I lie still. I won't sleep till Mother is back. I've made a promise. Instead I listen to the sounds of the night. An owl hooting, high as a flute, and behind it, behind everything, the roar of the sea. Ann lies awake beside me, but we don't talk. What is there to say? Finally we hear Father creak across the floorboards and heave down into the bed. I wait a moment for his snore, and then I climb out from under the covers and stand at the window, waving, in case Mother can see me and know that it's safe to come inside.

'Tommy,' Ann hisses. 'Stop that now.' And she leaps out of bed and pulls me from the window.

'What?' I go to fling her off.

But her grip is tight. 'What if the enemy is out there and takes your flapping for a sign?'

I thought I was cold before but now I'm so cold that my body shakes, and I'm too frightened to do anything other than crouch below the window out of sight. 'Get in, you fool,' Ann holds the cover for me, and I crawl to the bed and once I'm in, I let her fold her warm self around me, just as Mother used to do when I was small.

It's morning when I next open my eyes and the cock is crowing where the owl once called. Below the window is the sound of Mother sweeping and then the squeak of the well shaft as she pulls the water up. She must have stayed out, slept in the open like our nation's men, or more likely on the bench by the back door. I feel under the mattress for my growing bag of coins and I think of the day when I will surprise her with them. See the smile flash across her face.

Chapter 18

The same day two Liverpools are billeted at our inn the first refugees arrive. They come by boat, women and children mostly. A few old men. From Belgium. They dock at the harbour and Dr Collings goes aboard, but rumour has it that he's soon on dry land again. It was a bad crossing, that was for certain, and every man, woman and child is green as the sea, and the deck strewn with their suffering. But by the time I see them they're washed and clean and sitting round a long table at the Constitutional Hall where Mother helps to serve them a lunch of bread and ham. I'm there to help too. Bring in the plates and cups and fill the kettle with water, but really I've come along to gawp. I've never seen a foreigner before. Only Mac, and the herring girls, who, hard as they are to understand, are ruled by the same king. The Belgians, much as I stare at them, don't seem so different from us. The women are bare-headed, that's true, ours never go out without a hat, but their hair is tied back and twisted tight into a bun just like the ladies in the Constitutional Hall now that they're safely inside. It's not just me who's watching them. All around the hall there are men and women standing, staring, and under their gaze the Belgian mothers do their best to shush the children sitting on their knees and keep the older ones from choking on their food, so hungrily do they shove it in. The men, broken, with nothing to distract them, look the most likely to give in and weep.

By the time we've washed the dishes and dried them, swept the hall and moved away the chairs, the afternoon is wearing on, and I have to nudge Mother if we're to get back and open up the inn. Father can hardly be relied on, and Ann, with Jimmy gone to war, is as likely to get up at dawn and scrub the kitchen floor as she is to go roaming off across the countryside alone.

It's almost six when we get back, and Mr Mac is waiting by the door. It's half an hour yet till we can legally serve him beer, but he must have forgotten about Dora and the new opening hours, because he has his flask beside him, and he's tapping, impatient, with his stick.

'You still with us?' Mother asks, although it's clear he is. And she raises her eyebrows and looks him over as if to check he isn't one of the many things that's banned.

'I've been busy,' he says, 'working.' He doesn't seem to have taken offence. And still frowning he follows us round to the back door of the inn and comes inside.

Mac sits at the small table in the bar and lights his pipe. The tobacco gives out a sweet, warm smell. 'You'll have to wait.' Mother daren't go down and fill his flask, not till it's six thirty, but there's no reason, she says, softening, why she can't offer a gentleman some tea. She gives him cake too, a slice kept back from lunch, wrapped in a cloth to bring back home. He doesn't touch it, although he seems grateful for the tea. I keep my eye on it, hoping he will take one bite, so that later it might be considered ruined, and I can devour the rest.

'And your wife?' Mother asks. 'She still here as well?'

'Oh yes,' Mac looks troubled at the thought that she might not be. 'She's at home, just now, packing up our things.'

'Oh so you are leaving?' And the news forces me up straight.

'No,' Mac shakes his head. 'Not leaving. But Millside is to be given over for the needs of soldiers. We're taking the wooden house on the rise above the lea.'

'The rabbit house?' And I flush because it may be only me who calls it that, although there can't be anyone who hasn't noticed how rabbits swarm on the long slope of the garden, smoothing away like ripples the moment you come near.

'It was due to be demolished,' Mac taps at his pipe. 'But now there are to be no new buildings.' He looks up at us and his eyes are dark. 'Nothing new to be built in the whole of Britain. So it is to be left as it is. And we're to have it.' And I remember Runnicles telling me, and Runnicles knows a great many things, that Mac, our own old Mac, is a man who *makes* buildings. He's built a school and a church, in his home city of Glasgow. And houses, unusual houses, for gentlemen that don't care what anybody thinks. I glance at Mac's hands that don't look as if they've lain more than two bricks together, pale and long-fingered, nervously tapping as they are.

'Unless you have a room here for us to rent?'

The door slams and Father comes in. 'What'll you have, my good man?'

We all look at the clock ticking its way towards the half hour, but not there yet. 'A pint of beer, is it? With a whisky chaser?' And he steps down into the cellar.

'The good room's taken, I'm afraid,' Mother tells him. 'Soldiers. Like everywhere else. Is the Lea House not to your liking?'

Mac smiles. 'My wife finds the place a little eerie. With the sea rushing in below, and the wind roaring at the walls. But we'll soon be used to it. We're lucky to find anywhere with the village so full.'

Father lines up Mac's drinks beside his flask. 'The boy will help you move your things, if you need help. Isn't that so, Thomas?'

'I'll bring the handcart in the morning,' I say, and my heart begins to thump, for after all these years I'll have a chance to see the Millside ghost.

The next day I find the door unlatched and Mrs Mollett in the scullery, mopping at the floor. 'Go through,' she tells me and there in the parlour is Mrs Mac, wearing a fawn dress, with a red pin holding up her hair. 'That's so kind of you to help,' she says to me, in her good English accent, and she folds a coat and places it in the trunk. Mac doesn't seem to see me. Instead he stares ahead, frowning at a stack of books.

'What is it you're after?' His wife touches his arm. And Mac stands still as if he's forgotten even himself. 'I was thinking of the home I promised you when we married . . .'

Mrs Mac takes his hand. 'You made it for me,' she says. 'On Mains Street. No one could have had a more beautiful home. Unless they were lucky enough to have moved with you to Florentine Terrace.'

But he shakes his head, and I notice that one eye droops down at the corner. 'No,' he looks sad. 'We made it together.' And right there in front of me he leans forward and kisses her on the cheek.

'And Florentine Terrace is still there.' She smiles at him. 'Just as it was. Packed up and waiting for us when we return.'

'Yes.' The frown is back. 'If we return.'

'Shhh.' She lets go of his hand. 'We needed to get away, that's all. But once you're stronger . . . In the meanwhile we'll make another home. We can start now. Today. But only if you let me get on and pack his trunk.'

'Margaret.' He says her name so beautifully it's as if I've never heard it before.

'Toshie,' she answers with a little smile.

It seems they've forgotten that I'm there. I turn away and look around the room. As long as I've known Millside, it's been owned by a family – the Newberys, friends of old Mac's – who come from Glasgow every year to spend the summer here. They rent out this side of the house and when they're gone, and the lodgers too, the house is closed up for the winter. Now that I'm inside I want to run upstairs and peer out through the high windows to see that long-ago woman staring back at me. 'Is there anything you need bringing down?' I ask, all the time listening for the sound of apples falling, but Mrs Mac shakes her head and points to a box of letters on the table. 'You can tie that up with string,' she tells me.

While I'm knotting the string good and tight, Mac begins lifting boxes, carrying them out to the cart that I've propped up by the door.

'What's in all them boxes?' I ask, following with my own, and Mac tells me – books mostly, photographs. Articles about architecture and art. 'You can look at them if you're inter-ested.' And he gives a quick glance at my hands which I washed that very morning with water from the well.

When the cart is loaded I leave them to finish packing and push my way, careful as I can, back down the street past the Blue Anchor and to the right along the track that leads to Rabbit House. I have to wait for a herd of young heifers to lumber past, Mr Buck coming on behind with his whip as he brings them up from the low fields where they graze. What you got there? anyone else would have asked. But Buck only has eyes for the thin tails of his cows, swishing away flies, and for all I know he doesn't even see me.

The lane is rough with stones and troughs, and I catch the wheel of the cart more than once, nearly tipping Mac's books off to the side. I have to edge it up on to the rise, pushing through herb willow, hoping not to hit a buried brick. I'm quiet, though, the stems of grass softening the grind, so that when I come to the gate I catch a host of rabbits in mid-chew. They freeze, their ears up, their noses twitching danger. And as I push open the gate they turn, every last one of them in the same breath, and streak away over the grass like fire.

I bump the boxes of books up the track. No one has lived in this house since I've known it. It's made from wooden planks, its windows wide and peeling paint, looking out on every side. The key is under a pot by the front step and I leave the cart propped against a rain butt and creak open the door. Light spills in across the wooden floor. And a bee, heavy as a barrel, buzzes noisily around my head. I take a box and step inside. The floors are painted white, and there's a stove for a fire. There are no shelves or cupboards so I walk through into the next room but here there is nothing but a metal bed. I choose a corner and lifting the books out I arrange them, first in a tall tower and then, thinking better of it, leaning one against the other in a row. I go out for the next box. And the next. I leave the letters knotted as they are, but the last box is full of creamy pamphlets, and as I arrange them I open one and flick through. There are photographs – rooms full of furniture, chairs tall as a man, trees and flowers appearing out of the paper on the walls. I flick to the front of the pamphlet and attempt to decipher the unfamiliar words.

Waerndorfer. I think that's what it says *Carl-Ludwigstrasse.* And I wonder what it has to do with old Mac. But when I look more closely at the photographs and search the details of the rooms I see a vase of blackthorn just coming into flower. And that's when I see his name. Charles Rennie Mackintosh. Written clear as day. Who else would decorate their table with a bunch of sticks?

I get more comfortable, sitting cross-legged on the floor, and look at pictures of a tea room, with a cauldron of daisies hanging from the roof. Wrapped around each cauldron are circles of metal, like the pictures Runnicles once drew for us of the planets moving round the sun. A few pages on is a painting of two women, their hair spun wild about their heads, and at their overlapping hearts, a child lying, curled inside a rose. *Hertz am Rose*, it says. Margaret Macdonald Mackintosh. Although the baby is not the same one she was painting on her frieze. Might it be her own baby? And I wonder if it is buried in a short grey grave somewhere, like so many of ours. *Hertz.* I say the word aloud. *Dekorative. Wiener Rundschau.* And that's when I know, without knowing how I know, that the words I'm reading are in German. I've been reading German words! Looking at German pictures! And I throw the book down, scuffing it across the floor, and leap to my feet.

The handcart is waiting for me at the door, an old brown donkey, nose down for a bite, and I take it by the arms and rush the slope of garden, rabbits scattering as if I'm the devil himself. I scrape through the gate, dragging the cart behind me, and race with it down the lane until it veers off into a bog of sand. I leave it there and plough my way up through the dunes, the sharp stems of marram grass scratching at my legs, the sea roaring in my ears, and I have to swipe at the salty mash of tears that fills my nose and mouth. Once I'm at the top I lie down in the sand and wait until my heart has slowed, my eyes have dried, and then remembering my duty, I crawl forward, and taking a long, careful look along the coast, I check to see that we're still safe.

Chapter 19

No one thinks the herring girls will come this year, but there's nothing the fishermen can do without them, someone has to gut the silver darlings, as they call them, and soon the girls are flooding off the train, in a long crocodile behind their pastor, and making their way into the already overcrowded town. Most go to the lodgings they've had before, and a little troupe of them swoop over to us on the ferry. Mrs Lusher always takes some in. This year she packs in three above her shop, in a room she's lined with paper to keep the oil and fish smell from her walls. And Mrs Horrod fills Vic's empty bed with two sisters from the Hebrides, although what she'll do if the war is over before the herring season is done nobody knows, and I imagine the look on Vic's face if he comes home early and finds them squeezed in there like sardines.

Mrs Horrod stops in the street to tell Mother what she's done, and how each morning at five she bangs on Vic's old door to make sure they're up, and at work in time for six when the fishermen deliver their first catch. 'Bind your fingers,' she calls to them, quiet, so as not to wake the soldiers still sleeping next door, and she leaves a hot cup of tea out for them to drink while they take out their strips of linen and bandage up their hands.

I can see from the way Mother presses her lips together that she'd never want herring girls in her best room, and anyway the room is full of soldiers from the Manchesters. Three they gave us this time, with one sleeping on a straw mattress on the floor. But since they've been with us her bruise has faded, and there has been a gloomy kind of truce. It's the sight of their uniforms, I'm sure of it, that keeps Father on the wagon.

The sisters that lodge with Mrs Horrod are new this year. I know that as soon as I see them. They walk around with their eyes wide open, staring through arched doorways at the gardens beyond, sighing over hollyhocks and pansies, leaning down to stroke a snapdragon's velvety head. They clutch each other's arms as they pass the big house on the corner, and each time there is a slice of field, rolling away softly to the sea, they seem to say a little prayer. They're allowed to come as young as fourteen, if they are tall enough and strong, and although the older girl looks ready for any kind of work, the other's so small and slight she must have squeezed on to the train hidden in her sister's skirts. I see her dashing up and down the street past the inn, and once when she stops to look at the anchor, huge and rusted, that lies beached below our sign, I happen to come out. 'Dragged up from the bottom of the sea by one of our own fishermen,' I tell her. 'Father swopped it for a bottle of brandy. Danky it was, that dragged it up.' And I glance at her hands to see if she has suffered any cuts, for most of the girls are scarred with nicks from the sharp blades of their gutting knives. But this girl's hands are small and strong, freckled as her face, without a mark on them, and she catches me looking and holds one out to me. 'If you want to buy me a ring?' she wriggles her third finger, and I blush right up over the top of my head so that my blasted ears beat red.

'Come along now, Betty,' her sister takes her by the arm, and they whisk away together, laughing, down towards the beach.

The next afternoon that I have free I slip on to the ferry and steal over to the other side to watch the girls at work. I like to see the speed with which they gut and douse and pack the herrings into barrels, their bound fingers working, their bodies swaying to their songs. I look along the rows of girls, but I don't see Betty, or her sister. They all appear the same today, in dark skirts and aprons, with scarves over their hair, stooping down to seize their fish. And with the same quick twist of their knives they slit the bellies open and flick away the guts. They work in crews. Two gutters and a packer. And while the gutters are throwing the fish into one of three boxes, depending on its size, the packer lifts them out, douses them down and lays them in the barrel. Sometimes I forget about the gutters and only watch the packer. She is the tallest of the crew, able to stretch to the bottom of the barrel where she lays her fish so carefully, its tail meeting other tails, its head brushing the side of the barrel, resting below a scattering of salt. Then she starts on a new layer, placing each fish sideways, shoulder to shoulder, so that their skins shimmer like a slowly twisting flower. It's not long before a barrel is full, and then the cooper appears and twists it away to pour in pickling water and press more salt into the top. But the girls don't waste a moment looking up. And I remember the oath that they must swear to: I've stared at it often enough pinned up along the harbour. *You shall make oath that you will well and truly execute your office of a packer of herring within the town of Southwold and mind the laying of all herrings and that they shall be merchantable and that the vessels or casks shall be full and equally packed in every part. So help you*

God. They've started on another barrel. And another song. Without even taking pause to stretch. So I walk upriver through the harbour, careful not to look across to the far bank, where I might catch sight of Mac and his wife, sitting outside their shed. I've managed to avoid them since the move, slipping out through the back door of the inn when Mac comes in, lying low in the dunes if either one of them should pass by on a walk. Should I tell someone about the pamphlets? That's what I can't decide. And if so, who? And I worry that by staying silent I am going against Dora and it will be me who ends up guilty of treason. *Hertz am Rose*, I mutter, as I stumble along the bank. *Rose am Hertz, Dekorative, Ludwig*, until my eyes are blind. 'It's young Maggs!' Mr Mayhew, the owner of the jetty opposite Thorogood's shed, is calling to me. Each summer Mayhew and his wife live on this boat while renting out their house in Southwold. Now he's sanding down the perfectly smooth deck, and I'm reminded how I once asked him if he was planning on a trip, and he shook his head so fiercely his cheeks shook. 'No time, boy, no time.' And I look up at the mast, its sails bound tight as bandage, and I imagine slipping aboard in the dead of night, unfurling them, and steering out into the wind.

'Good day to you, sir,' I say, and it's then that I see her, not far from the jetty, working alongside her sister and a tall, broad packer with a squint. She's the smallest gutter I've ever seen, but her fingers flash as she slices open her fish, twists out its guts and flings it into the box. She's singing too, her eyes half closed, and as I walk by I peer at her round face, a streak of pale hair come loose from her scarf.

'It's the wee boy from the inn.' Betty's sister has spied me and Betty's eyes fly open and without losing her rhythm she catches hold of a new fish. I nod. There's nothing more for me to do, while they smile and nudge each other and without stopping their work they turn their heads and sing their song at me. There's not a line of it I understand. But all the same I feel the danger of the words. Waves high as a mountain, mermaids crying through a storm. I listen hard, and as I stand there I think maybe I can follow the story. A sailor, forsaken by his true love. The gulls about him, laughing at his despair.

I wait, because it seems I must, and as I listen I push those other words into their song, *Hertz, Rose, Dekorative, Rundschau*. And I flush to think that maybe the pamphlet I've been reading is not German at all but Gaelic. My heart lifts and I twist away and stare out over the water, to where the weathered wood of Thorogood's shed sits in full sun, but I can't see from here whether Mac and his wife are sitting outside or not. And if they are, whether they are working at pictures of flowers and babies, or whether they are writing letters to friends in foreign countries, reporting on the secret coves and currents of our coast.

There's a storm in the middle of that week, with hurling rain and lightning slashing down, and when it's worn itself out there are worms, dozens of them, lying stranded on the ground. They look so bald and pink, washed clean of their earth, that I'm tempted to help them back into the garden, but instead I gather up a few and put them in a box and I take them with a piece of string down to the river. The sky is clearing, although the light is lemony and sour, and I stare into the water and imagine the fish knocked senseless by the storm. They won't know which is up or down, and sure of my luck, I press a fat worm on to my hook and with a hag stone for a weight, I fling it out. But I'm wrong. The fish have swum too deep, and none are biting. I sit there at the mouth of the river, and watch the clouds roll back until the whole coast is bathed in light. There's the bald head of the lighthouse and Southwold pier stepping out into the sea. And behind me, the dark smudge that is the lost city of Dunwich with its one remaining church and pub, and the butcher's shop Father gave up when he came here.

It's then that I see him. Black against the sky. Old Mac. He's standing with his binoculars raised, staring out to sea. He steps forward, so that the tide must surely be running over his boots, and I look round to see who else might have seen him for it was only last week that Mr Gory, a newcomer himself, was asking what the man was still doing wandering about the place, when all the other visitors were gone? And his wife too, going about without a hat. And all that hair.

And what is he doing now? He's striding into the shallows as if he'd walk across the sea itself. And I watch him, fearful that he might be sending out a sign. I'll have to track him, it's my duty, and I'm pocketing my worms when a fish bites and I leap up and swing it in. It's only a dab, but I inspect it anyway, glittering and flipping in my hands. Dabs are never worth bothering with, Danky taught me that, so I slide the hook out from its startled mouth, and my heart swelling with my goodness and my power I throw it back in. When I look up Mac has turned away from the shore, and is stepping along the beach, his black back the only mark in the whole bay.

I wrap the babbing string, still wet, around my wrist, and scramble along the top of the dune. He's far ahead, and I'm sure I've lost him, but I keep down and press on, and then he appears, dragging himself up the scree, hanging on to tufts and strings of grass. He stops then and looks around, and as I duck down I can't help thinking, if he is a spy, then he's got some things to learn. But it's not long before he's off again, keeping to the high ground, winding along above the river until the old brick water pump comes into view. For a while Mac stops and looks at it, his head on one side, and then he steps off the path and staggers down towards it through the shingle.

I make ready to slide after, my heels are dug in, my back braced, when Mac stops again, and crouches down. What's he seen? I look around but there's nothing, just the empty day. Mac turns into the pebbled slope and lifts his binoculars to his eyes. 'Come and look at this,' he calls, and whipping round to check who else is there, I find there's only me. 'Beautiful, do you see?' He holds out the binoculars, and when I come close, he guides me with the tip of his cane, to where a dark purple straggle of flowers cling to the slope. 'Aubretia,' he says. 'Known as rock cress. The Campbelli or Parkinsii variety, I should think. See the white eyes?'

I nod. I do. And he leans forward and tugs at a spray, close down by the roots, and with sand and stones like tiny seed potatoes scattering, he pulls it free.

'I'll be off then, if that's all right with you?' And with the plant cradled in his arm he walks back towards the village.

Chapter 20

At the church gate George Allard stands back to let Mother in before him. But Mother never can go straight into the church, first she must make her visit to the grave. I sit on the wall and wait for her, nodding to my starlings, just once, so no one but they will know. I wait for Mary too, watching the people hurrying in, nodding and ducking their heads, keeping any news they might have gathered until after the service. Mac and Mrs Mac pass by, their heads together under an umbrella, Mrs Mac in a loose embroidered dress, Mac puffing on his pipe. I dip down and pretend to be studying the pebbles of the wall, and then Danky's sister pulls up in her little trap and waits while Danky carries in their mother. As they pass through the screen door the old woman catches her shawl on a knot and she looks up, so severe that I see Danky quiver.

Mary is usually here to meet us when we arrive, but today there is no sign of her. I wait out in the spitting rain until Mother hisses for me to come in, and we have already squeezed ourselves into a pew when she slides in beside us. 'What kept you?' Father frowns, and Mary puts her hands up to her mouth and her eyes are wide with fear. 'There's news from France,' her voice is hoarse, 'the Suffolk Regiment . . .' here she looks around at all the Suffolk men and women, talking, shuffling, preparing themselves for the soothing words of God. 'They fought for eight hours at Le Cateau – even the Germans begged them to surrender, they were outmanned from the start, but they wouldn't give in, not until nearly all were killed, eight hundred, Mother, out of a thousand, and then they only stopped fighting when they were rushed from behind, and the last few men were taken as prisoners.'

A woman in the row before us tuts, without turning, and Mother takes Mary's hands in hers. 'Where do you hear such terrible things?' she says as if it is somehow her fault.

'It's the truth, Mother,' Mary almost chokes. 'Sir Bly gets all the news, red-hot, from London. The Suffolks are slaughtered. It won't be long before the whole county knows it.'

The vicar steps up to the altar and the congregation rises. We rise too, although there is a cold chill in our row. Pale light floods in through the high-paned window, washing the vicar's head in white. Who will protect us now? I think, and I imagine the Suffolks lying on the ground like worms, writhing and dying, and I have to cover my mouth for fear I'll be sick.

We sing a hymn, *Father, we praise thee, now the night is over*, and as we begin, I glance at Mac who is sitting in the pew behind. He has tears in his eyes. Has he heard? Did he listen in to Mary's whispered news, or is he crying for some private Scottish grief of his own?

Our vicar has much to say about the war. The prayers and patience and the faith we must fortify ourselves with. I feel Father fidgeting beside me, twisting his fingers in his lap. If I dared I'd take his hand and hold it still.

We stand and sit and stand again. And then we kneel in prayer. I kneel on an embroidered sampler covered in a trail of purple flowers. Rock cress, is that what they are? And I stare at the creeping stitches as I mumble my own prayers. That Father will hold his temper, that Mother's garden will stay clear of blight, that Runnicles will never again test us on equations, but all the while I'm praying that Mary has it wrong, that the Suffolks are still advancing across Europe keeping us safe from attack.

The service is longer than usual, with prayers for the men who are abroad, the ones we know, from Westleton and Southwold, Blythburgh and Dunwich, for the regular army, and for the seven hundred and fifty thousand others who volunteered in the first week of the war. By the time the vicar releases us, the sky has darkened and the rain is clattering against the wooden door.

'Been fishing again recently?' Mac asks me on the path, and I look around, hoping that this time there might be somebody else he's talking to, but no. It's me.

'No, sir,' I tell him. And he reaches into the pocket of his cape and brings out a box.

'I have a wee gift for you,' his voice is low, and Mrs Mac lifts the umbrella and holds it over our three heads. 'It was most appreciated, the help you gave in getting us moved, and we haven't had a chance to thank you.'

I open the box and look down at the oblong blocks of colour. It's as if I've never seen colours before. They are so dense and clean they seem to burst out into the air, and fearful they will lose their shine, I flip the lid shut fast.

'It's a good box,' Mac says. It's much the same as the one he uses himself. And he draws out a book of paper and hands that to me too.

'Thank you,' I say. 'I'm sorry . . .' but unable to explain what I'm apologising for, I pull my jacket round me, and holding my precious gifts against my chest, I run down the street towards the inn.

Chapter 21

The next Saturday a package arrives for Mr Charles Rennie Mackintosh. Mac must have given out this address when he hoped our good room would come free. The writing on the brown paper is fine and silky and I lift the parcel to my nose to breathe it in. I'm hoping for the perfume, peppery as freesias, that floats about the bright head of Mrs Mac, but instead I'm startled by the smell of liquor. Brandy it could be. Or rum. I sniff again, but the smell forces me to put it down. And anyway, why would this parcel be from his wife, when she works alongside him so closely that when he finishes a sketch of flowers he marks her initials beside his in a pencilled box.

I'd like to take the package to Mac right away, but first I must make my inspection of the beach, and by then George Allard will be waiting for me. I daren't not go. He's still not forgiven me for taking the morning off to move the Mackintoshes' books, and the next day when I went to help him he said he'd got some other project to be getting on with, and he sniffed and turned his head away. Later I saw him walking through the village with a load of wood, and when he next had a use for me, there was a pulley, rusted and in need of oiling, lying on the ground by his back door.

Quick as I can, I climb the ladder to my room and prop Mac's package up beside the small picture of geese. I left the painting of the sea in the good room for the soldiers. The gold and green of it, the white frill of the waves. They'll need it to prepare them, they'll need it more than me.

As soon as I arrive at Mr Allard's, I see from his face that he's heard about the Suffolks. It's not his son that's lost – he's with the East Anglians – but all the same the news has robbed him of his strength. 'I'll do the turning today,' he says, and with trembling hands he wraps the strick of hemp around my waist.

I've not made rope before, but he seems to have forgotten that. 'Ease it out gently,' he says, sitting at the wheel, 'don't let it plait until each strand is twisted tight.'

I keep the yarn as taut as I can and tread back carefully. It's harder work than it looks and it's not long before my arms are tiring. At first I'm sure I've got something wrong, the three strands are spinning tight enough to curl into a ball, but when I'm halfway down the garden they catch against each other and I grin as the first coil of rope is formed. 'Keep going,' Allard croaks. Even his voice has lost its power and so I keep stepping back, down the long length of the garden, until I become entangled in the branches of a small sharp tree that grows beside the gate. 'On you go now,' Allard's voice is a growl, and my arms stinging, my jacket ripped, I reach out and tug open the door. I'm in the wide field, its furrows newly dug, a drift of gulls swooping away and then dropping down again when they see it's only me.

The rope is twisting together nicely now. I tread backwards along the narrow path, watching the village from behind, the shape of its roofs and chimneys, and the tower of the church looking down as I step blindly towards the sea. I've forgotten about my arms. The rope is golden, strong as wire, and it grips against itself, spinning and twisting as I feed it slow and easy with my hands.

'Helloo there.' A high voice pipes up from among the reeds, and turning, I see the sharp freckled face of Betty walking along the path. 'What are you doing?' She is laughing. 'Walking backwards across a field?' And I'm surrounded, for both girls are here, squeezing against me, peering at the strick around my waist. I'm about to explain when there's a whistle, and a sharp tug along the rope, and I look down and see that even in that moment the twine has bunched and twisted into kinks. 'I can't stop,' I say, taking a quick step as I speak, and the girls press themselves against the hedgerow, laughing while I pass. For a while they stand and watch me, as if I'm some rare animal or bird, and then they wrap their arms around each other and carry on. I stare after them as I back away. The tall strong sister and the sliver of herself, both with scarves about their hair, and shawls across their shoulders, heads together, chattering as they rush along beside my newly twisted yarn. They've forgotten me already, I think, as they dip out of sight over the rise of the small hill, but just then Betty leans over and flicks at the rope and I feel it travel, the touch of her finger, right down until it twangs against my gut.

I'm nearly at the start of the marsh when the hemp runs dry and the rope, still twisting, flies out of my hands. 'I'm finished!' I shout, lungeing for it, and I hear my voice sailing over the fields into the Allards' garden and down into the crook between the two arms of the building where the turning machine stops. For a moment I stand still. I stare up at the sky, the swirl of clouds, white shreds against the blue, and I gather up the rope, holding tight to its loose ends, as I stumble back along the lane.

'Good lad,' George Allard tells me when I come through the gate, and there's a soft look in his eyes I've not seen before.

Chapter 22

Mac isn't in his shed. The door is shut and locked, and Bob Thorogood, when I ask, tells me he doesn't know anything about where he might be. I walk down the lane to the Lea House, the package tucked under one arm, using it to bat away a swarm of midges that hang in the warm dip of the road. The gate is latched, the grass of the long garden singed with sun. 'I'm not here for you,' I tell the rabbits as they freeze, but I've not finished speaking before they are gone.

There's a window of glass set into the side door and I can see along the hall and through into the main room. There's a vase of honesty on a table, each disc rubbed free of its husk. I knock again, but no one comes. 'Mr Mackintosh,' I call through the slit for letters, but this parcel is too large to drop it through, and so I turn the handle and go in. The house is not so very different from before. But its emptiness feels purposeful. The white walls as if they're meant to be bare. There are plates, with fluted edges and a stark black flowered stem, arranged against a shelf, and below, to hide the pots and pans, is a length of cotton, printed with roses in an overlapping pattern of pink and black and white. I walk through to the next room. There are books on the table in two neat piles. And the stack of pamphlets I arranged against the wall. I pick a new one up and open it. I do it quickly, before I can warn myself off, but as I flick through for pictures I hear a noise – the twang of bedsprings as someone sits up, and a small, dry ladylike cough. I set down the package, and my heart leaping, I slip the pamphlet inside my shirt, the cool side of it against my skin, and I'm away out through the door.

The midges are waiting to get me as I race into the lane, and with my eyes half closed against them, my nose and mouth too, I run out over the marshes, and up through the fields to the line of trees that leads into the Hoist. There's no one else here. No lovers clinging together in the shadows, certainly not Ann who is most likely at home, waiting fitfully for the postman to pass by with a letter from Jimmy. I climb into the branches of a tree that's fallen sideways, a hornbeam that continues to leaf. And I give myself a moment to regain my breath before I slide the book out. There are more pictures than words, and I flick through the thick pages of photographs – brick walls and giant black-framed windows, and above the entrance to a building: Glasgow School of Art.

It's then I allow myself to breathe. These words are in English. I put my fingers to them. And there is Mac's full name spelt out. I flip over the page and find one side of the building is a fortress, with walls shooting up into the sky, windows as long and narrow as casements. And there's another house, with a tower, tall and round as a keep. Mac's not a danger. I can see that now. He may even have been sent here to keep us safe. Design us our own fortress, with battlements and arrow slits, and a drawbridge that drops down on to the beach. If he was allowed, I'm sure of it, he'd be starting on the plans right now. I nestle into the crook of my branch and turn another page. I am inside a house now, and there are roses, lamps, and for no clear reason, the long sweep of a woman leaning over in a kiss. Who is she? I trace my finger over the mass of her hair and down the long narrow body to the floor. But it is the photograph of the bedroom that brings blood to my face. The bed is white, as wide and deep as a hayrick, and the mirror at the foot of it has arms that curve out in an embrace. The curtains are white too, even the carpet on the floor is white, and I imagine Mrs Mac stepping across it in bare feet.

Is this the house they made together? The one that is waiting for their return? And I wonder what it ever could have been that forced them to desert it.

Chapter 23

Surely it should be against Dora, wasting good men like Runnicles on the likes of us when he could be somewhere important helping to run the war office. I think this every day as he oversees our copying and our crossing out, listening, his mouth turned down, while we recite our poems and our sums. But it was Runnicles himself who insisted the school open again. Said there was no greater good to man than education. And when this war is over smart young men will be needed to put the country to rights. 'But won't we still have our king and our prime minister?' the glazier's son asks, and Runnicles looks at us all but he doesn't say a word. He doesn't say what I've heard men saying in the inn: 'How can they know what they're doing, up there in London, if they allow the Suffolks to be slaughtered when they'd only been in France three weeks?' That was one of the Tilson men, the beer turned to tears coursing down his face so that by the end of the night he was raging and cursing, his brother's restraining arm around his neck. 'Robbed,' he wept, 'sacrificed, and no one with the courage to come out and say it.'

There was shouting in the bar that night, with others protesting that before they fell, the Suffolks had won valuable ground, a square mile at least, and without them Paris might have been taken, but Tilson wouldn't see it. 'Picture the eight hundred – they'd fill the whole of the field behind this house, and all gunned down or blown to pieces, and the others, taken away injured.'

No one and nothing could quiet him and I thought of the stir we'd made when that same field had been stripped of clover by the gypsies who'd rented out the inn. We'd woken the policeman, forced him to help us get it back. But now, with all this talk of bad government and wasted men, a policeman was the last man we wanted near. I crept down to the cellar and put my ear to the trapdoor. What if someone had found a way up from the beach and was hiding, listening for what was being said? Did Tilson's words come under the category of treason? Could anything he said be helping the enemy if the enemy was near? I screwed up my eyes and tried to see the printed words of Dora as if they were written there on the tiles, but all I could find were the old dust grooves of the hinges, and the splashes of beer lying stickily across the floor.

Runnicles is standing at the front of the room, marking up the most recent battles in chalk. Ground taken. Ground regained. Regiments in action. Regiments replaced. While he is busy I slide out Mackintosh's pamphlet and stare at the photographs inside. There is a picture here by Margaret Macdonald Mackintosh. It is of two women side by side, *The White Rose and the Red Rose*, and it is spun around with flowers. On the following page are the same women, their faces turned towards each other, holding out a baby as if they are not sure what they should do. I turn the next page slowly, for I know what I will find, but even so, when I see the nakedness – right there in Runnicles' own room – I jolt up so suddenly I knock my wrist against the desk.

'Battle of Liège. Battle of Mulhouse. Battle of Haelen. Invasion of Lorraine.' The voice is low, and I force my eyes away from the tilt of the girls' breasts, and the bald bare bumps between their legs. 'Battle of Stallupönen. Of Gumbinnen. Battle of the Ardennes. Of Charleroi.'

Runnicles turns back to the board, and I quickly flip over the page. Here the women are still naked, although they are unhappily naked now. *An Ill Omen*, one of the pictures is called. And I see it is not by Margaret, but by another Macdonald – Frances. I don't want to keep looking but neither can I pull away. *'Tis a long path which wanders to desire.* What does that mean? And there's another, of four women, shrouded by nothing but their hair, their fingers to their lips. *Truth lies at the bottom of a well.*

'Capture of Dinant. Siege of Maubeuge. Destruction of Louvain. Battle of Le Cateau.' Runnicles speaks the names as if they are his second tongue, and I try and imagine what he'd make of old Mac's pamphlets and whether all educated people speak another language as well as their own. *Hertz, Rose, Dekorative, Rundschau*, I mumble. And I wonder if it would be going against the rules of Dora if I were to recite these words for him and ask him to translate.

Chapter 24

Mac is working on his drawing of the rock cress, scratching it out when it goes wrong, sinking it into a basin of water when he can't stand the sight of it, and rubbing at the sodden paper till there is almost no colour left. I have his pamphlet in the pocket of my jacket. I've looked at every picture till my eyes are raw. But rather than return it, I sit and watch him paint. The paper he uses is thick. Whatman, he tells me it is. Named for an artist. But then he stops and seizing up a toothbrush he scrubs away at a raspberry-coloured blot until I'm sure he'll wear through to the wooden board. I lean closer and stare at the faded flowers and the mottled marks of the grey leaves. I want to tell him to leave it, to stop rubbing it away. I've never seen anything that looks more like rock cress, not even rock cress itself. Not that I'd taken much care to look at it before.

His wife lets him be. She's painting butterflies on a frieze. And she's written words along the top, in clusters, uneven as music, hovering in the sky. '*The little hills will jump for joy and the valleys will be filled with corn.*' It's a decoration for a tea room, she tells me. Up in Glasgow. And there's the baby again, repeated in a row, lifting its arms triumphantly above its head.

It's peaceful here. Now that Mac has stopped destroying his painting and set his board out in the sun to dry. 'How are you getting on with your boats?' he asks and I wish I could slide the sketchbook out and show him, but I only have his book of photographs scorching a streak against my side. 'All right,' I say. And I think of the paintbox, the colours smooth as glass, unused, for fear I might disturb them. Mac rips a sheet from his own large pad of paper, thick and grainy, good enough to eat. And without a word he hands me a board and a pencil, although I can see from the raise of his eyebrows he's surprised that I don't have one about me. 'Make a start, that's the thing,' he says then, and he turns back to staring at his own whitened work.

I sit on my upturned crate and watch the river. Opposite is Mayhew's jetty and further along, if I let my eyes drift, the straggle of the herring girls at work. I can hear their singing, the rise and fall of each verse, and I glance at Mac to see if he is listening, to check if he might even hum along. But Mac is smoking his pipe. Still staring at his paper. Although now he takes up his board again and without letting his eyes waver he makes a first new mark, and soon the only sound any of us can hear is the smooth strokes of his pencil.

'What do you have there?' It is Mrs Mackintosh, kneeling beside me, and I feel the blood rush over me as I move my hand away to reveal the small sketched face of a girl. Her eyes and mouth are crescents, her hair is covered by a scarf, but one small strand escapes and falls across her ear. 'I like it,' she smiles. 'Toshie. Have you seen this? The boy has made a drawing of something other than a boat.'

Mac looks up, although I see it is an effort. 'I started with flowers,' he says as if it is only now occurring to him. 'Then it was buildings, nothing but buildings, and now I have come back to flowers again.' His wife lays a hand on his shoulder and keeps it there, and I expect her to remind him about the barricade he's planning – the one that will stretch the length of the east coast, from Lowestoft to Aldeburgh, the one that will keep us safe.

'Yes,' she says instead, 'but it's not as if you ever left them behind. Nature is there in everything you've done.'

'Art is the flower.' He takes her hand. 'Life is the green leaf.' And he raises her fingers to his lips.

Chapter 25

Mother sends me over to the Kipperdrome for fish. I walk down to the river, and find I don't have to queue for the ferry, for there are so many herring boats jammed up in the harbour I can step from one to the next until I reach the other side.

The Kipperdrome is new. Newer even than the lighthouse, and inside its octagonal walls the stalls are heaped with every kind of fish. Sole and bass and whiting, mackerel, dogfish, cod. I look around for Betty and her sister but they are out on the river, gutting, and the herring that are here, gleaming shoals of them, are being sold by other, older women who have paid their dues.

It is cool inside the Kipperdrome with light that filters sideways through small high windows in the roof. If I close my eyes and breathe in deep I can imagine I am underwater, the shuffle and murmur of women, with hats tipped forward on their heads, making the same shimmery sound as the current. I squeeze my way between them and wait while they open their purses and close them again, while the fishmongers in their white aprons hold their knives ready to strip away the scales and slice open the bellies of whatever they might choose. I buy three skate. That is what my mother wants. She has a way of roasting them in the stove so that the meat falls lightly off the great sharp bone tasting of fennel and woodsmoke, and when I have my package wrapped and folded, I wander back along the beach, counting the longshore fishing boats dragged up on to the sand. The bathing huts have been rolled in, the boys offering goat rides have deserted, and the strip of high shingle is crowded with men at work, children climbing in and out of skiffs, dogs sniffing for a scrap of food.

I'm wanted back. I know it. But instead I walk along the harbour, one eye out for Danky. There is talk that he's been night fishing, trudging home by moonlight to his house, and for certain I've not seen him any morning this last week.

'And here's your friend, walking forward, come to pay us a call.' It's the sharp laughing voice of Betty's sister Meg, and I feel myself redden and I squeeze my package of fish until the squelch of it reminds me what it is.

'This one here's done,' the tall girl calls as she lays a last fish in the barrel, and a cooper comes and rolls it away. I step forward. The sisters will surely stop and stretch, but they are paid by the barrel, and they must begin again.

'Yes,' I hold up my packet of fish, 'I came out for my mother.' And I see a smile curl over Betty's face, a girl already three days' journey from her home, and no older than me.

'I'd best be getting back then.' My face is blazing, and to save myself I pick up a pebble and skim it out across the river. Its blunt edge chips the surface and it skips three times before it sinks.

'Bye then.' I can speak again, and with their eyes on me, I turn and hurry back the way I've come.

I've had Mac's pamphlet for so long I've almost forgotten it's not mine. I have my favourites now. The library in the School of Art with its soaring windows and its lamps. The Willow Tea Rooms, dark wood and bright white tablecloths, lit up by a cauldron of white flowers. It's on a street the name of which I can't pronounce. Sauchiehall. And I add that to my list.

I study Mrs Mac's work too. Her roses, which are Glasgow roses, wound about like balls of string. And her mysterious women, most of whom are clothed. But the picture that I look at till I have it off by heart is of a girl shrouded in a cloak so wide she could hide herself inside it. *The Mysterious Garden*, it is called. And along the top, as if they were trees, are the white faces of women. Are they ghosts? Or is the girl inside the cloak a ghost? And I have to turn over the page to keep from shuddering. But here, waiting, on the next page, are the tortured women Frances Macdonald paints. Naked or not, I fear them. Although the heat in my body rises if I look too long, and I calm myself by staring at *The Sleeping Princess*, a girl as beautiful as anything I've seen. As beautiful as Betty. She is lying in a silver frame, meshed around with spiderwebs and leaves, and moulded into it are the words, *Love, if thy tresses be so dark, how dark those hidden eyes must be*. I trace my fingers down the length of her hair, hanging far below her waist, and for all Frances Macdonald's insistence that she is sleeping, it's hard not to think she's dead.

I wait till both Mac and Mrs Mac are in their studio, checking on them downriver of the ferry where I can't be seen, and then, taking the muddy track that appears only at low tide, I cut past the Japanese bridge, until I'm in their lane. I don't waste time unlatching the Lea House gate, but climb over it, and scattering the rabbits with the thump of my landing, I streak up through the garden.

It's peaceful here in their house. I stand and breathe. There is a jug on the table filled with rosehip, and on the mantel are brambles thick with berries. The pile of books is still there, stacked and orderly, the spines lined up against the table's edge. They are the same books as before but in a different order and I slide my pamphlet in amongst them. I feel myself lighten, my conscience clear. I can go. But as I turn away I catch sight of an oblong purple box at the far end of the mantelpiece. There is a card tucked behind it and as I approach I get a whiff of that same sweet smell of liquor that seeped through the paper of the parcel I delivered.

Dear Herr Rennie Mackintosh, the card says. *Here is a small gift for you and your wife. I hope it gives you some pleasure in these difficult times. And that you do not see it as a bribe. As you know I await eagerly news of more flower drawings so that I may collect them together for a book. There are twelve you have been kind enough to show me, including those you did on Holy Island, but if I am to publish I will need considerably more as each one adds to and reflects the beauty of the others.*

Do let me know how you are getting on. And never imagine that our warring countries have altered my deep affection for you both.

In hope of better times.
With kind regards,
Your friend, Hermann Muthesius

Hermann Muthesius. I struggle over the name, trying to find the Gaelic in it, imagining it in one of Betty's songs. But I am stopped by the double Herr of Hermann and Herr Mackintosh, for I'm sure that it means Mr in German. 'Herr Mackintosh'. I shouldn't say it. And I lift the top of the oblong box and find, nestled there, six round chocolates resting in the paper.

They can't like them very much. Or maybe they like them so much they are saving them for best, and I count the four dented empty nests and imagine Mac and his wife limiting themselves to one each week. I slide my fingers into the box and draw one out. It sloshes hollowly, and the smell of the dark chocolate fills my nose, but when I put it into my mouth the taste of cherry brandy explodes there. I freeze, blowing my cheeks out like a bloater to avoid the risk of swallowing, and step as carefully as I can to the window where I force open the catch and spit it out. A dribble of chocolate runs down the wall and I spit again, leaking the syrupy mess over the sill. But all the time I'm coughing and gagging I know that I'll have to take another of the evil chocolates or they'll guess someone was here. If there are four, they might forget from one long week to the next how many they have eaten. But if there are five . . . And so with my nose pinched up I take its twin, and looking round to check nothing else is disturbed I slip out of the house, waiting until I'm in the marshes before I hurl the black bomb with its liquid centre far out into the grasses where a bittern might come across it and, cracking it open with her beak, feed it to her young.

Chapter 26

Our soldiers are being sent to France. Father slaps them on the back and stands them a drink, taking one himself, seeing as they're nearly gone. 'William,' Mother frowns across at him. But he ignores her.

I take out my copying. There are no boats in the margins now, not since I have my own sketchbook, and almost no crossing out and blots. Runnicles is pleased with me. He doesn't say so. But he's happy that I've stopped wasting my time with drawing and dreams of sailing off to sea, and I'm careful to keep the paper Mac gave me stored away out of sight.

'Thomas,' I don't realise at first it's my own name that's being called. 'Thomas!' Father's pint slams down on my table, sending a long pale splash of beer across my words. 'Tell these gentlemen about your friend old Mac. They've seen him in the village. Been wondering about him. Say he's out all hours.' There is a raised ridge of paper where the ale has settled and the ink I've used is bleeding from the words. 'Snooping around with those spyglasses of his.'

'Mr Charles Rennie Mackintosh', my heart is beating, 'is an architect from Glasgow. He built a school there.' I don't tell them it's a school of art. Because I'm not sure what that is. 'And a church. And he's made furniture too. Chairs taller than a man, and clocks like merry-go-rounds with the numbers upside down. And now he's here. Painting. He's taken over Thorogood's shed, down by the river. And he's made it into a studio.'

Father is staring at me. The soldiers too. And Gory, who is propped up in a corner, rolls his eyes. I drop my head and frown at the underwater writing like an inlet on my page.

'He uses the binoculars to examine things more clearly. Colours . . . and shapes . . .' I'm making this up now, 'so he'll know where the green of a leaf might change from one shade to the next.'

Father slurps his beer. 'We've had all sorts in here,' he turns to the men. 'Before the war. Artists and poets. A playwright even. All gone back to London now.'

'All gone,' Gory echoes him. 'Except old Mac.' And one of the soldiers spits, right there on the floor. He's a broad man with a meaty face. I don't like him. Or the other one either. 'Going about with his spyglass. A wonder no one's reported him.'

Mother says nothing and nor do I. Instead I run over the words I've used to check I've not betrayed him. *Hertz, Dekorative, Wiener, Rundschau.* No, I've not let any of these out. Nor have I told them about the requests from Hermann Muthesius to hurry up and send him more of our village's flowers.

'Ahh well,' the soldiers bend in to their beer. 'Probably harmless enough, although where there's smoke there's often as not fire,' and in the lull I rip out my page, and with my arm around the paper for protection I begin copying out my copying again.

I'm glad the next morning when the soldiers set off for their boat, their long cloth bags heaved across their shoulders like sorry-looking sows. When our first soldiers left we were down on the shore waving them off, and our second too, but today as we stand in the doorway of the Blue Anchor Mother says we can't spend our life on goodbyes. We'll have new men billeted with us by the end of the week and what will we do two weeks later when they leave?

Father catches hold of me as they walk away. 'You've been warned then?' He frowns down at my foot. I nod, although I don't know what he means. 'No more roaming about with your old Mac. You hear me?' And he thumps me hard on the shoulder, just because he can.

I was planning to do it anyway, but now I'm more determined than before. I take my paintbox, and after school I scoot along the river, ducking from one shed to the next till I come out by Thorogood's. There's no wind today, not even a breeze, and the sky lies crisp and blue above the boats. 'Hello,' Mrs Mac looks up, and I take a crate and sit myself in the shadow of their hut. I ease the lid off my squares of paint, the colours dancing, and I stare down at them, my brush hovering, too afraid of turning any one of them to sludge.

'What will you paint?' Mac swivels round, and when I hesitate, he shows me how to soak the board in a basin if the colours need a wash. 'You can even clean your paints,' he eyes me, guessing. 'Just take a cloth and wipe off the top layer.' And, relieved, I tell him that I'm going to make a picture of HMS *Formidable*, Jimmy Kerridge's boat.

'Has that not sailed?' Mrs Mac looks up. 'You'll not choose something you can actually see?' And I smile, because I can see it – Jimmy and his friends waving from the deck. I can see the hats they wore and the scarves around their necks, and the wide grins they had as their ship headed away, just as if I had been there myself. I wet my brush and dip it into blue, and once I've made the first line, it's easier to make another, so that soon my page is streaked across with colour.

There's a thick, warm silence as we work. I've sensed that silence, when I used to watch them, but now that I'm inside it, it's as solid as a coat. If it was flax you could twist it into rope, and I glance at Mac, growing the centre of an aster as if he's God himself and just created it, the way he sits so still and fierce in his dark suit. He is nothing like any of the artists that I've seen, certainly not like the Miss Bishops, who wore cotton smocks when they went out, and came home – at least the younger of the two – with paint in their eyebrows and their hair. But if Mac is neat then Mrs Mac is tidier still, standing, so sure and precise that not a drop of colour falls on to her clothes, not even on to the pale gloves she wears to protect her hands from the sharp sting of the turps. I imagine her painting on the white carpet of her Glasgow home, the white curtains hanging at the window, a glow of embers smouldering in the bed of the fire.

HMS *Formidable* has twenty-one sails. At least I imagine she must if she's to carry seven hundred and fifty men, and supplies for them all, and ammunition. I give her three masts, and a multitude of rigging, so that soon my page is one big shimmery mess of canvas, halyards and flags. There are portholes, cannons, lifeboats, oars. I take the paper to the tin basin and I wash it clean. Colours dribble off the page, but my boat remains there in a mist, and rather than ask for Mac's old toothbrush to scrub it off entirely, I take out the pencil I've brought and sketch in its shadowy shape.

When I next look up, the afternoon is gone. The sun, streaming downriver from the west, has turned the water turquoise and the sky is glittering with its last bright light. I stand up and squint behind me at the village. The inn will be about to open its doors, Mother may even now be standing on the street, waiting to give me a sharp word. And Father will be storming. Quickly I wash out my brush and taking the handkerchief from my pocket I wipe my hands, my arms, even my legs below the knee. 'There's a mark on your face,' Mrs Mac tells me, putting down her own tools, and when I clean it off, she laughs and points at my nose. 'Let me,' she shakes her head, and dipping the corner of the handkerchief in water she dabs at the smudge.

'Goodbye,' I say as I back away, but Mac is still working on his flower, his eyes boring into the paper, and he only grunts as I turn around and run.

Chapter 27

I'm up early to check the beach. The tide is in, and there are hoofmarks from the soldiers cantering across it at first light. But there's nothing sinister. Not that I can see. And so I head back into the village to do an hour with Allard before school. As I round the corner I see the herring girls hurrying to catch the first ferry, their shawls around them, their boots sparkling with dew. There is Betty, and Meg, and the two girls from the blacksmith's, and on the corner, Mrs Lusher's three, waving to them with high arms.

Allard is already muttering when I arrive: 'For all the nonsense they teach you at that school of yours, you could be here with me all day, learning a trade, it's high time you did something useful.' And I let him grumble because, after a year turning that wheel, there's nothing he can say that I've not heard before.

'If you let me twist the rope again?' I offer, but it's only jesting, because we both know I'd never risk missing even five minutes of school. Mother would hear of it, the news would reach her like a dart, and there isn't a single person in the village who wouldn't fear for my hide when she found out.

But even so, as I sit turning my wheel, I watch Allard closely, the way he measures out the twine, chooses the thickness, binds it smooth and slippery and strong. 'If only you had a brother,' he muses. And I hang my head, and wonder that he hasn't noticed there are other boys in the village. And some of them with brothers, as many as three. 'The other boys,' he shakes his head, as if he's heard me, 'they're not cut out for this work. They're rough and fidgety, with no patience for listening. It's a dying art, the rope-making, and one reason that it's dying is that those that have the patience for it are dying out themselves.'

I keep turning. It's not true that I have more patience than the next. But I've seen the look on Mother's face when I hand my money over, and one day I hope to surprise her, when she sees how much I've managed to keep back.

The Sailor's Reading Room is empty, although behind the partition door that leads into the snug, I can hear the low murmur of fishermen, their day's work done. Outside is bright and squally, the front door shivering when the wind whips in from the sea, but no one lifts the latch to enter, and for the most part the wooden room is quiet and still. I search the glassed-in cabinets for a ship which I can draw. It seems I do need to look at the *Formidable* after all, but without it, or any chance of seeing it, I settle on the *Wrestler* – a three-masted frigate, made over the winter of 1897 by the fisherman Sloper Hurr. It sits in a glass cabinet, its sails set into the wind, its bow curved to support the figurehead, made in miniature, a woman, her neck banded by a necklace of black beads. I kneel down beside the cabinet and take out my notebook, my eyes on the details of the ship – the keel, the stern, the square rig sail, while my fingers do the work.

It is a little like the copying I do at Runnicles', writing up the progress of the war, Battle of Tannenberg, Battle of Heligoland Bight, Siege of Tsingtao, without ever taking my eyes from the board. But today I count the lifeboats strung along the gunwale, the portholes below, the stays, shrouds and backstays of the rigging.

'Hello, old boy, what you doing here?' It is Danky, standing in the doorway to the snug.

I struggle to my feet, forcing my notebook into a pocket, sliding my pencil up a sleeve. 'Nothing much,' I tell him, 'just keeping out of the weather.' And as Danky pulls on his jacket, I give a last quick look at the *Wrestler* as I follow him out through the door.

The wind hits us hard as we step on to the path. 'Where you off to then?' he asks me, tugging his cap down over his eyes.

'Home, I suppose.' I look at him. 'You coming back that way?'

Danky winks. 'I'll stop this side of the river,' he tells me. 'Drop by the Lord Sandwich and wait for dark.'

I look around. There are soldiers in their uniforms walking in groups along the promenade, and the old rugby pitch is lined with tents in the same mulched colour as their clothes. A family of Belgians sit on a bench beside the cannons on Gun Hill, looking as foreign now as they did when they first came, staring back across the sea towards their home.

'Right,' I say, although I want to remind him night fishing has been banned, not that he doesn't know it. Not that he wants to hear about it from me. So I say nothing, walk with him past the town square where Mother and I came to read the rules of Dora, and I glance towards the place where amendments to the act are sometimes pinned, but today there's nothing new.

Danky trudges on beside me. 'Best not mention seeing me to Father,' I say. 'In the Reading Room and all. You know how he is about the sea.'

Danky touches his nose. 'We'll both keep to our own business.' And nodding in agreement, I turn and run, the wind behind me, to where the last ferry will soon be cranked home on its chains.

I don't see her at first. But Betty is standing tucked in beside Mrs Penny at the front of the ferry. She has her shawl wrapped right up over her head, but I know her by the narrowness of her shoulders. I edge past the other folk squeezed on board, and make my way towards her. 'Good evening to you, Tom,' Mrs Penny smiles across at me, and with the greeting Betty lifts her head.

'Hello,' I say before I lose my nerve.

'Hello,' she says back, and for once she isn't laughing.

'Where's your sister?' I ask. And a tear starts into her eye and, swelling, rolls fatly down her cheek.

'She's not well.' The girl bunches up her mouth. 'She caught her hand with the cutag – the gutting knife. Not so bad. But now it's swollen, and she has a fever. And Mrs Horrod's bound it up with cobwebs and given her a brew of herbs but she's not sure what more there is to be done.'

'Surely . . .' I start, and my head spins with offers of advice. An antiseptic from Mrs Lusher's shop. Or if anyone can find her, the old witch-woman that walked in from the country with her second sight. Surely she'd have herbs, or spells even, stronger than anything Mrs Horrod can provide. But all I say is that I hope she'll soon be well.

'Yes,' Betty gulps. 'Maybe she'll be a wee bit better tonight,' and she wipes away another tear.

We walk together up Fishers Lane, Betty trotting along so fast I have to take an extra, hopping step to keep up with her. She slows when we reach the Blue Anchor but I keep on, past Millside, where I don't waste a minute looking up at the high windows, and on to Mrs Horrod's. I wait there while Betty knocks and inches open the door, and I feel I'll know just from the sight of Mrs Horrod's face when she answers, how things stand with Meg.

'Away with you now, Tommy,' she says when she sees me. And I am right. Meg is no better, but neither is she worse.

The next morning I forgo my inspection of the beach, and watch for Betty. I'm rewarded by the sight of her hurrying towards the ferry, her shawl around her head. I am about to call to her, when Mother asks if I've let out the hens, and why I haven't drawn the water from the well.

I turn away, cursing the unfairness of my tasks while Father snores upstairs, and Ann sits writing yet another letter to Jimmy Kerridge to follow the others that have gone un-answered. But before I can say more I hear our new soldiers rattling on the ladder and I slam out into the morning and clank the bucket down into the well. I listen to the drop of it, the noise of the air rushing by, and the hard flat thud as it hits water. The bucket sits there for a second and then slowly, heavily, it begins to sink until with a last gulp it slips under.

Mother smiles at me as I slosh into the kitchen, and with-out a word I'm out to release the hens. 'Morning,' I say, as I slide open their hutch and I watch them shake their feathers, as one by one they step on to the slatted ramp. When they're out I duck into the dark stink of the shed. Usually they lay a little later in the day, but some may begin early, and I like to be the first to close my palm over the smooth, hot, newborn shells. Today there are three. I roll them into my shirt and bring them in to Mother who sets them straight into a pan of water on the stove.

'You'd best be off then,' she tells me. I've had my porridge, and a slice of bread – the eggs are for the soldiers

– and she moves towards me, her arms out for a squeeze. 'I'm going,' I tell her, and I slip away from her fingers, and I'm halfway down the street before I remember to tuck away my smile.

Chapter 28

As soon as I sit down at the wheel George Allard begins fretting. 'They want to bury the cannons on Gun Hill. They think we'll be safer with them out of sight. When what's the point of having them all these years if now that we finally need them, they'll be out of use?'

'Bury them? How?' I imagine a row of men, heaving sand up from the beach to turn them into castles.

But Allard isn't listening. 'Those six guns were presented to the town by Butcher Cumberland in 1746, given to the people of this region for helping him win the Battle of Culloden in which so many Highland folk were slaughtered.'

'Really?' I lift my head. And I imagine Meg and Betty, and possibly Mac too, their faces smeared with dirt, fighting for their lives.

'At least that's how people think they got here.' Allard smiles, as if he has fooled a whole gathering and not just me. 'Although there are some who date the guns from the time of James the Second, because they bear the Tudor emblem of the Rose and Crown. But this is not true either.' I begin to drift away, wondering how Meg is faring, how Betty is managing her quota of herring alone. Whether they have found another girl to help her fill the barrels or whether the tall squint-eyed packer is helping with the load.

'The real story', Allard pulls me back, 'is that the guns were cast in 1705 and given to the town to protect it from the Common Enemy. And Southwold has always needed protecting. In 1299,' he mentions the date as if it was only last year, 'the Earl of Gloucester's fleet was attacked and sunk whilst moored there, and in 1624 pirates seized the Blyth ferry boat and left it stranded at Margate.'

'Margate!' I want to laugh at the thought of the chain ferry clanking all that way south, and then I remember the ferry used to be a simple rowing boat, with one man at the oars, and if you wanted to take a cart and horses across the river, you'd have to drive six miles round by road.

'Two years later,' Allard is deep in history now, 'a French privateer captured a ship off this coast and fired its own guns back into the town. Destroyed two buildings on the front, killed a baby when the ceiling of its house fell in. But that could not happen now. Not with our cannons, eighteen-pounder muzzle-loading culverins. Although, it's true, they've not been fired for over seventy years, last used to mark the birthday of the Prince of Wales.' He starts walking backwards, as if finally remembering why we are there, and to keep to his pace, I begin slowly turning the wheel. 'But the story of that day is too sad to tell.' And it takes the rest of the morning to get it out of him. How a volunteer coastguard in charge of the first gun looked into the muzzle to see why it wouldn't fire, when at that moment it went off. He had a wife and three children and all efforts to obtain a pension for them failed. Allard frowns, remembering those children who might have been saved, the mother who was forced in to the workhouse, and I look away from him as I turn, watch the rope instead, twisting fine and strong between his fingers.

*   *   *

I wait for Betty to get off the ferry, and I walk with her up to the house. She doesn't speak and neither do I. But she seems to accept my hurrying along beside her. This time Mrs Horrod's face when she comes to the door is full of worry, and Betty puts a hand to her mouth and rushes away towards the stairs. 'Poor little thing,' Mrs Horrod says, 'she's very bad.' And she scuttles away too.

I stand at the open door with no one to tell me what to do. After a minute I step in and pull it to behind me. Mr Horrod is there, sitting in his chair. Too tired from a day's labouring to move once he gets home. I nod towards him but he doesn't seem to see me, so I stand and listen to the noises above, footsteps shuffling, voices low. Mrs Horrod appears again and goes to the kitchen where she calls for me, and I'm so glad to be of help I almost trip over in my hurry to assist her. 'Bring that up, would you,' she says, 'careful.' And promising myself I won't spill a drop I carry a bowl of water up the twisting staircase while Mrs Horrod follows with a poultice of herbs.

Vic's old room is narrow, with an iron bedstead pushed into the corner. The paper Mrs Horrod pasted up over the walls is peeling at the edges. I don't see handprints on it, but there is a dark and oily smell, herring mixed in with the scent of fever, hot and high. I flash a quick look over to the bed and there's Meg, her hair uncovered, her face waxy under a sheen of sweat, one hand red and misshapen, a cut in it, like a mouth, weeping yellow at the edges. She raises herself up, as if in search of something, and Betty takes a cloth and dips it in the water. 'Shh,' she whispers to her and she presses it against her forehead as she mumbles words to her in their own thick speech. I look away. I shouldn't be here. And when Mrs Horrod sets the dish down on the table and moves to the door I follow her, and in silence we tread slowly down the stairs.

'Tell your mother', she says as I reach the door, 'I'll call for her if she gets worse.'

'I will,' I say, thankful that she's not already worse, and I run back down the street.

Chapter 29

Runnicles has written a new list of battles on the board. Battle of Masurian Lakes. Battle of Bita Paka. Battle of the Aisne. Battle of Albert. We copy them down. 'I was wondering . . .' Ned Walpole from Flixton puts up his hand, 'how long it will take before we win?' And Runnicles looks at him in silence until we all begin to squirm. 'That is a good question,' he says eventually. And no one asks another.

I don't go to Thorogood's shed after school, but wait at home in case Mrs Horrod calls for Mother. But Mother stays where she is, kneading dough for three large loaves, and setting me chores each time she catches sight of me. Before the day is done I've swept out the fire, spliced a stack of wood and trimmed the hairy ropes of beard from a muddy bowl of beetroot. At dusk I creep up the street and stand outside the Horrods' house, straining for a sign of life from Vic's old bedroom window, but all is quiet and still, and I wander home again.

It's Sunday before I gather any information, for I'll not ask Mother for a crumb of news and risk my blood betraying me. Instead I roam out over the marshes, gathering leaves and flowers for Mac who has abandoned his aster and moved on to a stem of winter stock. I find a clump of clover, their tips tinged purple, and rather than pick one and watch it wilt to nothing in my palm, I lie down, sheltered by a wall of gorse, and taking out my notebook and my pencil I try and make a likeness of it. But simple as it looks, it seems I've chosen something impossible. There are a thousand little stems all making up this one smooth hood of colour and each one needs to be drawn in for it to look like itself. I'm slicing splinters off a pencil when I feel footsteps treading towards me over the grass. I look up and there's Betty herself, as if I've dreamed her, eyes streaming, walking blindly into the sun. I lie still. I don't want her to catch me watching. But just as she is about to pass, she stops, and covering her face with her hands she bends forward in a silent curl of pain. I don't speak. There's a chance she'll straighten up, and continue on, but after a minute her voice seeps through the slats of her fingers. 'They've taken her away,' and a sob bigger than herself rips open her chest. I carry on sketching, wishing all the time I could put out my hand. But instead I count the tiny greeny stems, and before I've even planned it, I'm putting each one in. I'm still drawing when Betty unfolds herself and sits beside me and I feel in my pocket for a handkerchief that I know I won't find there. 'Sorry,' I say. And I catch her red-rimmed eye.

'It's all right.' She has her own handkerchief, already sodden, and she blows her nose and scrunches it up and balls it into her fist. 'I wanted to go with her but they said no.' And a stutter of small sobs tilts her forward again. I scratch away, and I'm surprised to find that now I've stopped thinking so much about the clover it seems to be forming itself.

'Could you draw a likeness of me, do you think?' she asks then, with a sniff, and I'm tempted to flip over my pages and show her the picture I've already made – herself smiling, the pale hair escaping from her scarf. 'Maybe,' I say. And with this new permission I look straight at her. For a moment she holds my gaze. Her eyes, so flat and fearless. The freckles standing out against the paleness of her face.

'So,' she gets up and shakes out her skirt, 'I'll meet you here next Sunday,' and I watch her as she sets off along the path, walking fast, her shawl pulled tight around her.

On Sunday I wake early and slip out before church. I have my notebook, a pencil, my penknife and two hard-boiled eggs I set on the stove myself. I take a pinch of salt and twist it into paper, and packing everything into my pockets I'm out through the back gate.

There's been a grass frost in the night, and the blades snap stiff under my boots, but the sky is clear, and soon the sun begins to melt it back to green. I'd like to start straight away. But I can't start or she'll know that I've been watching her, and so instead I stand before the wall of gorse, and imagining that I'm Charles Rennie Mackintosh himself, I attempt to make a copy of the bright soft flowers that sit among the thorns.

When I look up the sun has risen above the sea, and if the bells were allowed to peal, they'd have been ringing out over the land for half an hour to call us into church. I pack up my things and run, pelting along the grassy lanes, crunching over acorns, snapping and popping, as I take a short-cut through the Hoist. The church is silent. The village packed away inside, and they must all be kneeling, bent forward in prayer, because as I tread along the path I'm sure that I can hear the rhythm of their breath. I stand by the oak door, listening, and when I hear the bustle of people standing, and the low voice of the vicar starting up, I creak it open and slide along the aisle.

Lunch that day is solemn. Father brings a bottle of whisky to the table and with every mouthful that we eat he takes a slug. My sisters turn on me, Mother too, hard-eyed as if to say: Now look what you've done. And they are right. It doesn't need much these days to tip Father into fury. We wait. My throat is tight, and by the time he slams his fist down on the table I'm ready to be hit. 'Sir Bly,' he says, surprising us. 'That scoundrel has turned down my application.' And steaming fit to bust he tells us his plans to build a smokehouse and sell smoked fish from a shack beside the inn. But first the shack must be built, and Sir Bly will not allow it, and in the terms of the lease of the Blue Anchor it is Sir Bly who has the final say. 'No new structures can be built.' This is his final word. And I remember Mac's face when he told us the same thing. *Now there are to be no new buildings.* But unlike Mr Mackintosh, Father cannot accept it. He is convinced this rule has been invented just to spite him, and not by the government at all, and as he takes another slug of whisky he reminds us of the rottenness of his luck, the torment of his life at sea, the knife-grinding business that refused to pay, until as always he comes to the glory of pork butchering and the empire it might have been. Mother, Mary, Ann and I keep silent. No one mentions the rent that is due. Or asks where the money would come from for bricks. No one mentions it or dares to even think it. In our silence we are careful to agree with him, for we've learnt that even through the fog of liquor his instinct for offence is sharp. Yes, I say inside my head, you're right, you *are* right, so that he might know, even though I wasn't born then, how convinced I am his enterprise at Dunwich would have flourished if he'd been given the chance.

I wait till he has fallen asleep, his head on the table, before I sidle out. This time I walk more slowly, the eggs cold in my pocket, the salt come loose. I sit in the hollow of grass and practise whistling through a fat green blade. It tickles my mouth and makes me shudder, but soon I am calling, low and loud, out across the sedge towards the sea. If I was a smuggler, in days gone by, I'd have used this whistle as my code. And I think of Betty at her outside sermons, standing on the common above Gun Hill, and I wonder what the parson says to them as his voice booms out in a foreign tongue.

'I'm here,' Betty startles me, 'no need to whistle for me like a dog,' and I spring up, the blade falling from my lips, and not able to think what else to do, I reach into my pocket for a boiled egg.

'Thank you,' she smiles. She unwinds her shawl and lays it on the ground. 'Here?' she asks, settling herself, and she tilts her chin towards me.

I take out my sketchbook, feeling the blood creep up over my face, and to gain time I flip open my penknife and slice a papery slither from the pencil. Now the other side must be evened up, and I sharpen it so thoroughly and for so long that when I press the point against the paper it snaps.

Betty doesn't move. She neither smiles nor frowns, but looks past me, her face so pale I can see blue veins below the skin. I open the pages of my notebook and look at the gorse sketch I made that morning, hoping to take courage from its splintery likeness, but all I see is a scrawl of scratches surrounding a dark shape that may or may not be a flower.

Turning away, I leaf back to the earlier picture of Betty and there at least is the shadow of her face. *Look, Toshie, the boy has made a drawing of something other than a boat.* Mrs Mackintosh's warm words come back to me. And glancing at her one more time, I force myself to begin.

Chapter 30

The news is all over the village when I wake. Danky's been shot. It must have come over from the fishermen at the Bell, for by the time I've clattered down the ladder Mother knows it, and Ann too. He was on the beach at Southwold, night fishing, when the constable took him for a spy. A bullet caught him in the leg, and another whistled past his ear, before he had a chance to put his arms up and shout his name into the dark.

'I want to see him,' I say. But Mother won't hear of any such thing. 'You'll go to school,' she says, 'and then, if there's no work for Mr Allard, you can go on up to the common and take him some fresh bread.'

There is work for Mr Allard but I stop by and tell him I'm not well, coughing for good measure, and looking at the ground. Allard backs away. 'You'll be the death of me,' he says, and he lets me go, but not before he's told me in full detail how the fools in charge of the cannons on Gun Hill are digging round each one in the hope they'll fall away into the ground. 'How will they ever get them out again?' he says. And he's still muttering when I hurry away.

There are two houses on the common, small stone cottages, their backs to the estuary. Danky's is closest to the water and

I approach, fearful of his sister's sharp tongue, as I knock on the door. There is no answer. So I turn the handle and look in. At first, all I see is a bundle of covers on a box-bed beside the stove. And then on the other side, his leg up on a chair, Danky himself, his eyes closed, his big old face naked without its cap. 'There you are,' he turns his eyes to me. 'Get me a smoke, will you. The old girl's gone out and left me. And to care for Mother too.' He nods in the direction of the blankets where I see, now that I'm actually looking, the yellowed curls of his mother's ancient head. The cheeks are sunken, the mouth is all bunched in, and if it wasn't for a gentle wheezing, I'd swear the woman was already dead.

Danky's pipe is on the table, out of reach, and I take it to him and his pouch of tobacco too. When he's packed it full, grunting and sighing with the strain, I light a splinter of wood from the fire and hold it until my fingers burn. 'That's better,' he says, and he sucks, spits and sucks again, releasing a billow of smoke into the room.

'So?' I sit down on a stool beside him.

'Not even a cup of tea?' He looks at me. 'How hurt does a man have to be to earn himself a bit of tender caring?' And I spring up while he laughs, and I put the kettle on to boil. I set the bread on a board too, bring it for his inspection, but he only waves it away and points instead to a bottle on a shelf. 'Doctor's orders. Even Lizzie can't argue with that.' And I look round fearfully in case his sister may have stepped, disapproving, through the door.

When Danky has his tea, topped full with whisky, I sit down again beside him. I want to hear the story of how he came to be shot. I've earned it, surely, even if he hasn't tasted the bread. I wait while he slurps at his tea and sucks happily at his pipe, and I glance at his leg which is bandaged round and wonder if the bullet is still in there or if it passed right through.

'Danky,' I try when his eyelids begin to droop, 'was it very bad when the bullet caught you?' But Danky only raises his hand and nods towards the old lady laying on her bed as if any talk of what had happened might disturb her.

I wait, unsure how to go on. Surely Danky can't still be frightened of his mam, and I imagine the beating I'd get from my own if I'd been caught down on the beach at night.

'Silly bugger thought I was a spy,' he mutters, and he chuckles round the stem of his pipe.

'But . . .' my voice is a whisper, 'does that mean there were other, actual spies, out there that night?'

Danky frowns and the corners of his mouth turn down. 'Bloody fool of a constable,' he mutters and soon his eyes are closing, his teacup, almost empty, hanging from his hand.

I take the cup and put it on the side, and stand above him unsure whether to loose the pipe from between his teeth or not – what if it falls and sets the room alight? – and I move a little closer to the old woman to see if for all her frailty she might stamp out a fire should it arise. She's rumoured to be the oldest person in the village. And I see now as I stare into her face that she is indeed more ancient than Mrs Lusher's mother who sits cheerfully outside the shop in summer wrapped up in a rug. Mrs Danky is pale as milk, there are grooves across her forehead in three swooping lines, and the soft skin of her chin is wild with wispy strands of hair. One gnarled hand protrudes from the covers, shiny and thin, but it is her scalp visible through the curls that frightens me the most – where is her cap, surely she should not lie here uncovered? – and as I frown down on her she snaps open her eyes. 'What is it, boy?' she says.

Across the room Danky starts as if it is he who's been addressed. 'Nothing,' I stumble. Her eyes are blue and unexpectedly bright and she looks at me so fiercely I take a step away. I glance at Danky but he has slumped back into his chair. And so bidding the old lady goodbye and whispering to no one in particular that I'll come again should I be needed, I slip out through the door.

The common is wide open and free. Bell heather bursts purple on its borders and clumps of trailing yellow flowers cling to the ground. I race to safety, spinning over the hard short grass, scattered with the droppings of muntjac and rabbit, glinting black to show where they have most recently been. I follow the maze of paths that lead to the river, and scramble along the shoreline until I reach the bridge. There is nothing coming so I skip across the track, stopping in the middle, listening to the silence of the rails, feeling my heart race, until I can frighten myself no more. Slowly I walk along beside the river, peering over to the Southwold shore and the beginnings of the harbour, listening for the singing of the herring girls as they pack their barrels. Germany was where the fish used to be shipped out to, but there's no fisherman who'd want to be feeding the enemy now, and no German who'd trust a herring caught swimming in water that is ours. Our fish will be sent out to the troops instead and I imagine the men in their smart uniforms, forking the pickled fish out of the barrels.

I count the sheds as I go by, the names of the fishermen scrawled above the door: Palmer, Upcraft, Watson, Hurr. And I think of Thorogood, bragging that he, of all of them, is still bringing money in from rent. It is Mrs Mac, apparently, that has the funds. There's nothing that gets by in a village this size. And Mother had it from Mrs Horrod, who heard the same from Mrs Lusher, that old Mac's business went down in Glasgow, and that when he fell ill, and ill he was when he first came here, it was she, his wife, who buoyed him up with money of her own. I think of Mrs Margaret Macdonald Mackintosh, her fine clothes, her high head, the thickness of her hair, and I imagine the proud look on her face if I ever manage to complete the picture of HMS *Formidable*. It's her smile that I'm after, and I smile so wide at the hope of it that I almost walk on past their shed. But today it is only Mac who is there. He has his board on his knee, and he is back on the winter stock, a thick stem in a jar before him, leaning so intently towards it that I daren't disturb him. I peer past him through the door, hoping to catch the flame of Mrs Mac's red bun, but the shed is empty and the panel she's been working on is leaning against the wall beside my board. I lift it, and together with the crate box I consider my own, I bring them both outside. I place the half-finished painting on my knee and sit with it, staring out across the river as I have seen Mac do. Battle of Yser. Battle of Coronel. Battle of Tanga. I find myself repeating that morning's list, although Runnicles has not set us the task, and my eyes wide with the horror of it I see the *Formidable* sailing into a battle of its own. I can smell the fire-ships and feel the cannons that blast into her sides, hear the cries of the sailors as they jump into the waves. I look down at my painting. The flatness of my ship. Its lifeless sails, and the portholes like bubbles with nothing behind them but thick rough paper and a wash of grey.

'Are you not going to start?' Old Mac surprises me. I hadn't thought he'd noticed I was there. And so I slide out my paintbox, and filling a jar with water I squash my brush against the paper and mash the colours until the surface of the page is raw.

I might have gone on like that until the picture was all chewed over if the light didn't desert us, and I look up to find Mac rubbing his eyes, standing, stretching, packing away his things.

'Where's Mrs Mackintosh?' I ask him, surprised to find she has still not appeared, and Mac tells me she is gone to Glasgow. 'This week her sister needs her more than me.'

'That must be a great deal,' I say before I have a chance to check myself and I bow my head and mutter an excuse.

'No,' Mac sighs. 'You're right. It is quite true.'

Together we lock up the shed and walk down towards the ferry where I slow my pace to see who exactly is getting on and off. There are a troop of soldiers, and a horse and carriage, with several people sitting on its box seat, and some girls with shawls about their heads pressed in against the sides. I think I see a flash of bright blonde hair but Mac, with his pipe and stick, is striding off ahead of me. 'I'll be along in a minute,' I say, even though he hasn't asked me to accompany him, and I wait there for a glimpse of Betty while he heads away towards the dunes. But Betty isn't on the boat. It is Mrs Lusher's girls who scramble off, and the two from the blacksmith's, and so I wait for the next boat and the next, until it occurs to me she might already have gone home. Foolish, I walk down to the beach, and there, alone, his stacked boot in the waves, is Mac, the binoculars raised to his eyes. 'Mr Mackintosh,' I shout, my arms flailing as I run. And when I reach him I tap sharply on the sides of the black frames.

'Yes,' he looks at me. It seems he has travelled out to sea.

'There's nothing there,' I tell him as strongly as I can. 'You can put the spyglasses away.' And with my arm flung wide, I sweep the beach. 'You've no need of them.' I can't seem to find another way of saying it. 'There is nothing there to see.'

'Nothing?' he mutters. 'No danger, you think?' And together with our bare eyes we scan the horizon to check that it is true.

Chapter 31

The next Sunday Betty is on the marsh before me. I hear the whistling of a blade of reed grass, stuttery and squeaking, even before I round the corner to our hollow.

'You have to keep it straight,' I tell her, 'stretch it tight between your thumbs,' but as I bend to strip my own leaf from a cane, I catch my foot against a root and I am down. Blood courses through me as the ground comes up to slap me on the back.

'Here,' Betty has her hand out to me, but I'm too ashamed for help.

'Thomas?' she says, as if to check that I'm alive, and when I still don't rise, she lies herself beside me, and together we look up at the sky.

'How'd it happen?' she says.

'How'd what happen?' But all the same my heart is hammering in my chest.

'Your foot?' And the air around me freezes, for as long as I can remember no one's asked me to explain. 'Why's it twisted?'

The sky is very pale. The crash of the sea is running in my ears. And all I want to do is get up and race away.

'It's not twisted,' I tell her. 'That's how it's meant to be, that's how it's growed.'

'No need to be angry.' She's up on one elbow.

'I'm not angry.' And it's then I hear that I am shouting.

'There was a storm,' I tell her. 'Three fishermen from Dunwich lost their lives. And Father was out after a rabbit. When he came in . . .' I drift off, because she doesn't want to know how he came in with a bottle of whisky, empty, in his pocket, and how my mother said it was the bells she could hear, pealing from across the marsh, and how she cried and held me tight against her and would never have let me go if she hadn't had to crawl to the top of the ladder and lower herself down to open up the snug.

'I don't mind it,' Betty says. 'Not for myself.' And we lie like that watching the seagulls flapping lazily as they arc in from the shore.

I try my hardest with the picture, but it doesn't improve. Even when Betty sets her narrow shoulders and turns her face to me without a flicker of difference from the week before. I strengthen her mouth, and work on the sad, bare outline of her eyes, and when she doesn't look away, I force myself to keep looking, just the same.

And then rain flies in against us, slanting down from a cloud that isn't even overhead, and I slap my sketchbook shut and slide it in between my jacket and my shirt. 'It'll have passed by in ten minutes,' I say, but Betty stands. 'I can't afford to take a chill. Not with . . .'

Shivering she wraps her shawl about her shoulders, and bent forward into the weather she walks fast towards the lane.

I've already been to church that day, but once Betty's gone I traipse across the marsh towards its pebbled tower. The graveyard is empty. Even the starlings have deserted. I stop by the back gate and look in at my mother's offering, a late-flowering rag of rose, quivering in its pot. I step inside, and kneeling, I put my nose to it but there is no smell. William,

William, James, William, James, Thomas, I whisper, and I huddle beside them and imagine it is James who is my friend today, the second James, alive till the end of his first year. We're alike as streaks, that's what I'm sure of, up to no good, clattering stones on windowpanes, scrumping apples from the orchard, daring each other to rush across the yard at Dingle Farm before Buck comes out with his fist raised. When I'm with James my foot is straight. And I can run as fast as any of them. It's crooked only for the sake of those who've gone before, and we race, the two of us, hurtling to safety under cover of the Hoist, admired by everyone who's quick enough to see us go.

The next Sunday I have a griddle cake for Betty. 'Here,' I say, but before I can even reach for it she dips her hand into her own pocket. 'Look,' and she draws out a narrow slip of paper, smelling as it does of fish. It is a letter, her name written on the envelope in thick black ink. And without a thought I speak it out. 'Betty Maclellan.'

'Yes?' she looks at me, her eyes as clear as glass. 'That's me.' And flushing, I steady myself by staring down at the familiar name of Mrs Horrod's house.

'Open it then,' she's nodding, and so I slide the thin page from its envelope. But I cannot tell one word from another. Only the last, and it's the word she's pointing at as she stretches her arm over mine.

'Meg.' I swallow. And I feel the shadow of her sister's ghost wash cold across my skin.

'Yes,' Betty smiles. 'She said she'd write as soon as she was well.' And she takes the letter from me and begins to read: 'I am still not allowed to step out of the house, and Mother is feeding me up with mash and mutton. I've promised to eat anything at all, as long as it's nae herring.'

Betty laughs and her mouth opens like the bow of a boat. If I could draw her now, I think, and I sit down on the grass and flick through my book until I find her.

'Ready?' I wait while she arranges herself, and I see that I will have to start again for there's nothing of this new glad girl in what I've drawn. I take a last glance at her old sad face before I turn the page, and with the blaze of happiness coming off her I sketch fast with quick upward lines until I have her, until I have the inside of her at least.

'Let me see,' she says when I stop. But I snap shut my book. 'It's not done yet.' I imagine the colours in my paintbox, and the mixing I will have to do to get the creamy denseness of her hair and the flecks of sun against her cheeks. 'Will you come next week?' I ask.

'Next week?' she looks surprised. 'Next week we'll be away. The train leaves on Friday and by Monday I'll be in Stornaway waiting for the boat to take me home.'

Of course. The herring season has to end. I know that. All week the weather has been closing in. And if the girls stay away too long they'll have nothing to show for their hard work, with the lodgings they have to pay for and the meals they must buy, and I remember the scone I lifted from my mother's baking, wrapped in a cloth for her and already crumbling in my pocket.

'Thank you.' Betty stretches out her hand for it, and breathing in the singed smell of currants, she breaks it open and offers back a half.

'No,' I shake my head, although my stomach winces, and I sit and watch her as she eats, pulling off small pieces and dropping them, one by one, into her mouth.

'Will you have the picture done before I go?' she asks, still chewing, and I promise that I will. That I'll bring it round to her at Mrs Horrod's before the end of the week. I think of offering up the use of the handcart too, and myself with it, to bring her trunk down to the ferry, but I daren't risk the laughter of the village boys as I push along beside her.

'Or if it's not done,' Betty leans towards me, 'you can send it in a letter.' She eases the pencil from me and writes her address in a large looped hand on the last page of my book.

Chapter 32

Mac is restless with Mrs Mackintosh gone. It's been three weeks and still she's not returned. I sit beside him outside Thorogood's shed and work on my picture of the *Formidable*, and I say nothing when he leaves the second winter stock half done and starts in on a sprig of gorse. In the evening Mac comes regular to the Blue Anchor now. He orders a pint of ale, and before he has drunk it, he's off, and word is he's down the Bell chasing it with whisky. Father saves his beer, slowly going flat on a shelf above the fire, for often as not he's back within the hour, needing more whisky to stomach the taste of it gone sour. I watch him from the corner where I'm working at my copying, and I watch Father too, topping up his own beer, which is never watered down. But Father's drinking is companionable tonight. And Mac, by the third visit, is in the mood to talk. Mrs Mackintosh, he tells us, is being held captive by her family, forced to intervene in her sister's wretched marriage. Frances Macdonald is an artist too, married to a man once feted, now overlooked, much as he himself has been. The lot of them once worked together, Margaret, Frances, Mackintosh and the husband, Herbert MacNair. They exhibited together, and much was thought of the promise of The Four, as they were known. But not everybody liked them. The Spook School, some Glasgow critics called them, hobgoblins in the cupboard, and MacNair took himself off to Liverpool to the art school there, to work as a professor.

Spook School. I can see Frances Macdonald's naked women, their fingers on their lips, and I watch my father listening, and wonder what he'd think if he knew. 'A professor,' he smiles encouragingly, and he nods in my direction as if four years with Runnicles will set me on my way.

'But MacNair,' Mac sucks the last drops of whisky from his glass, 'Bertie MacNair, he had trouble with his drink, too exuberant it made him, and unpredictable, and there were some at Liverpool who did not appreciate his work. After a few years, and he was a married man by now, the art school let him go. So there was no work for him, and no studio to paint in, and a young boy – Sylvan – to support. They travelled back to Glasgow so that Frances at least could teach embroidery at the art school there, but his wife's family, *my* wife's family, the Macdonalds, unhappy with his behaviour, came up with a plan to send him off to Canada on a one-way ticket.'

'Canada?' Father looks hopeful, as if there might be someone prepared to give him a new start.

'But now,' Mac sighs, 'he has returned. With less than no money. And so my poor wife has been called away to see if she can smooth things out.'

Old Mac closes his eyes as if he's said more than he intended. And indeed there's a pause while we gulp down our surprise at hearing so much of his talk. But the truth is, Father too has much to say on the subject. And soon he is telling a story that I've not heard before. It is a story about a man called Wideawake, a preacher in these parts who'd had no formal training and never was ordained because, for the first half of his life, he'd been a villain and a drunk. He'd had a rough start, that was for sure, his mother died when he was young, and he'd grown up in the harsh care of his father, who'd cast him out to live with the farm workers who beat him and taunted him and drew him into their bestial ways. When eventually he came into his inheritance – his father falling, drunken, from his horse – he used every penny that might otherwise have gone to his young family at home on drinking and whoring until they were all but ruined. And then, his daughter, a little thing who'd failed to thrive, for all he'd deprived her of his notice, sickened and died. Hearing she'd called his name in the last hours of her life, he felt so wretched he hardly cared to be alive, and he rode into town where he spent all day in the inn, and then, for nothing but the pleasure of seeing someone hurt, he picked a fight with a farmer returning from market. But he'd not reckoned on the farmer's strength, and with the first punch he was knocked down. As he lay reeling, he thought how he might find someone to teach him how to box, and surprise the man on his next visit to town, but he was too sore to do it now, and so he climbed on to his horse. Before he'd got half home, his horse, a docile animal that knew its way, turned off the road and took him into a glade of trees. And it's here the miracle happened. He heard music like a thousand distant trumpets. And as the sound increased, there came a blessed feeling of release. That's how he explained it, this man, Wideawake, as he later came to be known, for the evil simply fell away, and he was changed.

I glance at Father. And I can't but wonder what he has planned.

'From that day he made it his life's work to help others find peace.' He looks thoughtful as if he's pondered this story long and hard. 'He had to let them know it was never too late. And from dawn to dusk he could be found wandering the rivers and the lanes, or standing at night on the beach below the cliffs at Dunwich by a guttering fire, or by the shelter he put up for the soldiers who patrolled there in defence against Napoleon's army. It was those soldiers who gave him his nickname, Wideawake, because that's what he was, always ready to raise up his small flag and let them know a sermon would commence.'

There is silence while Father and old Mac drain their drinks.

'MacNair's not a bad fellow.' Old Mac's voice is slurred. 'But how can a man prosper when all doors are closed to him? When the life he is born for is made impossible.'

I look towards Father. You see? I want to say. But he is blind to me.

'The life he is born for,' he repeats instead. 'What's that then? What were you born for, eh, Mr Mackintosh? Or have you done it, with your buildings?'

Mackintosh frowns and pushes away his glass. 'Me?' he says. 'I've hardly begun. Just watch me.' And unsteadily he gets up and walks out into the night.

Chapter 33

I've never sent a letter before, although we've practised writing them at school – the address at the top, and the date below, and the envelope pasted down with spit or glue. If you have wax, then you can stamp it shut with your own seal. Runnicles melted a stick of dark-red sealing wax right there in the classroom, turning the air bitter, letting the slippery melt of it drip across the fold. While the wax was still warm he took from his pocket a small brass stamp and pressed, and in an instant the wax had dried, and there in the centre was an encircled R. We all strained to see over our desks. 'Sir,' Ned Walpole called. And Runnicles, instead of reprimanding him, passed it along his row.

Ever since that day I've wanted to make a seal of my own. I'll have it in gold, T for Thomas, and that night when I take the candle to my room I gutter wax on to the window ledge and press my thumb against it, but it must be a different kind of wax because it squelches and then cracks.

Betty's picture is finished, and for all that I inspect it by daylight, and by firelight and even by the light of the candle as I carry it to my room, there's nothing more I can think of to do. I'd like to show it to Mrs Mackintosh, for the kindness that's in her, but there's only old Mac sitting on his crate, trembling a little, using up all his energy on keeping his hand still. 'Do you think it's good enough to send?' I want to ask him, but I'm fearful he'll advise me to scrub the whole thing out and start again. Instead I set to work making an envelope to encase it. I use brown paper and mark out the address and for a long time I sit there, looking at the picture, before I write a message on the back. *Hello Betty. Here you are.* And I sign it fast as if she is watching me, laughing, as my ears turn red.

I take a penny from under my mattress and I go to Mrs Lusher's for a stamp. I have to wait, for there's a crowd of women already in the shop and they're talking up a storm. It's Mrs Cady – that's what they're saying, gawn and caught a cold after having her last baby. Too afraid she was to have it in the village, too close to the coast, what if the enemy were to land while she was pushing it out? And so she drove over to Wissett, to her sister's, but she couldn't stay there long because there were nine other children, needing her at home. The first thing she did, Mrs Gooch was saying, when she got home, was she went upstairs and checked on all those children lying in their beds. 'Whatever would those poor children dew without a mother?' she said when she came down. And now, a month later, she's a corpse.

'Caught a cauld-like on the long drive back from Wissett,' Mrs Lusher sighs. And the others shake their heads and frown.

'The husband weren't no good to her either.' It's Mrs Horrod's voice. I can't see her but I know it's her. 'He were fond of other women, and she knowed it.'

'That's it,' Mrs Kett agrees. 'It took away her strength. Nothing left to fight the influenza. Left all them poor children. What'll they do now?'

It's hard to breathe in Mrs Lusher's shop, and it takes me time to fight my way to the front and look in at her through

the window of her wares. There's nothing she doesn't sell –
even now, even with the war – bread, bacon, paraffin, lard.
There are china ornaments, cures for the toothache, candles,
soap. But it seems today she has no stamps.

'Peppermints?' she offers. 'Owdacious strong they are.' But
I'm saving my money and I thank her and say no.

As I'm shouldering my way out, the peppermint, just the
thought of it, burning in my cheek, I meet old Mac, coming in
with a letter of his own. 'You'll have to come back Saturday,'
I tell him, 'if you want a stamp.' And he looks so stricken that
I show him my own letter, and offer to take them both to
Southwold where I might just catch the late post. Old Mac
hesitates. I wait, as do all the women in the shop, to see what
he will say. 'If you're sure?' he agrees. And reluctantly he
places the letter in my hand. *Mrs Margaret Macdonald
Mackintosh*, it says on the front. And with the penny that he
gives me I slide it into my jacket.

The sun is sinking fast over the woods, striping the clouds
that hang above the sea. 'Will there be time, do you think?'
Mac asks as we look up, and having given my word to do my
best, I race towards the ferry. There's a troop of soldiers waiting to get on, crowding the jetty, stretching up past the ferryman's shed. And try as I might, elbows pressed against my side
to sidle forward, there's not a chance of getting on before my
turn. I wait, my eyes fixed on the river, the ferry gliding across
from bank to bank, until each soldier has been delivered safely
to the other side. I'm at the front now, and I'm stepping on.
But just as we're ready to set off Sir Bly's youngest son thunders up on his horse, and the ferry must wait, as he dismounts.
But however he coaxes, the animal will not move. It keeps
shying and neighing, he must lead it away along the jetty and
turn it around, twice, until with a grand swish of its tail, it
accepts defeat. I've only half an hour now before the last boat

sails back, but even so as we pull out into the river, the water is so still and pink that I fall into a calm.

It will be quickest to run along the beach, I tell myself, and with the tide in I keep to the high ground and jump between the tufts of grass. But I've forgotten how fine the sand is on this side of the river, and every time I slip, it fills my shoes. With each bogged step, the shops are shutting up, and as I struggle on I remember why I never take this route. I stop when the lighthouse sends its first beam across the water, and I turn and squint back over the river and across the common to catch the time on our church clock. But everything is in shadow and the sun is just the slither of a yolk above the trees. I sit down on a high hillock of grass and take out my letter. Betty Maclellan. I imagine her face behind the brown paper, smiling out at me. Behind it is the other letter. Mrs Margaret Macdonald Mackintosh. And on the back the address from where it was sent: Lea House, Rabbit Row, The Green. And I'm laughing. Rabbit Row! He's made it up, I'm sure of it, for me, and I push the letters back into my pocket and turn towards the ferry. I'll come tomorrow, soon as I've finished school, and I can only imagine George Allard's fury when I don't arrive as I've promised, to turn the wheel.

That night as I lie in bed I watch my letters glowing on the window ledge. 'What do you have there?' Ann is beside me, brushing out her hair, and I tell her I've been entrusted with a job. To take Mac's letters over to the post. I don't tell her one of them is mine.

'What do they say?' she asks me.

I don't reply.

'Have you not looked inside?' She sits upright, her eyes gleaming. 'If I could see how a proper letter is written, then I'd know. I'd know what to say to Jimmy Kerridge. Then maybe he'd write back.'

I try to stop her. I take her arm. But she's seized the smaller letter and she's out, past our sleeping parents, so fast I can't even catch the hem of her dress. 'Ann!' I follow, down the ladder and into the kitchen to where she's setting the kettle on the stove.

'You can't,' I hiss when I'm beside her. 'It's private property.'

Ann feeds more wood into the stove, and shuffles its inside with a poker. Even so the water sits like lead. 'Let's go back to bed,' I whisper. 'Come.' But Ann is determined. 'It'll only take a minute more.' And it's true, the water is already beginning to stir.

As the heat rises Ann holds the back of the letter over it, so that with the steam, the sealed edges curl, and with some nudging they begin to peel away, separating out the words of Mac's address. 'Shh,' Ann says when I protest, and she lights the lamp and we huddle together as she slowly inches out the damp warm sheet of paper.

My dear Margaret,

It's been four weeks now since you went away, and much less I hope till you return. I have your letter, I only got it when I returned late from a walk, and it is of great comfort to know that you are well. I'm sorry to hear the trouble continues between Frances and MacNair. And that the boy, Sylvan, is suffering – as well he might. They are lucky to have you there. And I am even luckier that soon you'll be back here with me. Today was grey and misty, but all the same I set off for our studio and managed to make some progress. I'm still working on the winter stock, the first is done, but the second is defeating me. I seem to paint so slowly and all the time I'm working I'm longing for it to be done so I can put it away and start on something new. I find I like that even more than saving money. Although if I don't sell something soon there will be no money to save.

You see, my Margaret, this is what I do when I can't come in to tea with you, I sit and write. For writing to you is how I best relax. I will write again tomorrow. Or maybe even tonight. Although there are only three important words that could take the place of all the rest. I Love You. I hope you find them here in every line.

MMYT

Ann, who has been reading, swallows, and tears start in her eyes. 'So that is how it's done,' she says. And she laughs and a small sob escapes her. 'I've been telling Jimmy how many apples we got from that one tree in the corner of the garden, and how poor Mrs Cady caught cold on the drive from Wissett and now her sister must move in and look after all ten children.'

'What's MMYT?' I ask. And we say it together and apart, in different voices, quiet, loud, but we still can't make it out.

Away from the steam of the kettle the envelope has curled and dried. 'Now what do we do?' I worry, and Ann mixes up a paste of flour and water and, matching the black edges of the words, smoothing the paper, she seals it up until it sets. 'What do you think?' and I have to admit it doesn't look too bad at all.

Chapter 34

'Maggs!' A book slams down on my desk, and I look up into Runnicles' red face. 'The dates,' he spits. 'Do you know nothing?' And I want to tell him that I may know something, but I've forgotten to listen for the question.

'Napoleon?' he prompts me. 'Or have you been asleep?'

'June the 18th 1815, Napoleon was defeated at Waterloo?' I offer, for I have to give him something and I know this is one of the things Runnicles likes to hear. For good measure, and to cool his fury, I add, 'As a result of the Napoleonic Wars, Great Britain became the foremost nation in the world.'

With a sigh Runnicles moves off and I am left alone again to try and decide whether I will run over to George Allard's to warn him I'll be late, or go straight to Southwold with the letters and get them safely to the post. I imagine them travelling side by side to Scotland. The first stopping off at Glasgow, the other rumbling on by train to the Kyle of Lochalsh, where it will cross the sea by steamer to Lewis and arrive finally in Betty's quick cool hands.

'Maggs!'

I yelp as the book slams down on my hands, and there is Runnicles glaring at me again. 'Lurkine doesn't know the contents of the Napoleonic Code. Can you enlighten us with your superior intelligence?' And even though I do know, somewhere, something about the code – is it to do with jobs going to the most qualified, rather than those of noble birth? – my fingers are throbbing so loudly my thoughts are mired, and I'm fearful that if I open my mouth even by a whisker tears will fall.

'You will write out, one hundred times,' Runnicles leans over me. ' "The Napoleonic Code has been the basis of European law for the last one hundred years." And Lurpine too. By tomorrow.'

'One hundred years, one hundred times,' I stutter. And I close my eyes to seal in what he's said.

I get a ride with the glazier's son as far as Blythburgh and follow the estuary around until the saltmarshes sinking into mud drive me back on to the road. It's a cold, clear day, the trees bare, the fields rough with stubble. My stomach grumbles for the meal I've missed, but if I walk fast I'll catch the post office just as it opens after lunch.

They say that Suffolk is as flat as a board, but if it is, then why am I toiling up this long hard slope of road? Every dozen steps I glance behind, hoping for a cart to speed the last two miles of my walk, but the only sound is the roar of the train as it thunders across the common. Maybe, if I'm lucky, I could climb on board at Southwold, and ride it home, and my heart lifts and my feet quicken at the thought of blasting fearlessly across that bridge. And then I remember Fred Tilson whispering in the pub that our train is the same one used for bringing in the wounded from the front. They ship them home to Lowestoft and take them to London overnight, although what they do with them there I'm not sure. I think of the Miss Bishops settling into their seats and I try and picture the carriage full of soldiers, arms missing, legs blown off.

Just then, when I'd stopped listening for it, a cart pulls up. It is full of men in uniform and one leans down and grins. 'It's our little cripple from the inn,' he says, and I recognise him. He's from the Cheshires and he's our most recent billet. 'Can we haul him on, sir?' he asks, and with a nod from their sergeant the man, Gleave, leans down and gives me his arm.

'So where you off to in such a hurry?' he asks, and I have to think fast if I'm to say something that won't make him laugh. 'I'm running an errand,' I say. 'For a friend.'

But Gleave laughs all the same. 'Running, were you? I should say not.' He looks at my foot. 'How old are you anyway? Fourteen?'

I'm so pleased I want to lie, but the blood that is always waiting starts throbbing in my ears. 'I'll be fourteen at the start of January,' I tell him.

'Another few years and you'll be about right to volunteer.' He looks me over. 'A chance to get fitted up with decent boots. Put a lift in while they're about it.'

'Another few years!' The man beside him grasps his crotch. 'Careful what you wish for.'

But Gleave opens up his chest and roars out across the blue water so loudly that a flock of gulls lift into the air. 'Let me at them. However long it takes.' And he prods me in the chest. 'Don't think a bit of a limp will see you sat safely at home, my lad. Don't let yourself be fooled into thinking that.'

It is a brewing day in Southwold and the air is dense with the smell of malt extracted from the grain. The whole town reels with it. Even the horses look befuddled as they lift their heavy feet. There's a stableblock behind the high street where the Punches go to rest when they've delivered their barrels, and I pause there to lay a hand against their muzzles and give them a scratch behind their ears. I think of our horse Kingdom, who we were forced to sell to the Grand Hotel one year when there was no other way to find the rent, and I run my mind over the weight of my money and think how much I'd have to save to buy him back.

I take my leave of the horses and head back towards the post office, where, having sent my letters on their way, I walk towards the sea. I drop down on to the beach and inspect the boats, check which have been out, and how long since they were dragged in. I'd stop here if I could, go into the Sailors' Reading Room for news of Danky, take a quick look at the yawls for anything I've missed, but Allard will be waiting for me. Even now he'll be standing, fretting by his wheel. And so I cut across Gun Hill, jump over the patches of rough turf that mark the spot of each buried cannon, and run along the towpath beside the canal. Here, the sky is reflected in the water, sheets of it like washing fallen to the ground, and to see it clearer, I climb the bank above the path, and my head in blue, my feet snagging against grass, I march along until I reach the ferry.

At first it seems George Allard isn't there. 'Hello?' I call as I step through into the garden. 'Mr Allard?' I wait beside the wheel. 'I'm here,' I try again. I see his wife, scurrying away around the side of the house.

When Mr Allard does appear he's got a streak of oil across his face. 'So there you are,' he says. And he stands there looking at me as if he may not have a use for me after all. 'Right then.' It's rare to see him so distracted. 'We'd better make a start.'

I sit at the wheel as Allard gathers up the hemp, and I catch him glancing from me to the loom as if he's measuring us against each other with his eyes. 'Is something wrong?' I ask, and startled, he tightens the strick around his waist, and takes a step back.

He's halfway across the garden and he still hasn't spoken a word. 'The cannons are gone now.' I hope to rile him. 'There's nothing there but mud.' But he only nods and checks the tension of his twine, and motioning for me to turn the wheel faster he backs towards the gate.

Chapter 35

If it takes three days for Betty to get home by train and boat, how much longer would it be before a letter arrived if it travelled the same way? It's the kind of question Runnicles might ask us, but as the days pass by this is a question of my own which I ask each morning as I trudge along the beach.

Mac's letter has arrived. I know this because when I next see him he's reading Mrs Mac's reply. He thanks me, and asks if I'm going that way again, because if I am I might take another letter to the post for him. He has a theory, which he tells me between puffs of his pipe, that letters mailed from Southwold arrive more quickly than from here, and that Mrs Lusher, for all her helpful ways, may forget on occasion to actually hand them over to the postman when he calls. 'Although,' and here he lowers his voice, 'it seems no one is above the censors, for my wife thinks my letter to her may have been looked over, although nothing was crossed out.'

I feel myself go pale, and I ask what the censors might be looking for when they read people's post.

'Signs of disaffection.' Mac shakes his head. 'Fraternising with the enemy. Information that may lead to an arrest.'

I try to remember what was in Mac's letter. There was something about his work going slowly, saving money, pictures in a drawer. And what was it that had so impressed Ann that she had set herself down and written to Jimmy Kerridge right then and there? Something about three important words hidden in the letter. Words that could be found in every line. But Mac's not as slow as he's pretending, because he's started on a new painting and it's growing fast. Not a flower this time, but the view of the river, a stretch of pale water, and the groynes, ground down with weather, shrinking as they sink into the sea. He's pasted it to a board and set it on the table where his wife usually serves tea.

'When will Mrs Mackintosh be back?' I ask, looking round hopefully for the sandwiches she would have cut, but Mac doesn't speak, he has pen and paper and he's writing in a fast and fluid scrawl.

My dear Margaret.
Ann and I read later by the light of the lamp.
It is teatime and as I can't come in to tea with you, I'll have to write to you instead. I've worked hard today and I feel I deserve a little relaxation. It feels good to have made a start, and it's never so bad as before I begin. It was a perfectly glorious morning, cold and bright, the sea absolutely flat, just as I painted it at Holy Island. I took my three-legged stool and tried to do three things – to look about me, to paint, and to think. I must have looked about me, because I did start to paint, although it is only a start, but I did think a lot, and particularly about you – wishing you were there beside me – although after ten minutes you would have complained that your delicate behind was not made to sit on for so long.

Heat flushes to my face, a vision of Mrs Mackintosh's white skin appearing so forcefully I can't see the words. But Ann is still reading.

I've caught the light, I think, that is the most important thing. Which makes me wonder, how are you finding the fog of smoke up there in Glasgow? And have you managed to make peace at all between MacNair and your family? I know poor Frances is still attached to him, however he behaves, but that of course is what the others mind so much. And I would too if she were my sister, which of course she is. And how is the dear boy, Sylvan? How much of a confusion must he be in? But more importantly how are you? You do not say that you are in good spirits, which worries me, but then I'm also secretly happy that you are not too light of heart when you are away from me. So there is nothing else for me to say except that the only reason for writing this letter is so that you know that I miss you and I want you and I look forward to the time when I don't need to write because you will be here.

MMYT

I don't tell Ann about Mrs Mackintosh's worry over the censor, but watch instead to see how carefully she sticks the envelope back down. I wonder if now she'll write to Jimmy Kerridge about it having been a glorious morning, the sea flat, or even of her own delicate bum. 'Have you heard from Jimmy?' I ask instead as she smooths the curled edges of the paper.

'No,' she lifts her chin. 'Nothing from him yet.' And she snuffs out the light.

Danky is fishing again. He's back in his old spot on our side of the river, and if it wasn't for his stick you'd never know that he'd been shot. Now I have to queue up if I'm to talk to him; he has so many people asking what it feels like to be mistaken for a spy it's almost as if it is summer again and he's modelling for the lady artists on the bridge.

On Sunday I see his sister at church, and I hear her say to Mrs Horrod that she'd have tried harder to get him to come along himself, to give thanks to our Lord for sparing him, but she needed a rest from all his bossing. He's worse now than he ever was. God bless him.

Later that day, I find him on his bench outside the Bell. I sit with him while he sips his beer, and I tell him about my picture of HMS *Formidable*. How I've swapped my matron with her stern black beads and chosen instead the figurehead of a red and gold princess. I count the portholes for him and check over the lifeboats, the gunwale and the boom, and with my hands I sketch out the long curve of the keel, made from one solid piece of wood. But Danky isn't in the mood for listening. Being shot has lost him his patience for it, and after a few minutes he takes his pint and moves inside.

It seems our man from the Cheshires has taken a fancy to Ann. I find them by the back door, Gleave smoking, leaning towards her, while Ann listens, one foot ready for escape. I don't need to, but I throw the bucket into the well, hard, so it clangs against the sides and I wait there as it fills and then, slowly, slowly I turn the handle to draw it up.

'There's a foxglove, foxglove in my pansy patch,' I sing,
'Decked so brightly by the rain, there never was its match.
It is made of velvet petals, russet blots and lovely smells,
And the wind he is the ringer for its peal of bells.'

The bucket is up. Ann bites her lips together in a laugh. And I wish I'd chosen a different song, for now the next verse is in my ears.

'There's a foxglove, foxglove, in my garden ground,
Never mortal listeners shall hear its tinkling sound . . .

'Coming through,' I warn them, and the water sloshes so that Gleave must stand back if he doesn't want to be soaked.

'What's all this?' Mother asks when I push open the back door, and for once I would have welcomed Father's interruption, but he's over at the brewery haggling over the cost of a barrel, and so I shrug and leave the bucket in the middle of the floor.

With Mrs Mac still away, old Mac comes over to us to take his supper at the inn. Mother gives him a rabbit stew and a serving of turnip and he sits in the small bar by the fire and drinks his first drink fast.

'My father was a religious man,' he tells us. 'Aye, and an ambitious man too. Worked his way up from clerk to superintendent in the police force. But what he loved more than anything in this world was his garden, not that he'd allow himself the pleasure of spending even a minute of his time there on the Sabbath.'

'What would he grow?' Mother asks, while Father brings him a fresh pint.

'Flowers,' Mac says. 'A few wee vegetables. But it was flowers he was good with. I'd go in there as a boy and draw them.'

In our house it is Mother who tends the garden. Marrow, beans, carrots, potatoes. Although she edges it with marigolds to keep away the pests.

'So how'd you get started on the buildings then?' I ask because I can't see how you'd go from drawing buttercups to building a tower.

'Well, I was apprenticed to an architect. A Mr Hutchison. That was the deal I struck with my father when it was clear that I was only good for one thing, and that was drawing. With my mother ailing – my ma who indulged me in all things – I had to choose a line of work for it was clear she would not be there much longer to defend me.' He takes another long drink, and I look at my own ma and try to imagine his.

'Mr Hutchison was a good man, and he agreed to release me twice a week so I could take classes at the art school.' Mac shifts round in his chair. 'But however much I loved the classes, and love them I did, once I'd started with him, taking measurements, working out the pitch of a roof, the angle at which a window might catch hold of the light, I found I couldn't stop. I entered competitions. I entered the Department of Science and Arts annual competition when I was barely twenty.'

'Did you win?' I ask, sure that he must have, but Father's scowl drops me into silence.

'No,' Mac looks amused. 'But it gave me the idea. And from then on I entered every competition I could. That's how it happened. I was still attending night classes at the art school. Our premises were in the basement of a gallery, a low dark space and with not enough room for all the students who were pouring in. Painting, metalwork, embroidery, architecture. There was no one who didnae want to study there, under the new man, the new headmaster, Francis Newbery.' Mac takes another slug of beer, and the taste of it seems to drift the thoughts out of his head. Go on, I want to say. But the sight of Father, leaning up against the fireplace, his fingers restless for lack of a glass, stops my tongue.

'It was Mr Newbery', Mac shakes himself awake, 'that pushed for a new school, and with his chivvying they found a site, a steep slope of hill between Renfrew and Dalhousie Streets, and put it out for competition. There was a budget of fourteen thousand pounds . . .' Father's eyes flash wide at such a sum '. . . and eleven architects submitted plans. I'd left Hutchison by then, was working for the firm of Honeyman and Keppie as a junior, but it was me that drew up the plans, and submitted them, and it was my drawings that won the commission to design the new Glasgow School of Art.'

'You won!' I'm grinning. I knew he would have.

'Aye.' Mac drains his glass. 'I say I won. And it is generally accepted, now at least, that the school is my design. And everything inside it, from the light fittings to the forks used in the students' canteen. But I put my drawings forward under the name of Honeyman and Keppie – I'd been working for them since I was twenty-one, and so it was in their name that the award was given, and when the first phase of the building was finished, it was the firm that was acknowledged. Mr Honeyman, and Mr Keppie. And your man was left out in the cold.'

Father takes Mac's empty glass and goes down to the cellar and soon he is back with one fresh pint. 'What is this *first phase* then? What does that mean?' he asks, and Mac tells him that fourteen thousand pounds was not enough for the whole building, or even for half of it. They'd started at the eastern end of the plot, at the corner of Hope Street and Renfrew, and worked their way across, but before they'd even come to the front door they were running out of money.

'Fourteen thousand pounds,' I whistle. I imagine that would be enough to rebuild our whole village and put back the church to the splendour of its ruins, but Mac turns to me and he is scowling. 'This, my boy, was to be no ordinary building. It was to be something special. Something to inspire the great work that would take place inside.' There is sweat standing out on his brow and his hands tremble. 'And even though by the time we stopped work twenty-one thousand had been spent, I was determined to go on. Ten years, it took.' He thumps the wooden table. 'Ten years for the rest of the money to be raised. But raised it was, another twenty-five thousand, to get the art school finished, and by that time I made damn sure it was my name on the design.' He is pale, and I remember what he looked like when he first arrived here. 'The finishing off of it', he says, quiet, 'nearly finished me off too.'

'A drop of whisky,' Father offers and he fills a glass, and watches thirstily as Mac raises his chin and swallows the liquor down.

'And what did Mrs Mackintosh say when you was overlooked?' Father asks, for he must distract himself with something, and I imagine her standing in the doorway, her back straight, her eyes fierce.

'Well,' Mac pauses, 'when the first phase of the school was built I was not yet a married man.' He stops as if he's noticed who his audience is, but there's no one else, so he goes on. 'Although there was an understanding that I was to be married, but to another lass. To the sister of a partner in the firm.' He swallows. 'To John Keppie's sister, Jessie.'

Father sighs as if the whole sad business is falling into place.

'But Margaret Macdonald and I, we were friends already.' Mac stares past him. 'She was a student at the art school, and we'd exhibited together. A very talented artist she was. Still is. And yes, Margaret Macdonald went to the opening ceremony, and she stood in the street and saw the silver key that I'd designed, sitting on the pearly silk cushion that she'd made herself, and she listened to the speeches, on and on while everyone huddled under umbrellas. She told me how the chairman of the board took up the key and opened the door, my door, and that everyone hurried in with great enthusiasm – even if it was just to get out of the rain – and how once inside there were speeches, and more speeches, nine in all – including one by John Keppie himself – but she never did tell me what I'd guessed, that my name was not once mentioned.'

Mac takes his whisky and tips up the glass, although even I can see that it is empty. 'Not a mention of me in that whole damn building. Not in the heating ducts, or the double-hinged doors, not in the sculpture studio, or the boardroom with its hanging lights – you know it is the first building in Glasgow to have electricity? No one commended me for the drawing gallery with windows divided into even panes, to better frame the views of the city and the Clyde, or the rough brick of the entrance hall to stop students from lingering and wasting time. There was not a whisper about the long white corridor of the basement that made you think you were up on the top floor.'

Father pours more whisky, and then in one quick movement, his resolve breaking, he pours one for himself. I watch the two men drink. And when they have finished they drink more until Mac, mumbling about the work he must get done, tomorrow, at first light, sways to his feet and looks round unsteady for the door. I take his arm and help him out, and our heads bent against the salt wind from the beach we struggle down the road, arriving at the gate of his garden, ghostly with its shadows, and I wait there and watch as he stumbles up the path and, after some fumbling, forces open the door.

The bottle is empty when I get home, and Father is asleep on the seat by the fire.

'No letters for me tonight?' Ann whispers as I climb in beside her and I shake my head and close my eyes and think of the photographs I've seen of the fortress of Mac's school, the windows that rise high as a whole wall, and the wide black doors that open like a flower.

Chapter 36

The Cheshires are in no hurry to move on. Not that they have any choice in the matter, but if the war is to be over by Christmas, they'd better get across to France soon if they're to see any kind of action. Instead they practise manoeuvres on the common, steaming and grumbling in the cold, their boots stamping in the early-morning frost. They're not the only soldiers in the village, Mary has half a regiment of Lancasters up at Blyfield House. But whenever I see a division it seems that Gleave is always at the front, waving to me, winking, and when his sergeant's back is turned, dragging his foot behind him, twisting his body round so that he's grimacing like an oaf. I don't wave back. I can't. Although it is against Dora for all I know. Instead I turn away as quickly as I can, and when I see him at the inn I do my best to stay out of his way. 'How can you stand to talk to him?' I ask Ann, but she shrugs her shoulders and says he's not so bad. And I notice she's not so frantic when the postman walks by empty-handed, although she still waits eagerly to see the letters I collect from Mac.

My dearest Margaret.
    We read them together.
    How much longer must you be away? I woke this morning

early, the sun was shining through on to the bed and for one moment I thought you were there beside me, a russet darling on the pillow. To distract myself I went straight out to the river with my board and I sat there, wrapped against the cold. It's strange to think of you being in Glasgow, my home before it was ever yours, and now I've been gone from it longer than at any time in my life. Even when I went to Italy on the scholarship money I won, I was only away three months, although, if they'd had the decency to pay both parts of it to me, I could have stopped in France instead of rushing back, half starved, through Brussels, Antwerp, Paris and London, before catching that last slow train up to Glasgow to claim the second half. What did they think? That if I took the whole £60 I'd have stayed away for ever and deprived my home city of those countless sketches of Italian churches that I'd drawn?

So how is Glasgow? Have you been past our school? Is it bearing up? Are the doors swinging back and forth as busy students rush from class to class? And have you seen Miss Cranston? If you do, please say to her your frieze is ready, wrapped against the damp, sitting in our studio, which you may or may not tell her is actually a shed. I wonder – has anyone asked after me up there? I expect you would have written if they had.

This landscape drawing is now practically finished and I think it is quite good of its kind – I shall give it another short morning as there are one or two things that might still be done – little points of closer observation – I find that each of my drawings has something in them but none of them have everything. This must be remedied. But enough of all this chatter. I hope you can read the meaning in these pages, for there is only one, and that can be said in three short words.

Ann sighs and seals up the letter, and then, just as I'd hoped, she starts in with a letter of her own. I stand behind and look over her shoulder but she keeps her arm around it and I can't see what she's written. 'Shall I take it to the post for you?' I offer, but she eyes me sharply and answers shortly.

'No.'

There's not always time to go over to Southwold, however firmly I tell Mac I'll do so, and there are days when I pass Mac's letter on to Mrs Lusher, with a promise from her that she'll hand it to the postman herself.

'What else am I likely to do with it,' she leans forward to stare into my face, 'eat it for my tea?' and flushing and mumbling, I back out of the shop.

'For thousands of years,' George Allard has been fierce of late, 'people of all kinds have relied on rope. They've used grasses, vines, hair, weaving it together to make twine. They found a fossil in a cave in France, from twenty-eight thousand years before Christ, although how they knowed that is beyond me, but it was marked with the twisted threads of rope. You see?' His voice is a challenge. 'And now they don't want rope, they want metal. Even at Bridport,' his mouth is bitter, 'they're twisting twine from manufactured oil.' He is disgusted, but it's true, our orders have dwindled to almost nothing, and each day I come to turn the wheel Allard warns it may be my last.

'And how do you think they made the pyramids?' He turns on me again. 'Dragging all those stones across the desert? With rope of course. Could never have done it without. Rope, and nets of rope that pulled across the sand.'

'I thought they used elephants.' Runnicles must have told us this, and after all my copying, I feel duty-bound to repeat it now.

George Allard glares at me. 'Maybe they did use elephants. But I'll tell you one thing, the elephants used rope.' And he warns me that he can't pay my shilling if there's no shillings coming in.

But today when I arrive, he's waiting by the wheel. Stamping his feet and restless as a horse. 'We have an order.' He is triumphant. 'A rode for an anchor. Double-braided with a braided core and cover. We'd better make it fast, before they change their mind. Sit down. Hurry now. There's no time to lose.' But there's only so fast we can make a rope that must drop one hundred and twenty fathoms to the sea floor, and I wonder if Mr Allard will have the strength to walk all that distance backwards, and backwards again four times, with the strick of hemp like a great thick skirt around his waist.

Even when times were good we didn't often get an order this large. Usually for an anchor rode they went to the factories where engine-powered machines sat in great covered walks as long as streets. 'My father was the man for making rodes for anchors,' George Allard tells me, and not for the first time he describes the run his father had at Southwold. 'Spinners Lane. Stretched from the high street right down to the common. It's known by that name even now, although nobody works it. There were so many orders he had to hire three boys, in rotation, to turn the wheel. Glad my own son has gone into another way of life,' and he's distracted for a moment by the thought of Abb, out there in France, fighting, with so much more to fear than the end of rope.

'Everything that's worth anything', Allard teases out the dense gold hemp, 'comes from God's own ground. And now this war has turned men towards unnatural things and we'll see no good in it.'

I want to say the world will soon turn back once the fighting's finished. But I've stood on the cliff path beside the strings of wire, and I know, because I've felt the jagged barbs, that this new rope will outlast us all.

*   *   *

There's nothing much flowering to put on the grave, but I glance in anyway to see what Mother has found. Sometimes she gathers leaves, or bracken, their edges rusting, their stems still green, and today when I walk through the churchyard, I see a twig of acorns, the shells open like a row of bells.

There's nothing on the new grave. It's been dug behind the church, and the turf looks lumpy and uneven where they've laid it back. I kneel down and place my hand on it, and hope poor Mrs Cady isn't watching from on high, and will never know that her children are wandering snot-nosed through the village with holes in their clothes and all wrapped up in strips of cloth for that they don't have enough coats to go round.

I hear a noise behind me. It is Mac, inspecting the ruins of the old church walls, stepping through a priest's door in the curtain of the chancel. I go and stand beside him but I don't speak for he's murmuring calculations under his breath. When he's done he moves around the churchyard, reading the inscriptions, pointing out to me the carved angels, the clasped marble hands, as if I'm the stranger and not him. That's enough, come on out now, I will him towards the gate, but his attention is caught by the nodding heads of Mother's acorns, and he hobbles down towards our plot. *William, William, James, William, James, Thomas* . . . and underneath in larger letters, *beloved sons of William and Mary Maggs*. He looks over at me then. A studying sort of look. And he tells me that he had brothers too. The eldest of which was Billy. William like his father. And mine.

'What happened to him?' I have to whisper. And he frowns as if it'll help to get the memory back. 'He ran away to sea. He can't have been much older than you. It's true to say I hardly remember him, being so much smaller. But the years went by, and we hoped for news, my mother especially who had taken to her bed, and stayed there, but when the letter came, it was from South America, written by a seaman who'd befriended him, and the reason for the letter was to tell us what we most feared to hear. That Billy . . . William was dead.'

'And your other brothers?' I didn't mean to ask so fast.

'Just babbies' he says. 'There would have been eleven of us if they'd survived. But as it was, the house was full of girls.'

'And you.'

'Aye. And me.' And I hear it, the sad note of the *mee*, and I know that he is thinking about his foot. I look slantwise at it. The black boot, laced and stacked into a club. And I wonder why the foot is called a club. For it only looks like one when it's laced into that boot.

I shift uneasily. My own foot is forced into a leather shoe, worn down on one side where it drags out from the ankle, and I wonder if he's heard the story, that in every seventh generation there is a boy born with a deformity, who brings with him a gift. A gift that's cursed, some say. But Mother says that's not to be believed.

I listen for my starlings. I'd like to hear from them, one whistle or a squawk, and I close my eyes and ask them for a sign. But they've grown big, their feathers and their beaks turned dark for winter, a scattering of white across their backs like snow.

'Will you look at that,' Mac's head is raised, and there, above us, like a great black mass of sand, a thousand birds have gathered. My starlings are among them, I can see them, I'm sure of it, the undersides of their wings silver, their backs black, and as one, they turn, and glide out across the marsh. I hurry after them. Mac is by my side. 'A murmuration,' he says. 'Like nothing that I've ever seen.' And my ears are so full of their hard fast beating that I can't say a word.

'Look at that now,' Mac gasps as the starlings darken to a knot, there must be more than a million of them, and soaring up they are off again, each bird taking its place so that the lines they make are perfect, a question mark, a heart. We stand still to watch them. And although each winter I have seen them, scissoring down into the marshes, swooping round again as they prepare to nest, I've never seen so many or heard their wings so loud.

'Who's giving the orders, do you think?' I ask, and Mac shields his eyes to stare up at the sky.

'Aghhh.' A dropping catches the peak of his hat, and as he wipes it clear, he sighs. 'If our army was like that, we'd have nothing to fear.'

I look at him. I didn't think we did have anything to fear. Not really. Not with our own prime minister, and our king, and the likes of George Allard and myself keeping a close watch on the sea.

Another dropping catches Mac's shoulder. 'They say it's good luck,' I tell him, but even so we stumble out from under the cloud and watch as the starlings draw together, as dense and shifting as a shoot of coal, and then with a pause as if preparing to amaze us, they swarm away in the shape of an arrow-headed kite, one tiny silver bird fluttering at its tip.

Chapter 37

Ann has hopes that Jimmy Kerridge will be home for Christmas. She has seen his mother at the Monday market, and although she has no actual news, Mrs Kerridge tells her that is only because no one is allowed to know the exact whereabouts of his ship. They could be sailing the rivers of Egypt, or round the tip of Africa, but the information must remain secret in case it is intercepted and a submarine picks up the news. The town is still reeling from the men they lost when the *Aboukir* went down, her back broken by a single torpedo, two other ships destroyed when they went to her rescue. Fifteen hundred men lost in an hour. And our men, the ten that were from Southwold, their names are pinned up outside the town hall, and there's talk of putting up a memorial to them in the market square.

'Did you tell her Jimmy's not written?' I ask. But she scowls at me and slams out of the door.

Mrs Mac is back. I pretend to be surprised, although I know from Mac's letters to expect her. He has worked hard to finish his painting of the harbour and I stop by the hut to see how it came out. He has an oil light lit and there's a jar of holly on the table, and both he and Mrs Mac are drinking tea in their coats.

The picture is propped against the wall. 'Can I?' And I stoop down before it.

'What do you think?' Mrs Mac asks.

I keep looking. There are no people in the picture. Just the chain ferry in the middle of the river, too far away to make out who is on it, or to see the ferryman drawing it across. The tide is out and there's the island at the mouth of the harbour, and the mud of the path, with its puddle, broken up by sky.

I look over at him. 'You like it here,' I say. And I smile because he's painted the river as if it is his own.

Mac leans down to see what I have seen. 'Yes,' he says, 'I suppose I must do.' And he puts an arm around his wife's shoulders.

'And how have you been getting on?' Mrs Mac asks me. 'Toshie says you've been working hard, at school and at the rope-making, and hardly time to spare for your ship.'

They've been talking about me? And I force myself to lift out the big picture of HMS *Formidable*.

We look at it in silence. The outlines are all in, the boards and sails, the lifeboats and the cannons, but it sits stiffly, going nowhere on a bed of solid sea.

'He's got an eye,' Mac nods, and I slide it away quickly before either one of them thinks it necessary to say more.

A week before Christmas our soldiers get leave to travel home. Gleave and his friends, without having even strayed from our coast, are heading north again. The night they go I find Ann in our room, unrolling a gift of sheer stockings up over her ankles. She stops when she sees me, one leg outstretched, like a cat mid-wash. And then she carries on, the blotched skin of her shin disappearing under silk. I sit on the bed beside her and feel for the moles on the back of my arm and imagine Ann and Jimmy's wedding. Ann in a hat piled high with flowers, Mother in her good blue dress. Is Father there? I can't see him, hard as I look. And so I will him to be there, his cap at an angle, his eyes straight ahead as if to say that he's done nothing wrong. And it's true. He's been calm and quiet these last weeks with the Cheshires in the house. But now, as I sit beside Ann, watching her slowly roll the stockings back down her legs, and replace them in their box, I wonder what tonight will bring.

It starts quiet enough, although the wind is up and howling round the door. Mac and Mrs Mac come in for their tea. Mother gives them a stew of pork and beans and Father brings them up their stout. I listen while they talk: about the war, and then about the weather, wet and wild as it has been these last few days, with more rain lashing down. The Tilson brothers blow in. And James Ladd, and Mr Gory from Lowestoft. And Father tells them how he's sure that the guns across in France are bringing down the rain. Shaking open the clouds, he tells them, angering the heavens, and the talk moves back to the war and how they'd better hurry up if it's to be over by Christmas, and then just as I'm thinking of climbing up to bed, Danky bursts open the door, and shouts to us there's been a wreck, the lifeboat's out, and all the men from the Bell are down on the shore. I curse as I snatch my coat – if only Father had taken the lease of the fishermen's pub when he came back to the village, for despite the name above the door, often as not the adventures of the sea go on without us.

'Not you, my boy,' Mother tugs at my collar, but I slip from her hands, and I'm out into the dark, Danky beside me, our heads bent into the rain. I glance behind, and I see our drinkers streaming out in the light from the front door, and Mother with them, and only Father standing coatless, a bottle of beer clasped by the neck.

We hurry towards the harbour, our boots splashing in the street. And when we get there we find most of the village waiting on the shore. The tide is in, the waves are high, and the lights of the wrecked ship are glinting at us through the storm. I wonder for a minute where our lanterns are, the ones we use to steer our men home. And I'm turning to Danky when I remember the enemy may be out there too, waiting for a signal, looking for a place to land. I stare out through the dark for a sighting of the lifeboat, but the water rises high and the moon is sunk behind the clouds. 'Here,' I'm scrabbling for a foothold, 'help me,' and I lock my feet against the wooden struts of a groyne and with one arm on Danky's shoulder I hoist myself up. I'm glad I've been up here before, because the narrow ledge is less of a surprise to me, and I wrap my arms around it and steady myself before I stand. 'Get down. Do you hear me?' It is Mother, shrill, below, but I stare into the water, raking my eyes back from the dim lights of the ship until I see it. A shadow on the water. Our lifeboat, with Shrimp the coxswain crouching in the prow. I can't tell if it's coming back towards us or heading for the ship, for it's moving sideways, its hull against the waves. And then the clouds fray, and the moon beams through, and I see the boat sheer up a wall of water, and as it tips towards me I make out the cowering heads of a cluster of people, dark against the sea. 'They're coming in,' I shout. 'They need a light.' I don't care anything for Dora now. Or the enemy who'd be fools to risk the sea on such a night. And as I shout, the sky meshes black over my head and I lose sight of the boat.

It is Mac who passes up his lamp. I crouch beside it, willing it to take, the wick flickering, small as a fly. 'Go on then, boy,' Danky calls from below and just then it blooms into a light. I stand, unsteady, and raise the lantern high. The boat is nothing but a black shadow on the sea. Lost and found again.

Spray bursting over its sides. I hold my arm up till it screams. I want to shout and call into the wind but I know it's of no use. Instead I wait, the rain soaking into my clothes, my hands red raw, the fingers stinging. The cloud breaks up again and I see the crowd of heads, their faces towards me. 'They're turned this way!' I shout and there's a cheer from below, and Mother's lone voice demanding I get down.

Spray slams into my face, the wind catches at my clothes, and I switch the lamp to the other hand. I could stay up here for ever, my arms stretched to the sky, but the boat has reached the harbour mouth and I can hear the oars pulling below me. Slowly I lower the lantern, passing it to Danky who snuffs it out, and in the sudden blackness I jump down to the ground.

'Foolish boy,' Mother cuffs me, but I'm so cold I hardly feel it. Other hands tap me on the shoulder, pat me on the head. 'Well done, boy. Well done.'

All night I dream the lifeboat's coming in. I can see it, sliding on the steep slope of the waves, crashing and vanishing in the swell. Danky is there, telling me how once the fishermen of our village formed a human chain, more than thirty men, hands linked, to haul a lost man in. 'If they'd had rope,' George Allard is bellowing, but someone tells him, and it may even be me, that there are times when only a man's hand will do.

I'm cold, out there on the shore, and I twist and turn and pull the blankets round me, meshed up in seaweed, the cool soft weight of it dragging me down. And then I wake. And Mother is leaning over me, her hand on my forehead, her face concerned. 'You have a fever,' she says and she strips the blanket off me. 'Sit up now,' and she peels away my wet shirt, and with no warning, pushes a flannel under my arm. The cloth is cold as blades, and all around it I am jumping with the shock. But she dips the flannel into icy water and splashes it against my back.

I'm dreaming again. Mac is swinging his lantern through the dark, his wife beside him, her red hair loose. 'The boy has an eye,' they say to each other. And they write the words on a shred of paper and with their joint signatures in a rectangular box – CRM MMM – they place it in a bottle and hurl it out to sea.

It's Sunday morning before I'm strong enough to come downstairs. And even then I'm excused church service and told to stay by the fire. Father's face looks bruised with drink. And the two smallest fingers on Mother's hand are bandaged together in a splint. But they leave the inn, dressed in their best clothes, with Ann, head down, behind them. I sit in the big chair and stretch my feet out to the fire. My legs are thinner, my foot white as a root. I examine my knees, wide and bony, and lift my shirt to inspect the hollow of my stomach. A pure clean hunger flashes through me, and I imagine the first fat blackberry of autumn, and the sweet milk segments of a beech nut as I scoop out its insides. I could get up and search for something. But I can't seem to move from my chair, so I sit there, breathing in the smell of our dinner cooking on the stove. Pearl-barley soup with nubs of mutton. Mother has asked that I keep one eye on it. And I wonder if this is what it feels like, to have been on a long sea voyage and finally come home.

I'm woken by the crash of a chair falling, and the clatter of a cup flying across the room. Mother has her hands over her face and Ann is crouching by the fire. 'Get down,' she whispers to me, and she takes my hand and pulls me to the floor. Father stands in the kitchen doorway. There is a dark, singed smell. 'If you hadn't stood about outside the church rabbiting like an old woman . . .'

'The food is not ruined,' Mother dares. And she takes the lid from the pot and peers inside. 'It is only the base of the pan that's burnt.'

Father turns his eyes on me. 'And whose fault is that?'

But I don't look at him. I will do. One day. I'll rise up and fight him. But today my legs are trembling and my head spins and I stay crouched on the floor.

'Let's be grateful,' Mother says, 'that the fever has broken and the boy is well enough to come downstairs.' He turns away from me and moves towards her, and I swear if she didn't have the hot soup in her hands, he would have knocked her down. But she stands before him. The pot raised. And there is a silence before he slumps down in his chair.

'Grateful,' he says. And the fight goes out of him.

Mother sets the pot down on the table and ladles the scalded soup into bowls, spoon by spoon, until she reaches the thick burnt sludge. Ann takes it from her then and pours in water to lift the crust, and I pull myself up from the floor, and heave myself into my chair. But when the grace is said, and Father nods his head to show we can begin, I find for all my longing, I can't lift the spoon to my mouth.

Chapter 38

I lie in bed, the days tumbling by, darkened by the rain that falls outside the window. I am roused by Mother, spooning broth into my mouth. To please her I try and swallow, but more often than not I cough. 'Try again,' Mother urges, but eventually even she gives up and lets me be.

Ann sits and talks to me from the end of the bed. She has a letter. I'm not sure if it is the letter I've been waiting for, the one from Betty thanking me for the likeness that I made of her, asking me to wait through spring and summer for the herring season to start up, when she'll be back. Her trunk is already packed, her kist she calls it, her gutting knife – the cutag – wrapped in her shawl, her apron and her boots ready to go in. Or is it a note from George Allard telling me he'll have to find another boy if he's ever to finish the line for his anchor? But as I watch Ann's face I think that maybe the letter is not for me at all, but is word at last from Jimmy Kerridge, telling her he loves her, and the war is nearly done. He'll be coming home to marry her. Is that it? Or why does she look sad?

Ann makes stars from strips of straw and hangs them across our window. 'You need to eat,' Mother's eyes are dark, and from the shadow behind her, Mrs Horrod appears. It's strange to see her curious face under my sloped roof, and she sits by the bed and feels my pulse and puts a rough hand on my forehead. 'Peppermint and elderflower,' she says. 'And whisky for the heart.' And later that day I twist and turn my head as the hot stinking liquor is pressed against my mouth.

The next morning I wake early. There is no sound but the birds, calling. A pure clear whistling and a high *peep peep*. Ann is not in the bed beside me. She must have fled from my scorched limbs to the big room in which the Cheshires have left their smuts and smells. A weak light seeps through the window, and the roar that has been in my ears is gone. I look out at the day and a calm washes over me. I wrap a blanket round me and walk through the slumbering room next door, and down the ladder to the main bar where the ash of the fire is still warm. I push some sticks against it and breathe it into life, and with the effort of my puffing, the whole world spins. I steady myself and pull open the back door. It's cold. A shroud of frost brightening the yard, and the air is sharp and sweet. I step into boots and stumble outside. The well is open, the bucket silvered, and I drop it down, waiting while it fills, and when it comes up, I raise the water and I drink. I'm as thirsty as a newly planted tree. I feel the water spreading through my limbs, so hungry am I for it that I can hardly swallow. I splash my hands and face, and then I tip the last drops over my head and feel my body start with life.

'Tom!' It is Ann at the door. 'Come inside, you lunatic.' She holds the blanket that I've dropped there and she wraps me up and sits me by the fire. 'Happy Christmas,' she laughs. She can see that I am better. And she goes out into the yard to release the hens, and bring in the eggs, which this morning we'll keep for ourselves.

*   *   *

The letter, when I find it, is from Mac.

> *My dear Thomas*, it says. *I'm sorry to hear that you're not
> well. Please, as soon as you are better, come and call on us,
> as we will be very happy to see you. There may even be a
> wee gift for you here. A surprise. Which means I cannot let
> you know what it is now.*
>
> *With very best wishes,*
> *C R Mackintosh*

I trace the initials of his name, the round black flowing letters.
C R Mackintosh. Charles Rennie. But hard as I study it I'm
still no closer to discovering the secret code – MMYT – he uses
in his letters to his wife.

I'm excused church, although I would have gladly gone,
ready as I am for any kind of life. Mother has prepared a side
of muntjac, although she won't say where she got it, but there
is nothing for me to watch this time as she is going to roast it
with stewed apple when she gets home and so avoid the chance
of burning. 'You'll keep yourself warm?' Father mumbles, by
way of farewell, and Mother runs back in and kisses me on the
top of my head.

I sit by the fire and wait. The service at Christmas is always
longer, for the vicar must bring the whole village closer to God
on this day if not on any other, and so I rifle through my
schoolbooks and look down the margins at what I've scrawled
there. Wherries and winklebrigs, smacks and yawls, and then
later, in the clothbound book Mac gave me, the sweet smiling
face of Betty. What would she have written if the letter had
been from her? And I imagine her words curling across thin
paper. *The whole island of Lewis has gathered here to take a
look at your picture. So cleverly done it is, and so like me. The
winter here is harsh. With snow thick as a blanket, and*

nowhere to go but to sit by the turf fire. I'm in a hurry for the spring. And after that the summer, by the end of which will see me setting off for Suffolk and the work and fun that is to be had gutting the herring.

I close my eyes. What else might she have said? *My sister is well again and will be my companion, although this year she'll bind her fingers doubly tight before she takes hold of her knife. I'll write to Mrs Horrod, to keep hold of the rooms, and I'll let you know too what day we shall arrive.*

I pull a page free from the binding of my book and start on my reply. *My dear Betty,* I put the pen in my mouth and then remove it fast before Runnicles can rush over from Wenhaston and swipe it away. *I'm glad you're keeping well. I've had some kind of fever, stayed with me a while. But thanks to the cheering words of your letter I'm well again. How is it in the Highlands? Is the war very bad for you there? There are rabbits aplenty here. And we still have eggs and food from Mother's garden. There are others a lot worse off than we are. I heard of a ship – the* Hawke, *torpedoed by a U9 in your waters, overturned in fifteen minutes with only time for two lifeboats to be lowered. There weren't many survivors, but some were taken to Aberdeen. That's not so far from you, I think?*

I picture Mac's letters as I flounder for anything else to say. And then, trying for his words, I write: *I'm sitting alone here at the inn, but if the door were to open, there's no one I'd be happier to see than you.* No. I shiver with the horror of it. And quick as I can I blot out that last line.

Chapter 39

Mother is up at first light and ready to go poltering with Mrs Horrod. There have been gales through the night and they want to get there early to see what's been washed up. 'You might as well stay home,' Mother tells me, 'poorly as you've been.' But it's weeks since I last checked the beach, although I've heard of nothing unusual come in, save for a cask of stout, discovered by the Cheshires who broached it and drank it out of buckets where they stood.

I pull on my coat, and a scarf of Father's, and running off ahead of them I slide on the ice of each thin puddle as I tread down the lane to the beach. The dunes as I climb them are threaded with snow, scattered stiff as lace across the sand. We're the first here, I'm sure of it. But as I reach the top I can see other figures, crouched over the sand, stooping and searching with gloved hands. 'Quick,' I call to Mother as she ambles behind, Mrs Horrod smaller and stouter by her side, and I take the bag she's brought and run with it, my eyes searching for any black shape against the white. The tide is low now and the beach is half a mile deep. A charred stick sits on the sand, and beside the stick an orange stone gleaming up at me. I lift it and weigh it and knowing as I already do that it is not a piece of amber I throw it far out into the spit. It lands with a small glug and sinks into the sand.

I turn to find Mother talking to two women. Their sacks, from the strain of their arms, are at least half full. How have they found so much coal when until ten minutes ago the sky was dark? Have they used lamps? I narrow my eyes, and heavy with suspicion I tell myself it must have been the snow that led them to it. I daren't think anything else. I stare for a moment at the rising sun, test my eyes before they become dazzled, and then, while the women are still talking, I run, nose down, across the beach. At last I find some. Smooth and black, scattered high up on the shingle, and with my back to the others I scoop it into my bag.

'That's a good lad you have there.' It is Mrs Virtue, the sneak, coming to see what I have found, and she bends down and from under my hand she snatches up the last splinter of the coal.

'Yes,' I hear my mother sigh. 'God saw fit to bless us.' I feel their pitying eyes follow me as I hobble away along the beach.

I tread the waterline as far as the groynes and search amid their limbs. Seaweed glows wetly in the light and I imagine octopus and starfish blinking at me from behind their waving arms. I'm always hopeful I'll find treasure here. It's where I'd hide it if there was any to hide. But there is nothing, just a length of planking half buried in the sand. I tread closer, my footsteps springing up behind me, and that's when I catch sight of it. A mound of a shape, lumped up behind the wood. I can hardly breathe. My boots are sinking, but as I come closer, there's no doubt it is the body of a man. His face is down, his hair pasted thin across his scalp, and his ear, the one that I can see, is nibbled to a frill. 'Mam,' I shout as I bend over him. He has boots on, the leather swollen, the laces stretched, and his trousers are ripped and ragged to the knee.

I kneel down and touch him. There's something there. A canvas pouch, bound with twine, strapped around his leg below the knee. I look behind me. Mother is a black silhouette, stooping low against the snow. But Mrs Horrod, with her eager ears, has heard me, and she is hurrying this way.

Quick as I can I slide out my knife, and I slice through the string. A trail of seaweed has caught up in it, and the canvas is slimy. I hold it in my hand. I weigh it. There is gold inside. Or better than that. Gems. I slip it into my pocket, string and all. And I glance at his leg, the grooves of it, like slashes, where not so long ago he must have bound his treasure to him tight.

'Tommy?' Mrs Horrod is upon me. Her small eyes blazing. 'What have you found?' And she comes closer and bending down she slides her fingers under the man's shoulder and lifts him just enough to see into his face. It's terrible. A wide-open mouth and the nose smashed sideways.

'That's enough now, Tommy,' she says. 'Look at you. White as a sheet. Hurry away and find the coastguard. Or James Ladd up at the ferry.' And as I go I see her bend low again to look into his face.

I don't see the coastguard but I tell James Ladd and he sends news of it across the river, so that by the time I find the harbour master and lead him back, there are a crowd of people round the body, and Mother and Mrs Horrod frantic with the telling of the story.

'There's no name on him. No papers. Nothing to tell us who he is.' It's Shrimp the coxswain, never happy to let a man perish in his waters. And he pats down the man's clothing, and checks his pockets once more to prove the truth of his words. My face flushes hot and cold. And my body too. I feel it prickling below my shirt. And the canvas packet, wet as it is, is forcing a green stain through the wool of my jacket. If only I'd had the quick thinking to slide it into the poltering bag instead, and I take a quick look down, my heart beating, and cover my action by the mumble of a prayer.

'Thomas Maggs.'

My head jerks up.

'You're proving to be quite the little lookout. We'll be relying on you in future. Although you missed that cask of stout and a box of margarine that was hauled in last Monday.' The harbour master laughs, and I give him back a smile.

'Yes,' I say. 'Is it possible . . . do you think . . . might he be a spy?'

'Whatever he was, he's nothing now.' Mrs Horrod is quiet, and I look across at George Allard, and I see him nodding, as if to say, you see, I've trained the boy well.

A roll of canvas arrives, and the man is levered on to it and carried up the beach. We all walk with him, and when we're on firmer ground he is lifted on to the back of a cart, and taken away to the mortuary at Southwold, the ferry silent as he takes his last voyage. I'm tempted to go with him. Feel I owe him that much at least. But Mrs Horrod is inviting us to breakfast, and I'm so hungry at the mention of it, I can hardly stand up. She has a pan of porridge, she says, waiting in the oven, and a spoon of cream sitting on the sill.

'Thank you,' I say, but Mother hesitates. 'Your father may be up,' she looks at me. Her fingers are still splinted together inside her ragged glove. But then – I see her reasoning – we haven't found enough coal to be sure of his good cheer anyway, so . . . she shrugs, we might as well risk his fury after breakfast, as before. She laughs. And Mrs Horrod laughs with her. And the two women link arms. And pressing my hand against my pocket, I let it rest there against the corner of the canvas package, as I walk along behind.

The porridge is fine and silky. And the cream that's stirred into it, with a spoon of honey, tastes so good I sigh. 'What do you say, boy?' Mother prompts, and I shake my head and, just as if I were a child, I chant, 'Thank you, Mrs Horrod. It's so good. Can I have more?'

'Wait till you've finished that bowl first,' Mother shakes her head. But Mrs Horrod laughs. 'I'll be saving some for Vic when he comes down.'

'Vic is home?' How is it possible I didn't know? And the days that passed while I lay feverish in my room hit me like a slap.

'Yes.' Tears spring sudden into Mrs Horrod's eyes. 'He's home all right. Just for a few days. He'll want to know about the drowned man.' But although we sit over a second pot of tea he doesn't come down.

'Poor little old boy,' Mother whispers later when I ask. And when she catches my surprise, she says she's sure a bit of rest will give him back his strength.

George Allard's son Abb is home too. I've seen him in his uniform striding through the village. Chin up, chest forward, the tips of his boots striking the road. He must have fought in a different battle, where the enemy were driven back, and not as I hear now, in Vic Horrod's regiment, where Girling, Spence and a score of others lost their lives within the same half hour.

'The anchor rode is finished, thanks to Abb,' Mr Allard has told me, and he's promised to send word for me when more orders come in.

There are chores to be done and logs to split before I'm free to climb the ladder to my room. I shut the door tight and, having nothing else, I push the chamberpot in front of it. Carefully I draw the package from my pocket. The canvas is still damp and there's a tide of salt washed up at its corners. I lay it on the floor and unwrap it. Over and over, the material unfolds, and finally, at its centre, just as I'd thought, there is the chink of gold. My heart leaps and then it plummets. It is not a coin but the gold edge of a painting made on china. And beneath it are two others. Portraits in miniature. The first is of a woman. She has a stiff collar, and her hair is piled high, but her eyes when I squint into them are warm and chestnut brown. Two children stare from the other frames. Soft curls and polite smiles. I take them in my hands and I hold them, the cold painted china, the hopeful faces, until they are warmed.

Later, I pull up the mattress and I tuck them with my coins into the safety of the bed. And then I kneel beside them and I offer up a prayer. To keep my mother and my sister safe, wherever I am. And I renew my promise to check the beach each morning as soon as I'm awake.

The snow has gone but it's still cold. There's a wind that whips in from Siberia, without a mountain range between. Out at sea a naval flying boat shoots along the coast on its patrol, and I follow it with my eyes, raking the waves for what it might have missed. I tread the shoreline, jumpy as a coot, fearful I'll find another body hidden in the sand, and as I near the harbour wall, I tell myself low murmuring stories, to stop the terror racing in my heart. But there's nothing here today. Just seaweed, and the low, clumped stumps of groynes, with the water rushing away from me, silver in the sun.

Now I've made my inspection I'm free to visit Mac and his My Margaret, for I've not forgotten there's a present waiting for me there. But if I do, I'll need to take a gift of my own. I search the shingle for a fossil. I found one once, the shape of a shell pressed into flint, thousands of years old, and another time, collecting stones as weights for bait, I came across a hag stone lined with crystal. I gave it to Mother. And I try to picture where she might have stored it before I force away the thought.

I crouch down and inspect the stones. I try to see them as Mac would. There is one pebble shaped like a heart – or almost – and I think of the pamphlet of Mac's designs. There were hearts carved into a bookcase, and a cluster of them floating high up in the panel of a bedroom door. There were small dropping hearts in lamps, and most beautiful of all, a square of metal moulded to the rise of a heart with a doorway at its centre for a key. But my pebble is lopsided, and only glows when wet, so I leave it on the beach and turn my thoughts to flowers, the twigs and sticks Mac likes to draw, the willow his wife weaves into globes.

I walk through the reedbeds, their stems ash grey, and consider cutting down a bunch. But they are more than six feet tall and their heads, once fine, are tattered and worn. At the fork where the path turns I inspect the stubby twigs of blackthorn as if they are quite new. Their thorns are sharp as razors and even as I reach for one it rips a corner from my cuff. I look around. There is nothing but chaff and grey and silver in this whole low land. What could I find here? What could match a surprise? And I turn towards the church to see what Mother has found to put on the grave.

The churchyard is silent, the last of the snow unmelted here. My footsteps crunch as I walk between the graves. At first it seems there is nothing for our boys, but as I get closer I see the pot is full, the leaves in tiers, white and bowed. I give them a shake and they unbend, grateful, three stems of glossy green. I lean close in and smell, but all scent has frozen away. And so I stick out my tongue and lick a leaf and there it is, the bitter taste of bay.

*　　*　　*

It is Mac himself who comes to the door. It seems to take him a moment to tell that it is me, but I unwind the scarf from my face and pull off my hat. 'Tom Maggs,' he says. 'I heard you were up and about the place again. Come in.' He holds the door wide.

Mrs Mackintosh is sitting by the fire. She has a cloth over her knees and a needle in her hand. She rises, a long red thread dangling. 'Look at you,' she says, 'nothing but skin and bone.' And holding the needle high, she puts her arms around me. I blush, scarlet. And I feel the heat of her blazing through the room.

'Let's get you something to eat,' she is releasing me. 'Don't tell me you're not hungry?' She slides the needle into her work and laying it on a pile of silken threads she moves out to the kitchen to see what Mrs Mollett has prepared.

I stand still with the bunch of bay I picked on my way here. My coat is on. Old Mac has vanished too, although I didn't see him go, and so I stand where they have left me and I look around. There is a picture hanging above the fire that I've not seen before, the surface of it rough as sand, the shapes raised, as if by sandworms tunnelling from below. I move closer. There are two women, one upright, the other curved, and at their ears and throats are roses made from jewels. I put my fingers out but just then Mrs Mac comes in with a tray.

'Ah,' she looks pleased. 'So you've seen my gesso.' She sets the food down on the table. 'I couldn't leave it behind in Glasgow. Not again.' She comes and stands beside me.

'But what is it?' I want to know. 'How is it made?'

Mrs Mac looks at the picture in silence as if, for once, she's seeing it through my eyes. 'Well,' she says slowly, 'you mix plaster of Paris, and stir it together with rabbit-skin glue, and you paste it on, layer after layer, until you have the surface that you want.' She's staring at it, hard. 'Then, just as if you were piping icing on to cake, you make your marks on it, form shapes, press stones and glass, into its surface.' She is smiling, looking up at her own work. 'It's not easy, and takes a lot of strength, and the wretched glue stings your hands if you don't wear gloves. But . . .' and she looks closely at the jewels studding the picture, the fast swirls of the paste, 'I'm pleased with this one. There are not many people doing gesso, and it's been said,' she colours slightly, 'mine are some of the best.'

'Yes,' I say. I badly want to touch it.

'I made a larger version of this picture. To go above the fireplace at Florentine Terrace. But now I've rented out the house,' her shoulders lift, 'I worry for it. And for all the furniture Toshie designed. Even after a week, when I stopped by, I found the house was not as orderly as when we left it.' She is fretting, twisting her hands. And to help her I suggest she pluck the emeralds and the rubies from the surface of the picture, and then surely she wouldn't have to rent out the house at all.

She laughs. She laughs so hard her mouth flies open. 'I would, believe me. But . . .' and she whispers in my ear, 'those precious stones are only coloured glass.'

'Oh.' I am ashamed. But she takes my sprig of leaves from me, and my coat, and leads me towards the table. 'Come and have something to eat. Toshie and I were just about to have our lunch.' There is a plate of cold mutton. A pot of mustard. And three slices of thick bread.

Mr Mac comes in from the next room. He's trailing a string of orange wool, although it's not clear that he's noticed. He sits down beside his wife and as he does, although he doesn't wink or move his mouth, it's clear he has told her something, and it is something that she's understood. I eat slowly. My stomach is too shrunken to gobble. So that I have to chew, and sip and take my time, even if the others have left the table and started on their chores while I hold tight on to my bowl in case anyone gives up on me and wrenches it away.

But everyone eats slowly today. And between mouthfuls there are questions to be asked. They want to know about my illness, if I'm truly well, and each time I answer, they rest their knives and forks and listen while I talk.

'And you are twice the hero. Is that not so?' Mac asks. 'What is this news about a body discovered on the beach?'

I gulp. And nod. And tell them what they haven't asked. 'We don't know who he is,' I say. 'There was nothing to be found on him.' I feel myself flush as I lower my voice. 'It's possible he might have been a German spy.'

'Is that a fact?' Mac leans towards me. 'What makes you think so?'

But there is no evidence and I have nothing more to say.

Mrs Mac brings in a plate of seedcake, and dutifully I eat, forking in small mouthfuls, as Mac takes up a letter.

'It came this morning,' Mrs Mac tells him. 'My sister, wondering if you'll be able to help with the fees for Sylvan's school?'

'I had a letter from my own sister last week, asking the same thing. Although she couldn't resist adding that I was too proud and stubborn for my own good.' He shakes his head. 'Although what she thinks grovelling and begging would have done to help the situation I don't know.'

Mrs Mac pours tea. 'How much longer is her boy in school? It can't be long now. Surely not much more than a year?'

It's clear Mac doesn't know.

'And when he leaves? What will he do then?'

'The police. That's what he's planning. To work his way up in the police force like my father.'

'Assuming that the war is over.'

Mac lays a hand over hers. 'And it will be. Surely.'

'Yes,' Mrs Mac agrees. 'It must be. In another year.'

It seems they've forgotten about me. I reach out for more cake. I've eaten so much that my stomach aches, but even so, I know if I don't force down one more piece I'll wake in the night, regretful.

'Now, Tom, my boy,' Mac's black eyes are resting on me, 'we have something for you.' He stoops down to the floor and picks up the ball of orange wool that must have fallen there.

Mrs Mac looks over and she smiles. 'Take it,' she says. 'And see where it will lead.'

'Really?' I stand, the wool in my hands, unsure what to do.

'This was our Christmas tradition.' Old Mac is smiling too now. 'Every year my sisters' children would come over for a party. And they'd each take a ball of different-coloured wool and follow it. Go on, start winding,' he says, and I see that the yarn is trailing off across the floor. I follow it, feeling foolish. Imagining the other children. A crowd of them tangling up in a spiderweb of thread. But I keep walking, winding as I go, turning the ball in my hand as it leads towards the kitchen.

In the kitchen all is neat, the plates on their shelf, the cups with their fine china stems, the pans hidden by the strip of cloth, black and white and pink. The wool runs under a table, round its leg, and out again, through the main room, along the floorboards, winding round Mac's desk. I stop there to untangle it. Noticing as I do a tall blue book, wide as the desk itself, tied together with a ribbon.

'Keep winding,' Mac is impatient, and I free the wool and follow it over to the fireplace, around the legs of a footstool and back on itself into the bedroom. I stop. The room could hardly be more different from the photographs. No white carpet, no flock of hearts in the panel of the door, but all the same the bed is tucked in with a white cover and there is a silver mirror moulded with the leaf shapes of two women on a ledge above the hearth.

I step into the room. The bright wool leads me to the foot of the bed, round its brass legs, and over to the window where it disappears into a wooden chest. I stop and stare at its orange tail and I imagine throwing open the chest to find a hoard of treasure, briny and glinting, dragged up from the sea.

Both Mac and Mrs Mac are waiting. What can it be? My breath comes fast as I creak open the lid. Inside is a package wrapped in brown paper. It is flat and hard. And my heart sinks to think I'll be given a picture of a flower, but when I fold away the paper, there is a painting of a boat. It's a small boat. Upside down and beached on the shore. Blue, with a stripe of white below the rim, and on the white, in curled black letters, is my name. Thomas. 'I wish I had the real thing to give to you,' Mac says. But I can see from his face that he believes that this is more.

'Thank you,' I manage. And I hold the board in my hands and turn it up so I can see how the boat might look when it is tipped into the water. 'Thomas,' I say, for I must say something. And I wind up the last skein of the wool.

I put my boat on the window ledge beside the geese, and from my bed I watch it in the shadowy dark. Ann is asleep beside me, her face turned away, her breath so quiet I can hardly hear it. I close my own eyes and imagine the *Thomas* floating on our river. I see its blue bottom gliding on the high flat water, its strip of white catching the sun. If you can make a building like the Glasgow School of Art, I think, then surely you can build a boat? And I drift about on a tide of tree trunks, each one wide enough to curve into a hull. If you can design air-cooling vents and lamps for electric light, then surely it must be possible to carve a rudder from a plank of wood? I'm so disappointed I have to hold my breath. But even then I see the *Thomas* as if she were alive. And by the time I fall asleep I've fixed two riggers to her sides, drawn the oars up into the bow, lain down in her polished hull and, with the current rushing in, floated downriver to the sea.

Chapter 40

It's New Year's Day and the Cheshires are back. They stamp into the inn and sling their bags up the ladder and through the open door into their room. They're shiny with home and a week at a training camp in Stafford where they learnt to throw grenades. They have the story of one old sergeant who took it upon himself to give a demonstration and promptly blew himself up. But the Cheshires are laughing. They heard the explosion, they say, while they were digging latrines, and when they arrived they saw the tree under which the man had been standing, scorched and split, with just a strip of uniform hanging from a twig. Some other men, from another division, were asked to clear things up. And in the mess that night they raised their glasses to his memory.

'Lost in the service of his country,' Gleave says now, and he takes a noisy slurp of beer.

Later I hear him in the yard, lighting up a cigarette, talking in a low voice to Ann. I want to go out to them, and warn them about the red glow of the tip, sending signals to our enemy through the dark. But when I creak open the door I see their two shapes, close together, moving out across the field, and the cigarette, if he still has it, must be cupped close in his palm.

I stand by the well. There is a crescent moon, silver, hanging above the sea, the shadow of its rocky stomach lying in its lap. I listen for a whisper of them, my eyes closed, and then a bat soars past my ear, a tiny shriek from both of us splitting through the dark. Afterwards I laugh. The well is open, I feel the chill of its damp brick, and I stop myself from throwing my voice down into it. *Hello, lo, lo, lo, o.*

'Where are they?' I remember why I'm out here, and quiet as I can I walk towards the trees at the far end of the field. 'Ann,' I call, but there is silence, and then the muffle of a laugh, and as I stand I see the one black shape of them, tangled together against the arms of the yew.

The next day when I come in for my lunch Gleave is sitting by the fire, the newspaper spread out before him, while the other man, Booth, tall and awkward with a red, raw Adam's apple, grunts as he leans forward to cover the front page.

'What's the news?' I ask. I'm hoping it will be a call for rope production across the whole south-east of Britain but Gleave nudges his friend and the man, with his thick fingers, flips over the page. I move closer. There's a picture of a ship. 'What's that?' I say, straining to read, just as Ann comes in with a stack of bowls for soup. And I laugh. They've got it wrong. That can't be HMS *Formidable*. That grey metal monster without a single sail? And it takes me a moment to catch the words beneath it. *More than 600 men lost.*

I swivel round to look at Ann. 'What?' she asks. She knows my face too well. And she glances at the soldiers who have folded the paper into squares. Not one of us says a word. 'Come on,' she holds her hand out for the news, and when no one offers anything, she screams so loudly that even Gleave's face goes pale.

Ann rushes the paper into the kitchen. 'No,' she sounds as if she's being hit, 'no, no, no.'

Gleave leans back in his chair and frowns. 'Sunk in the Channel by a German submarine, although it does say seventy-one men were picked up by the skipper of a trawler.' I wait for more news of what they've read, but when the men fall silent I slip out of the room and into the kitchen where Ann is crouched down by the stove. 'Not all were lost,' I whisper into her ear, but she is shaking, her eyes glazed, and I put my arms around her and I tell her, 'Seventy-one were pulled out of the sea. Seventy-one, Ann, seventy-one.'

Father finds us like this on his way to the cellar. 'What you two doing snivelling down there?' he says and that's when I know I'll do it. One day. I'll take a mallet and I'll knock him into the ground.

Our soldiers never get their paper back. Ann takes it up to bed and reads over every word. 'Yesterday.' This is what most distresses her. The boat sank yesterday and she didn't know. '*In the early hours of January 1st...*' Her hands are icy and her body shakes. And I think of hens and how they can die of shock. '*... The battleship HMS* Formidable *was sunk by two torpedoes from a German submarine 20 miles off Start Point. The first torpedo hit the number-one boiler port side, a second explosion caused the ship to list heavily to starboard. Huge waves 30 feet high lashed the stricken ship with strong winds, rain and hail, sinking it in less than two hours. One pinnace with seventy-one men on board was picked up by the trawler* Provident, *15 miles off Berry Head. There are no other known survivors.*'

Ann falls asleep sitting up, the paper in her arms. I lie beside her trying to decide what could have happened to the other lifeboats. Would they have not been lowered, and wouldn't men have leapt down into them? And I wonder, were they swamped by waves or did they cast about all night, looking for land? Are they out there now, with their captain, Loxley he was called, and the ship's dog, whose name, apparently, was Bruce? And I picture Jimmy Kerridge bailing water with his cap, straining his eyes for a torch to guide him towards the coast, a beacon, or a candle, even the red-hot tip of someone's cigarette.

Chapter 41

With Abb gone back to his regiment I try George Allard again, although he's sent no word to me.

'He's busy just now,' his wife calls when she finds me at the door, but I catch sight of him through the hall window, stepping backwards through his garden with the hemp around his waist.

'Who's he found', my heart stutters, 'to do my job?' And I peer round her to see who is sitting at the wheel. But Mrs Allard spreads her arms to block my view. 'That's enough now. Best for you to go on home.'

'Home?' I'm having none of that, and I duck under her arm and I'm off round the side of the building to the garden.

But there is no one sitting at the wheel. There is no wheel. In its place is a small windmill and it's standing out by the corner of the house where the breeze can spin its sails.

'Good day to you,' Mr Allard can't help but look proud. And as he moves backwards the strands of the hemp twist together into twine. I nod but I can't speak. I can see the pulley, polished to a shine, the pulley I once saw resting by his front door, and there are the shafts of wood he's been collecting, and the strips of cloth, stitched and held, full of the days and weeks and months of work that must have gone into them. I stand there, my mouth open. Backwards he goes, the wheel turning without any human help, and I think of the three boys his father hired, the pride of it, and I wonder if maybe now he'll find another job for me to do. If I stand here long enough maybe he'll forget and tell me the story of the Saxon founder of our village, or how the Vikings sailed down the River Blyth in their canoes. He may tell me again about the church that used to stand in Chapel Field as long ago as 1400, and how it had been near as forgotten until the farmer Robert Gooch ploughed up its cemetery, raising the old worn names out of the ground. But George Allard has nothing for me today. His lips are set, and his tongue is still.

'What if there's no wind?' I shout to him. But he shrugs his shoulder. 'Then we'll read about it in the *Gazette*, and take our tea, and sit down on the beach.'

I flush then. At the mention of the paper, and not a word to me about HMS *Formidable*. Although he must know that it went down.

'You owe me a shilling,' I say.

'I can't stop now. You can see that.' He's walking away. 'But Mrs Allard will give it to you. Go round to the back door and tell her why you've come.'

Up in my room I untie the knot of my handkerchief, and drop the shilling in. The rent is due. I know it. Mother has been fretting all week. I dip my hands into the coins and run them through my fingers. I choose a sixpence which I shine against my cuff. I'll hand it over, but I won't tell her about the wind-powered wheel, not yet. Maybe I'll find some other job before I do, and I stare into the faces of the miniatures and think of the work available to a boy with one lame leg. Apprentice clerk. That's what Mother wants for me. But I'd rather go down to the brewery and offer my services as a bottle sniffer, checking each container that has been returned to see that it is clean. Or I could ask for work at the mill on Field Stile Road, sorting feathers into different weights. Someone must blow them up into the air and, as they float down, catch them and drop them into tubs.

They are advertising at the Homeknit factory on Pier Avenue. For a five-day week and a few hours on a Saturday they offer board and lodging, and a small wage, although, just like the herring girls, they ask their staff to sign an oath. *To faithfully serve the master, his secrets keep, his lawful commands everywhere gladly do.* I know they make underwear for troops – socks and vests and longjohns – but I know too that however glad I'd be to keep a secret, it is only girls they hire.

Ann is out. She has gone, on her unsteady legs, to visit Mrs Kerridge, and as soon as she is through the door Father begins griping. 'What has the girl got to be upset about? It's not as if she was planning to marry the lad. A sailor? I could have told her how that would end. War or no war. She'd be stranded like my brother Wilfred's wife when his ship hit the sands at Happisburgh. Body never found. Now she's taking washing in. If Ann's looking for misery and danger, she'd be better off marrying a soldier.'

'A soldier!' Mother sits heavily beside me. 'And where would that leave her, eh?' And she puts her head in her hands and weeps.

I think of Gleave and his leering grin. And it takes all my strength to keep the secret of the witch-woman, and the lies that she has spread.

The next day I don't go to school. I wait as usual for Mr Button to come by with his cart, but after I've jumped down, I turn around and cut back across the edge of Wenhaston Common, and on along the heath road towards Minsmere.

That old witch-woman must live here somewhere. If I can find her I'll ask what she meant by not telling us that the *Formidable* would sink. How can Ann marry Jimmy Kerridge if Jimmy Kerridge is lost? And I'll shake my fist at her and pull her spindly beard.

But Minsmere is wide open and barren, and after tramping over the fringes of it for most of the morning, I follow a sheep track that leads towards the cliffs. The patrol boats are out again, I scan the waters for anything they might have missed, and climbing over the barbed wire, I slide down the chute of crumbling earth, until I'm on the beach. There's no one here. The fishermen have headed north, if they've headed out at all, and eager to be useful, I search the tideline for anything that's been washed up. An empty tin, the lid of a barrel, a leather boot, so soft and blackened you could burn the thing as peat. I'm not sure what to do now. I daren't go home, or on towards the village, for fear that I'll be seen, and so I hug the shoreline, peering into caves to see where they will lead, waiting until the cliffs smooth down to the level of the land, and then I scramble through the undergrowth to the cover of the Hoist. I spend the day listening for woodpeckers, tracking the echo of their drill, hoping to catch one hammering its beak against the bark. *Crrrrrrrrreek.* The sound is like a tree falling. Every time. And even though I tell myself it's just a bird, I stand still and check there's not an oak coming down towards me, its roots tearing up out of the ground.

Having missed one day of school, and not been punished, I decide to miss another. But today as I trudge across the marsh, a fog rolls in like water. I'd know which way to go with or without sight, but even so I stand quite still and pretend that I am lost. A bush becomes a mountain, the sedge a lake, and I close my eyes and let my feet lead me, over tufts and down worn, known hollows, so that soon I'm winding up Lea Lane from the coast. There is no one to see me. Not unless they stand by my side, and so I creak open the Lea House gate and walk up through the garden.

Maybe it's because the Mackintoshes have no children of their own, but they don't mention school. 'Come in,' they say when they see me. 'Warm yourself.' And they sit me by the fire. Mac is working on a stem of witch hazel, one flower snapped off and floating in the air. 'Will you look at a book to keep yourself amused?' Mrs Mac says gently. She knows about the *Formidable*. I can hear it in her voice.

'Thank you,' I say, and not wanting to disturb them further I head towards the desk where the large, blue, clothbound book is propped against a shelf. I rub my hands clean against my jacket, and careful as I can I carry it back to the fire. It's tied with ribbons that must be unlooped and as it falls open I look up, startled by the sound of paper moving so loud in the quiet of the room.

The book is full of separate sheets. On the first is a picture of the outside of a house. It is white with tall windows, cut up into squares, and at one end the building curves like the prow of a boat. There are rose bushes set against a fence, their heads like bubbles on thin stems, and on the far side of the entrance, in the same leaf shape as Mrs Mac's tall ladies, a row of poplars disappear off the page. The whole picture is made in black and white and green, with studs of raspberry for the roses, and I look at it so long I don't notice at first the words in pen along the top. *Deen Wettbewerb ... für ein Herrschaftliches ...* I'm breathing hard ... *Wohnhaus eines Kunst-Freundes.* It takes such effort to read these words that the stilted sounds come out aloud. I look up to find that Mrs Mac has looked up too. 'Competition for a grand family house,' she translates. 'For an art lover.'

'For an art lover.' I blush. It seems somehow this phrase should remain private. And I glance over at Mac and I remember how much he loved to enter competitions. 'Did you win?' I ask him. But he is staring at his stick of witch hazel, a bright gold slick of paint quivering on his brush.

Mrs Mac comes to stand beside me as I turn to the next page. Here there is the dark interior of a dining room. A table long enough for knights, but with only two chairs, high-backed and cane-bottomed, and two vases, one at each end, both filled with heavy-headed roses. From the ceiling, which is domed and white, hang green bulbs of light, eight of them, fringed with feathery-tipped tassels. But most wonderful of all, around the walls, are Mrs Mac's pictures, each one featuring a woman with a rose, or many roses, scattered across a cloak, tucked into a swirl of bright wild hair, wrapped around her women in a cocoon. 'Made from gesso,' she tells me. 'Twenty-four panels. *The Life of the Rose.*'

Very carefully I lift the sheet of paper to reveal the one below. And I laugh. I'm so surprised. There must be nothing like this, surely, anywhere in the world. I turn to Mac again. 'So you did win!'

'*Das Musik Zimmer*. The music room.' Mrs Mac leans over me. 'Toshie's idea was that you move from the dark hallway into this room full of light.'

The music room is sparkling. Windows high as the walls, pillars like a glade of trees leafing at the top with green. From the ceiling hang white lamps in squares, each side painted with a raspberry-coloured heart, and there is a cluster of king's thrones in blue, with globes like drops of sky between each clutch of lamps. I want to go there, roll over its white floor, sit at the white piano on its bench for two and listen as music fills the room.

Mrs Mac lifts the next page, and takes me into a smaller room, with a white oval table, and a silver mirror, and two window seats tucked into alcoves, facing each other like a pair of doves. She leads me upstairs to the children's room, and we stand there together and look out through the windows and I'm sure I can hear the seagulls calling, the same ones I hear now.

'Is this house in Glasgow?' I whisper, for Mac is still working, his breath shallow, his movements sudden as he dips his brush.

'It could be,' she answers. 'It could be anywhere.' She sends me a secret smile.

Mac stands abruptly. His face is dark. 'It seems I didn't submit the required number of drawings. They needed a certain amount of interior perspectives, and I only gave them . . . Well, they weren't able to give us the first prize.'

'Who did get it then?' There couldn't be a building more beautiful than this anywhere in the world.

'No one.' Mac paces the room. 'Although there was a reward for a mock-medieval castle, perfectly acceptable, orthodox in every way. They're sticklers for etiquette, these Austrians, well, the architectural society in general. But in Vienna everything must be done just so. Instead they gave us a special commendation. A consolation prize. To say "There, there".'

'No, Toshie.' Mrs Mac looks pained. 'A special commendation is not that at all. It means they commend you. They admire you. You know how revered you are in Europe.'

'And to who did they commend me? To my own country? To my own city? Who still treat me with hostility and suspicion. So that these last three years I've not had a single commission.'

'Kate Cranston still asks you to design the interiors for her tea rooms,' Mrs Mac tries.

'Yes,' his eyes are bright with fury. 'And happy as I am to do so, I'd rather be designing Liverpool Cathedral.'

I hold the book on my lap. *Deen Wettbewerb für ein Herrschaftliches Wohnhaus eines Kunst-Freundes.* I try the words again. And as Mac, the fire gone out of him, sits back down on his stool, I ask him what language they speak in Glasgow. 'Same as you speak here. Give or take a few words.' He looks at me, bemused. 'Although my family was from the Highlands originally, and they speak Gaelic there. But it's not me who's good with languages. I can hardly write legibly in English, it's my wife here who is the clever one. Speaks French, and German as if it was her mother tongue.'

Mrs Mac laughs and shakes her head. They're friends again. It was as easy as that. And she moves to her easel and the twin women who are waiting there, and pulling on her white gloves, she lifts her brush.

'How did you learn?' I ask.

'At school,' she murmurs, 'and my parents liked to travel.' She steadies her eyes and I can feel her drifting, tunnelling back down into her work, until she is lost to everything but herself.

I look at each room again. The dining room. The music room. The library. There seems to be no drawing of the stairs. Is that the picture that was missing? But I'm on the top floor anyway, in the snowy softness of the bedroom. And I'm lying in the boxed-in bed, the feathers plump around me, Mrs Mac's embroidered curtains at the window. My head droops before the fire, my eyes swim in the warmth of woodsmoke, and I'm kneeling by a sea of bluebells, snapping them up by the roots, tugging at their spongy stubborn stalks. There's a sloe bush on the corner of the cemetery, whipped into white blossom, but then I must have taken a wrong turn because there is Runnicles, asking what is the capital of Moldovia, and when I don't know, I'm jolted upright by the smack of his ruler as it slams down on my hands.

'I'm sorry,' my head jerks up. But Mrs Mac is before me, stooping to catch the book which has fallen to the floor.

'It's all right,' she says. She has it clasped in her arms. 'I've got it.' And she carries the book across the room and places it in its position on the desk.

Chapter 42

I'm glad to see the Cheshires go. They are being called to the front. But first, and for the last time, Gleave tries to talk to Ann. He waits for her by the back door, and I hover in the kitchen to hear what he might say. 'I'm sorry,' he starts. There is no word from Ann. 'For your loss.' And I can feel him through the boards of the wood, struggling to go on. 'I'll think on you,' he says, 'when I'm out there facing the Boche. And if you would think on me . . .' But just then the door flings open, nearly knocking me off my feet, and Ann comes running in. I wait there, my back to the wall, and after a few moments I hear the crunch of Gleave's boots going away round the side of the inn.

'Ann,' I call up the ladder. I can hear the gasp of her sobs. But I'm due at school – I'll not risk Mother's fury again – and if I don't start running Mr Button will have passed by with his cart.

Battle of Dogger Bank.
Battle of Bolimov.
Defence of the Suez Canal.
While Runnicles writes on the blackboard I make a sketch of the *Formidable* in the margin of my book. It's not the

many-sailed, wooden frigate, abandoned in watercolour on its board in Thorogood's shed, but the real ship: the 15,250-ton pre-*Dreadnought* battleship with its gun holes and its chimneys and the lookout towers halfway up its masts. We know the story now. It was written in the paper. How calmly the men waited for the lifeboats to be lowered. How someone played a tune on the piano, while others started up a song. We read that the chaplain went below to find cigarettes for the men so that they could smoke while they waited to be rescued. And it was then the ship gave a tremendous lurch, and the captain shouted, 'Lads, this is the last, all hands for themselves, may God bless you and guide you to safety.' And then he walked to the bridge and, with his terrier on duty at his side, waited for the end.

The piano was thrown overboard. Boats smashed as they were lowered, or else they were swamped by waves and sunk. But we know now that it was not just one pinnace that got away, but a second, half full of water. One seaman sat over a hole in the boat from the time they started to the time of rescue. For rescued they were, but not until they'd seen dawn break out of sight of land, and been passed by a liner and eleven other vessels, as the sea pounded and waves as high as cliffs hid them from view. Night fell again. They were surely lost. But then through the blackness a light shone out from the shore, a red light, for two bright seconds, guiding them to land.

The boat was first seen at Lyme Regis, an outline on the horizon, by a Miss Gwen Harding, walking with her family along Marine Parade after dining out with friends. The alarm was raised. And so began the rescue. But by the time the pinnace was brought in there were only forty-eight men still alive, from a total of seventy, six of those that had perished still lying in the hull. Miss Gwen Harding, I repeat to myself. And although Jimmy Kerridge was not among those that were saved, I wish it had been me who'd been walking on Marine Parade. That it was me who'd seen the outline of that boat.

A shadow falls over my desk and Runnicles looks down. He sees the ship but he doesn't raise his hand. Instead he shrugs and moves to the front of the room. On the board are a scrawl of facts about the history and construction of the local church. How it was destroyed and rebuilt in 1696, the year of our Lord King William the Third, by two church-wardens whose names are commemorated on a plaque on the north side of the ruins. 'Copy this,' he says and he sits at the table and bows his head.

The billeting officer calls round to inspect our room, and although he promises more soldiers, the weeks pass and none arrive. 'What'll we do now?' Mother frets, for she's come to rely on the money they bring in. But Father is on the run, his face scorched, his eyes roving, and he has nothing useful to add.

Mother treads around him, careful, shrinking with the effort not to rile him, while Ann keeps mostly to her room. She's turned our bed into a nest of tears, and although I long to sleep at least one night in the good room I keep my place beside her. Ann needs me. She clings to my back through the long dark hours, and in the mornings when she wakes I'm there to hold her hair while she leans over the chamberpot and vomits. 'It's all the crying that's ailing her,' Mother says, and she blinks and turns away. 'Just keep out of his sight,' is what she advises. 'And wrap yourself up well.' And I'm glad sometimes that I'm not still turning the wheel for George Allard, so I can help Mother with the chores Ann leaves undone.

As winter edges towards spring Mac tries painting a snow-drop, dug up at the roots, and then a tiny sprig of violets, but they wilt before he can bring them to life. I find him a pinecone, newly fallen, springy with life. 'This is a cultivated specimen,' he tells me happily. 'The nearest indigenous Scots pine are in the Highlands.' And I think of Betty walking through woodland, the cones falling like rain about her head.

Thorogood's shed is still too damp for working in, and Mac has settled himself by the back window of Lea House. I watch him closely. A north light is what he needs, while his wife is happy with the view of the garden. 'Will you not start something?' they ask, but my heart is still heavy with the failure of HMS *Formidable*. I'm fearful that by imagining her to be made of such fragile things as wood and rope and canvas I had a hand in her downfall.

'Not today,' I tell them, and I shake my head.

I'm at Southwold reading a poster that's been pinned up outside the town hall.

Instructions:

For the guidance of the Civil Population in the event of Bombardment from the Sea or by Aircraft.

1. Inhabitants of houses should go into the cellars or lower rooms. If the houses are on a sea front where they are exposed to direct fire from the sea, the inhabitants should leave by the back door and seek shelter elsewhere.

2. Gathering into crowds or watching the bombardments from an exposed position may lead to unnecessary loss of life.

3. If an aircraft is seen or heard overhead, crowds should disperse, and all persons should if possible take shelter.

And that's when I think I hear them, the whirr of the starlings. I look up, but there's nothing there, and I'm still searching the sky when a regiment of cyclists wheels into town. 'It's the Royal Sussex,' someone shouts, and every man, woman and child in the street stops and stares. At first it looks as if they'll just keep riding. They'll speed on up the high street, past the Lord Nelson and on over the promenade into the sea. But at the top of the road, outside the Sailors' Reading Room, they stop. The crowd presses in on them. The Royal Sussex Cyclists. They're dressed much like any other soldier, their trousers tucked into boots, their rifles resting on their handlebars. I push myself forward, wriggling between bodies until I'm at the front.

'They're here to do coastal patrol duty.' It is the butcher, who's beside me.

'Dangerous work,' a woman adds.

Behind us someone sniggers. 'I don't know what use they'll be in France against the guns.'

The door of the Reading Room slams open and Danky comes out on to the steps.

'Danky,' I hiss across to him. I raise my hand and wave. But he's pulled his peaked cap down over his eyes and he's looking away from the cyclists, out over the sea.

Chapter 43

On Sunday Mary comes to us for lunch. Sir Bly's two sons are captains now, and the news from the front is good. We sit and listen to her talk, and as I watch I see how cleverly she looks away from Mother's swollen lip and the pallor of Ann's face. 'It's quieter up at the big house now,' Mary says, 'without so many recruits.' And keeping her eyes on the table, she tells us how she'd like to free herself from service and go over to the hospital they've made at Henham Hall, and train as a nurse for the Red Cross.

'You, a nurse?' Father snorts.

Mother, safe in numbers, flashes back at him. 'And who was it who tended to me all those years when I was ill after the boys?'

Mary is quick to change the subject. 'Have you heard news of the blockade? There's to be nothing at all taken to Germany by boat, from any country, not even from the United States of America. Starve them into submission, that's what the government is saying. Weaken them for the attack.'

We nod, and spoon up our stew. And I think of the Royal Sussex Cyclists surging through the ranks of the enemy, butting them with their high handlebars, slicing through them with their wheels.

'So what are you saying?' Father sneers. 'That until now we've been sending them our finest goods? Crates of apple cider. Barrels of pigs' trotters. Goose fat in screw-top jars.' And Ann, bent at the middle, runs from the table and out through the back door.

That night there's a spring tide and the water rushes in over the shingle, up the dunes and on to the marshes where it makes a lake knee-deep. At first light I walk down to its shore to see what I can find. I inspect the horizon, flat and still and no sign of an invader. I kick off my shoes, and roll my trousers high. Mud and silt squelch underfoot, and there's sand too, between my toes. There are stones and tiny shells, and I wish I'd woken in the night to see the waves tumbling up over the beach, rolling the sea bed with it. I peer into the water, but it's murky, brown as a canal, and I can't see anything, so I take a step. And that's when I feel it – a fish – in the mud below my feet. I bend down fast, it's slithered away, but when I take another step I graze my toes against it. I wade out to the bank and find a stick. It has one sharp end that I make sharper, and once I'm in the middle of the flood, I slam it down. Nothing. I step again, nothing, and then I come across a shoal of flounders, their bodies flat and shadowy as cloud. I crouch low and raise my spear. And I've caught one, pinned it by the neck. And thinking suddenly of Betty, and how I might tell her of my triumph, I drop it into my sack.

We have fish stew for tea that night. While Mother is preparing it she makes me walk along to Mrs Horrod just as it is getting dark. I glance across at Millside as I pass. There are men from the Duke of Westminster's unit stationed there now, and an armoured car parked in the yard. They'll have scared the tall ghost woman right back inside the mill, with their marching and their drills, and taking courage I edge into the middle of the road, and look up at the top window, right at the place that I once saw her peering in through the glass. Nothing there, I almost laugh, remembering how I was a boy then, holding tight on to my mother's hand, but even so I feel the air around me shift. What is that? I spin around, and before I can stop myself, I'm shivering hard enough to shake my teeth. 'Hello?' There's a shuffle on the verge, and I almost scream as a figure looms out from the hedge.

'Good evening.' It is Mac.

He has his cloak on and his hat, and if it wasn't for the white puff of his pipe, I'd still not see him. 'It's a good bit milder tonight,' he says.

'Yes.' And to steady myself I tell him how I caught half a dozen flounder and I'll bring him some if he and Mrs Mackintosh would like.

'Thank you,' he nods. 'Will you come by tomorrow? I'm not sure when I'll be through with my walk.' He turns down Palmers Lane, and I watch him go, his hat casting a black shadow in the darkness around.

I walk on to Mrs Horrod's. I hadn't known it but I'm to collect herbs for Ann.

'Wait here now, will you,' Mrs Horrod takes the fish, and so I stand by the fire where her husband sits.

'Full moon last night,' I say to him, and his mouth twitches just once so I know he's still alive.

Mrs Horrod's herbs smell bitter, even through the muslin of the bag. 'Tansy, parsley, penny royal and angelica,' she mutters as she ties it tight. 'Tell your ma to boil them up, strain them, boil them, and then strain them again. Then when they are cool, they can be swallowed. On an empty stomach, mind.'

'Boil, strain, boil, strain,' I murmur to myself, and I thank her and I run back down the street.

*   *   *

The next day the water is lower but I wade in anyway, spreading my toes wide. Mud, silt, stalks, sand. I walk slowly, lifting my feet high to avoid a splash, out across the marsh, my stick resharpened. I imagine the flounders, burrowing into mud, their boot-noses snuffling, their fins hovering like wings. I raise my stick high, and close up my heart. I'm determined to bring fresh fish to Mac. I want him to see the camouflage of their bodies, feel the flip of their tails in his hand. I go more slowly, the sky above me sodden, the land turned to sea. And there it is. A shiver in the mud, and I bring down my stick so fast I nearly spear my toe.

Mac is working on a bright purple grape hyacinth. He has it laid out on a sheet of paper and is examining its tiny solid head. 'No,' he mutters to himself, 'no.'

I've let myself in, but now I'm not sure whether to disturb him.

'Hello.' He looks up and catches me at the door, and he tells me that never has he spent a morning with a flower and known less about it when he was through. 'Look,' he lays it out. And together we peer at the dense purple blocks of it, solid as wax above its stalk of blazing green.

I reach into my bag and draw out a fish. It's the smallest one I've caught. Just long enough to cover my hand.

'Well,' he smiles, and he leans down and inspects its sandy coat, the dark dots that might be pebbles, the menace of its lower jaw.

'Will you paint it?' I ask, and he looks back at his hyacinth. 'Eat it, I think,' he says. And he takes the bag into the kitchen where he leaves it in a tray for Mrs Mollett.

I sit with Mac through the afternoon, hands scrubbed, insides warmed with tea. It's not long before he's battling with his flower again, and with Mrs Mac gone over to Southwold I tiptoe to the desk and bring the blue art-lovers' book over to the fire.

Speise Zimmer, Musik Zimmer, I watch for a break in Mac's drawing and I ask him, 'What does it mean, this word, *z-i-m-m-e-r?*'

'*Zimmer*', he says, 'is room.'

'*Zimmer,*' I murmur. And there it is, I've said it. If Mac is the enemy then I'm the enemy too.

'*Freundes?*' I ask him later. And he tells me. 'Friends.'

I could skip to think that it's that easy. 'If you could teach me a word a day, then one day I'll have a whole other language, and when I go off on my travels . . .'

'Yes,' he nods. 'In about two hundred years you'll be fluent.' And when Mrs Mac comes in, he tells her, 'This boy here wants to learn German.'

'Really?' she checks to see that we're alone. 'Why is that, Tom?'

I shrug. 'Or Gaelic?' And then I blush, because even as I say it I'm thinking of Betty. Betty, Betty, Betty. Since the start of spring her name has filled my head, and last night while Ann slept, I wedged the candle near and drew her a flounder. *Dear Betty*, I wrote below it. *I hope the winter's easing up. We're managing all right here. Although we have Zeppelins flying over now. They're on their way to London and don't bother with us. You'd like these little fish I caught, although they're not as simple as herring to gut. Carnivores they are. Do you have them in your part of the world? They stick close to the sea bed.* I wondered then how Mac would fill a page, and as I did, I chewed my pencil until the wood was pulp. *Let me know. There's nothing more I'd like than to hear some news of you.* And after another long chew, I signed, *Your Tom.*

Your Tom, I doodled, knowing that I'd never send it. *My Betty. My Betty Your Tom. MBYT.* And I had it. The secret of Mac's message. *My Margaret. Your . . .* what was it that Mrs Mackintosh called him? *Toshie. MMYT.*

The day is nearly done when I get home. The hens are out, chortling by their coop as if they'd prefer to be inside, so I stamp them into a line and clap my hands until every last one of them has run up the ramp. 'Ma?' I call, as I push through the back door, but the stove is out and there's no warm smell of food.

'Ma?' I call again and Father walks through, unsteady, from the bar. I glance at the clock on the mantel and see it's more than an hour before opening. He catches me looking and his face darkens, but the hand he lifts drops to his side. 'It's not any of your business', he turns away, 'how I run this inn.' And I see it across his shoulders. Why waste the effort it would take to raise my hand to you?

I climb the ladder. I'm thinking I might count my coins. Last time I counted there was a pound, five shillings and sixpence. There's no reason to think there might be any more today but the counting is soothing, and it's possible I may have got it wrong. But as soon as my head comes through the trapdoor I'm distracted by the smell. The bitter smell of Mrs Horrod's herbs. 'Keep calm now,' Mother is kneeling on the floor of her room, and Ann is hanging off the bed, retching out a filthy stream of brown.

'Oh Lord,' Ann cries when she has breath, 'help me,' and she clutches her stomach and curls into a ball. Mother looks up and sees me. 'Shhh,' she puts a finger to her lips. And slowly, calmly, she tells me to go down and light the stove and put a pan of water on for boiling. I nod, but I don't move. There's a sweat standing out from Ann's face, and her skin looks thick and greenish.

'Quick,' Mother hisses, as Ann retches again. And I clatter down the ladder and throw wood into the stove. There's half a pan of water already standing, but just in case I run out into the yard and throw the bucket down the well. It's darker now and silent, and the night is sharp with cold. The bucket hits the water and is sucked under, and I'm heaving it up when the back door opens. 'Where's your mother?' Father's silhouette sways, and I'm so frightened by the light spilling out from the kitchen that I shout at him to get back inside. A fury sweeps over his face and I imagine he might take me and hurl me down the well, but something stops him. He staggers backwards and slams shut the door.

It's blacker now than it ever was, and every minute that I stand there new stars crack open the sky. An animal screams. A fox I think it is. And I imagine the hens tucked up inside their hutch, their feathers swelling, their eyes swivelling with fear.

'A watched pot never boils.' I've heard Mother say it but I've never waited so long to find that it is true. I go back up the ladder. 'How is she?' I ask. Ann is lying on the bed, her face the colour of old candle. 'Please,' she murmurs, 'God forgive me.' Her lips tremble in prayer.

Mother looks at me, and I see that she is scared. I've never seen her scared before. Not of Father, not of travellers brawling in the bar, not even of the man who came across one year from Southwold Circus with a bear on a rope.

'Is the water hot?' she asks, and I tell her it's close to being boiled but not there yet. 'Bring it,' she says, and as I turn away I see her lift Ann's cover and adjust the bloody cloth that's clamped between her legs.

The water, away from my scrutinising, is grumbling in the pan. I roll down my sleeves and lift the handles, and step by heavy step I heave it up. I want to wait there, see how this water will be the thing to save my sister. But Mother wishes me away, and with nowhere else to go I open the door into the best room. It's cold and clean in here. And I can hear the talk of men in the bar below. Father must have opened up. Or have they been here all the afternoon? I listen to Father turning over his old theory that the guns in France and Belgium are drawing down the bad weather, flooding the land, freezing it, keeping winter with us when spring should have settled in.

'But it won't be long now . . .' Is that Fred Tilson? '. . . with Germany starved into submission.'

And Father cursing. 'So God damn it, why didn't they have the blockade before?'

'They did, they did have it. But America was still to agree. There's a lot of money to be made from a war.'

'Not so that I've noticed.'

'Someone's making it. Right now.' Gory is there too. 'Big business. That's why they'll keep it going.'

'No.'

There's no one wants that.'

The voices overlap each other so I can't make out the words. I take off my boots. I'd lie on the bed but my feet are black from the rot of the marsh and so I stand at the window, and with no light behind me I look out through the curtain. At first it's as if there's nothing there, but the longer I stand, the more clearly I can see the shape of the village, the row of houses opposite. Victoria Cottage, Holly Cottage, Thorncroft. I can see down to the end of the street where the road breaks up into a lane, and the sky above it, lit up by the sea, wide open and white. The other way is dark. Large shadowy buildings, and beyond it the arms of the mill, and before I can stop myself an image of Mr Allard's wind-powered wheel stabs me in the gut. How is he getting along? I wonder, telling his stories to those sails of cloth, and I imagine him looking hopefully towards it and asking, 'You want to hear what happened next?'

I lie down on the floor at the end of the bed. I fancy I can feel the glow from the fire below, warming the boards. And I listen to my father's voice telling the men about his days as a pork butcher and the business he was building up. I roll my eyes. And then I remember how he can sniff out disagreement even through a wall, and I turn on to my back and I listen instead to the rats tumbling and thudding in the roof.

When I wake it's dawn and I hear wailing. I stand too fast, forgetting where I am, and crash against a chair. I open the door, and rub my eyes in time to stop myself falling down the shaft.

'Ma?' There's no one in her room, and so I climb down the ladder. The snug bar is empty save for a few sour glasses striped with beer, and the main bar too. I open the front door and look out. Nothing but last night's moon, sinking low towards the sea. And then I hear it, the low, pained moaning, and my blood stills. It's Father. I've never heard him so much as sniff, but I know his crying all the same, and it's drifting through the outshot window of our room. I climb back up the ladder and push through the low door. Father is sitting by the bed, his face sodden with tears.

'Thomas.' My mother looks as if she's forgotten who I am, while Father, at the sight of me, puts his head in his hands.

I kneel down beside Ann. Her face is white and empty. Her eyes closed. And high up in her chest is the last tiny scratch of her breath.

I sit on a bench by the wall. I sit there through the morning and into the day.

The doctor comes, and shakes his head and, frowning, writes something on a square of paper, and might have said more if the man from the brewery hadn't arrived, delivering barrels, his horses steaming and stamping in the cold. Father splashes his face and goes out to talk to him. And with promises and more promises, and no money exchanged, together they bring the barrels in. Mrs Horrod hovers in the kitchen. She comes out when the doctor is gone and puts her arms round Mother. But Mother has frozen, her face is set, and as soon as it is polite to do so, she shakes her off and goes upstairs to Ann.

Dear Betty, I write when I'm alone *Now my sister is ill.* I don't tell her the truth. That Ann has slipped into unconsciousness. Too much blood lost, the doctor says. That she's unlikely to pull through. *I'm helping to look after her. Feeding her up with broth and rabbit stew. She's getting married in the summer. To Jimmy Kerridge who's been home on leave from the navy. How are you? How is the war treating you up there?*

I draw her a picture of a hen. I don't know why. Maybe because Ann liked to name them – Mirabelle was one, Clemency another, and Father once clouted her on the ear and said, now there'll be tears when I wring their necks.

I put my hand up to my own ear and I think of Father, and although I know there is no use in it, I go over every thing he's ever done that's pitiful and mean. But this time I stand up to him. I'm a warrior, David to his Goliath, and I shout the truth so that he staggers, and while he's off his guard, I knock him down. Yes. I raise my arm in triumph, and Betty's letter falls to the floor. I pick it up, and I read it over, but my thoughts are frayed from fighting and I have nothing more to add. Instead I fold it smooth and slide it into my pocket, and I lie down on the bench in the main bar, and close my eyes.

Chapter 44

It's Mac who finds me. Sitting by the grave. His tread soft on the grass. He has flowers in his hands, a drooping hellebore, that Mother calls green winter rose. At first I think the flowers are for Ann. She already has a spray of them, but then I see that Mac has his plant by the roots and from the way he's looking at it he's not letting it go.

'Will you come and have some lunch with us?' he asks me. 'Mrs Mollett has made a leek and potato soup.' And although my stomach tightens at the mention of it, I tell him I'm needed at the inn, for I can't leave Mother on her own for long.

'I'd best be away then,' he tells me. The plant is folding in around his hand. 'But don't be a stranger to us.' And he pulls his cloak round him and walks across the churchyard and out through the gate.

No one mentions going back to school. Without Ann I must do my best to help with the running of the pub, for it's not possible for Mary to give up her work at the hospital and come home.

On Sunday she cycles over and helps move Ann into the good room. 'It's the shock, I'm sure of it,' she says, 'that's frozen her,' and she sits and strokes her hair.

The shock of what? I want to ask her. Of the *Formidable*, or the sight of so much of her own blood? I squeeze Ann's cool hand, and I look at her body, shrinking, as the thin soup Mary feeds her slips down the side of her face.

Mary stays that night, tucked up beside me on Ann's side of the bed. I look over at her, her eyes open, and I wait, but she has nothing to say. Later we hear a Zeppelin coming in across the sea, thundering above us, making its way inland. A beam from the searchlight flashes across the window and I leap up and stick out my head and in the arc I see it, a fat, slick, gold cigar. A spray of gunfire bursts after it, jolting me so that I hit my head. But Mary doesn't shout at me to come in, not as Ann would have done. Instead she lies still, the covers pulled almost to her eyes, while the Zeppelin keeps on its journey, the boom of its engine fading, and the sparks of the guns falling to the ground.

Ann's work is never done. And there are my own chores to do besides. I let the chickens out, plucking up the eggs, warming my hands on them before I bring them into the house. I pull the water from the well, sweep and wash the floor. Lay the fire. And while I do so I think of Mr Button on his cart, and the sharp rattle of the horse's hooves knocking against the road. I'd be at school now, copying battles from the board, and I find I even miss old Runnicles and the flash of his ruler as it thwacks down.

Mother is in the kitchen making bread. Kneading and slapping the dough on to the table, her tears leak into the creases as she pummels in the air. When I was small she'd give me a lump to scratch my name into, or mould into a boat, and even now, if the morning's work is done, she'll cut off a crust for me when the bread is baked, and let me have it with a scrape of jam.

As likely as not it's then that Father stamps in. 'What's this?' he scowls as if it's a party that we're having, and Mother gives an excuse to get me out of the house.

'Get over to Mrs Lusher for some pepper,' she tells me today. And I take her coin, and I'm out in the street.

'There's liquorice come in,' Mrs Lusher offers, 'put a smile on your face.' But I'm having none of it. 'An ounce of pepper-corns is all,' I tell her and she disappears from the window of her cave and I hear her scooping and weighing until she returns with a small white paper bag. 'Thank you.' I unroll the paper to peer in, and the smell of a distant heat-soaked land bursts up and makes me sneeze.

It's April, and as cold as winter, with hardly a dry day. Father may be right about the guns in Flanders stirring up the rain, for there's a squall blowing in across the German Sea. My jacket up around my ears, I walk the long way home. Buds sit shrivelling on branches, and the sheep come trotting towards me, their black faces hopeful, so hungry are they in their barren fields. 'I've nothing for you,' I tell them, but they cluster by the gate, their knees knocking together. A swoop of birds fly overhead, their shadows patterning the ground, but the sheep keep the stripes of their orange eyes on me, and even though I have nothing to offer, they follow me, on the other side of the fence.

I hand Mother the bag of pepper and watch her mash a pinch of it in the mortar. There's no one in yet. Although Gory usually comes for his lunch. And Kett. And sometimes Tibbles too. But I take my bowl of soup and I sit in the snug bar, beside the fire, and I spoon up the soft diced potato and the veiny cabbage, and as I wait for the hot explosions of pepper to surprise me I forget for a moment about Ann, up above in the good bed, so far away and lost.

Chapter 45

It's the middle of April before the weather lifts, and Ann still in her bed. It's been so cold that Mother has taken to wearing her coat indoors and gloves too, and if she can manage it, a blanket like a shawl around her shoulders. 'It's your spirit,' Mrs Horrod says, 'that's weakened.' And she mixes up a tonic and brings it round. But Mother doesn't take it. She leaves it wrapped in muslin on a shelf, and after a week or so when the smell is faded she tosses it away.

I want to be like Mother and shun Mrs Horrod too. But I can't. It hurts me to see the bright look in her face when she calls round. 'Cooee,' she stands in the door, unsure whether to come in, and Mother looks at her, bare-eyed, as if she's speaking a language that she doesn't know. 'Fancy a spot of poltering tomorrow,' Mrs Horrod tries, 'I could call for you at first light?' but Mother frowns and turns away, and Mrs Horrod saves herself by remembering that tomorrow after all there's something for which she's needed at home. I ask if she has any news of Vic. I don't like to, but someone has to say it. And Mrs Horrod smiles and says that yes, he's doing well. They had a letter from him only last week. And then she falls silent because Mother has left the room.

*   *   *

On the first warm day I stand in the yard and let the sun fall soft against my face. I've let the hens out and my chores are done, and so I walk along the river with a bucket and a length of stick, thinking I might go babbing for an eel. The sunshine is stirring the harbour into life, and there is a queue of people for the ferry. I keep on walking. There's a jetty that's not been used all winter, and if I lie down on it I can keep both hands on my line without the risk of slipping over. But as I pass Thorogood's shed I notice that it's open. Mrs Mac is inside sweeping with a broom and Mac himself is struggling with the shutter of its window. I pause but I don't stop. There's a jar of worms in my pocket and I don't like to think of them there, twisting and turning, while I sit to eat a sandwich. I have a length of woollen worsted too, and when I reach my spot, I thread it with a worm, lowering it down into the river, staring after into the dark water, watching for its flicker. I've not long to wait before there is a bite. I jerk the stick up, but it's only a dab, and I let it go. But after the third bite I feel a weightier pull, and there's the narrow head of an eel. Quick as I can I toss it on to the bank, where, with no hook in its mouth, it begins to slide away into the grass. But I'm too fast. I throw myself at its long body, and grabbing at the slimy skin, I hold steady. 'Got you,' I say, and without looking into its ancient face I lie it in the bucket where it thrashes in the water.

I wait longer for a second catch. Are the others warned? Did they see its body disappearing upwards? But then another eel bites, and I have it, up on the grass, and I'm wrestling with every bit of strength to keep a hold of it. It's a strong one, muscled as an arm, and I think it will get away from me but I slide my fingers up the length of it until I reach its neck. 'Yes,' I say aloud. And I hold it there, its tail twisting, before laying it in the bucket with the other.

*   *   *

Mrs Mac is sitting on a chair outside the hut when I pass by again. There is a clip of blossom in a vase beside her and she's leaning over a letter. I lug my load a little closer. 'Would you like an eel?' I ask her and she looks into my bucket and gives a start.

'Toshie?' she calls, and he comes out of the hut.

'Wait there,' he says, and he goes back inside and returns with his pad of paper, and a pencil, which he sharpens to a point. 'May I?' And he sets the bucket at his feet and folding over a new page begins to sketch.

I wait. And watch the eel through his eyes. There are four of them now, and as Mac draws, they form the stems of a mysterious plant. 'Any news of Ann?' Mrs Mac asks, and when I shake my head she goes back to her letter. Who is she writing to? And I think of offering to take it to the post for her. But how would I steam a letter open without Ann? How would I seal it up again? A plague of loneliness drops over me. Don't cry, I tell myself. Not here. But my throat is like a thistle and my eyes sting. I leave my bucket and step into the hut. The walls have been repainted white, the air is thick with the clean new smell of it, and all around are hung Mac's flowers. Each one on its own grained page of Whatman, the colour bursting from the pencilled lines. I start at the beginning, by the door, and stare at the ragged pink and purple of the larkspur. Next is hung the borage, two blazing blue flowers, and two unpainted buds to show what might have been. A little further on I find the rock cress, the one I'd thought he'd given up on, although now I wonder if Mac hadn't always meant to leave it like that, with its innards exposed. Both winter stock are here. As different from each other as two breeds of dog. And I feel my heart quietening. Maybe I can go on. Maybe I will. And I think of my brothers, imagine Ann flying through the sky with them, and I stare at a petunia and see the face of a bird in it. A comical bird with a yellow beard and two beaky eyes and I laugh because I'm sure I've conjured it, but when I shake myself and look again, it's there. 'Mr Mackintosh?' I turn, but he's bent over the eel, and I can only see the hunch of his back.

I find our pinecone, and a stick of rosemary I picked for him. There is the hard purple pillar of the hyacinth, and at the very end, the hellebore green. I see it as it was, wilting at the grave, and I think: this winter rose is holding up better than Ann. I'm about to turn away when something pulls me back – two baby birds, hidden in the centre of each hellebore. And without warning the tears are sliding down my face, catching on my lip, dropping from there into my collar.

I go closer. I look at everything again for what else is hidden. There's the head of a duck folded into a sunflower's stem. A cockerel perches on the sharp branch of the gorse, and the larkspur, when I examine it, has three chaffinches sitting amongst its papery blossom, their heads tucked down, their long tails preened. There's a mother bird too, it is clear to me now, a trailing scarf of purple floating out behind her hat. And a smaller bird, her chick, happy, riding along behind.

I stumble from the shed, my face swollen with tears, and forgetting I ever offered Mrs Mac an eel, I take my bucket by the handle and I run back to the inn.

I stay with Mother all the rest of that day. I take one end of each sheet she's washed, and twist it with her till it creaks, and once the water has been wrung out I help her peg them to the line. I sweep under the beds for her, and wipe down the window ledge in the good room where Ann lies motionless. I take the wood ash from the fire and spread it in little humps between the rows of seedlings, leaving it in mounds too high and soft for slugs to climb. When the fireplace is clean I sprinkle it with water to dampen down the bricks.

That night Mother fries the eel with our last precious onions, and serves it up with mashed potato and a pale green sauce of sorrel. It smells so good even Father comes to the table, and we bend our heads and listen as he tells us, as if he's not told us before, that if it wasn't for Sir Bly's pigheadedness, he might have built a smokehouse out by the side of the inn. 'I could have smoked these eels, and any others that you cared to catch,' he says. 'We could have gone in together and made money.'

I look at him, but I don't mention that it's not Sir Bly who makes the rules. It is the government who has declared no new buildings can be built while we're at war. Why do you think, I want to ask him, as I pull the backbone from the eel, that Charles Rennie Mackintosh himself is here, in our village, painting flowers, when he might be off, anywhere in the world, building palaces and spires? I wonder about the cathedral that he designed for Liverpool. Were there birds secreted amongst its towers? And I wonder too if after the war, he'll make new buildings to replace the old ones that have been destroyed, and if he does, whether he'll take our village with him and press its grasses and its twigs into the walls.

I help Mother clear the table, and scrub out the pots, and when all is done, and I've looked in on Ann, I step out into the night. It's not dark. That's the first thing I notice. It's after seven and the sky is pale with light. I walk towards the common. It's higher here, and the stars are nearer your hand. When I reach the tufted heather of the heath I lie down. Spring fever, I've heard them call it. But whatever it is I can feel it in my blood. A restlessness. A hope. I scan the sky, stretching my eyes, further, up beyond the clouds. Where are they? I ask myself. Are they looking down? And I search for my brothers in the shapes that wing above me. But it's not them I see, but the old witch-woman, her sharp nose marked out by the Milky

Way, and I close my eyes and still I see her, sitting in a cabin with her hunger and her fleas. She's in the woods on the other side of Dunwich Forest, and I stand up and begin walking, knowing even as I start that it's too far. I follow the railway line until it closes in towards the road, and cross it below the corner where two smugglers – long ago – were strung up on gibbets for their crimes.

I hurry along a sheep path, the marsh whispering white on either side, the sky a black dome above. The later it gets the brighter it becomes, the moon a night away from fullness, the stars so sharp they burn. I'm sure I've never seen so many stars, thousands of them, millions, and the harder I look, the more of them I see, bursting out from the unfolding skies behind. If I can find the witch, I tell myself, she'll explain what she meant when she told Ann that she'd be married. She and Jimmy Kerridge. And I run my hand up inside my sleeve to feel the soft edge of the moles that she discovered there. Liar. My mouth is bitter. Letting her think it was a sailor that she'd have. And I wonder, did she plant those moles on me, like the black spots that are delivered to pirates, did she tell Ann what she most wanted to hear for the sake of some tatters and a herring?

I'm on the edge of Dunwich, by a glade of larches, beyond which for mile after mile the woods stretch in a dark streak along the coast. Now I've come this far, I falter in my purpose, but I go on anyway, roaming along the lane that leads into the village, and out again down the high street, where cottages huddle together, their latticed windows and porched doors keeping the forest out. I skirt past the lepers' church and the Ship Inn, and trudge back up towards the wooden house where Father had his pork butcher's in the shed beside. The waves are lapping at the cliffs, and the ruins of All Saints stand out black against the sky. They say it won't be long now before the church tower drops into the sea, and Mother has told me that when she was a child there were twice as many headstones in the churchyard, and I think of them splitting off from their moorings and sliding down the cliff into the sea. I shiver. The wind is creeping in across the marsh. 'I'll not find her tonight,' I tell myself, although I've always known I wouldn't. And slowly, tired, I stamp back towards home. But with the wind come clouds, and soon whole swathes of sky are blotted out. A hill rises before me, dissolving through the blackness into a bush, and the ghostly flank of a muntjac slides away into a copse. I can no longer see the shoreline that has guided me this far, and I take a wrong track and come out high on the lane above the Hoist. But I'm so grateful to have my bearings I hurry past Dead Man's Corner with hardly a nod, and crossing back over the edge of the marsh I head for the spire of our church.

I'm running downhill now towards home, hoping I've not been missed, when I hear a low rumble, humming in from the sea. I stop. There's nothing there, just the roar of thunder through cloud, but I wait all the same, staring upwards, straining to see, and there it is, the round belly of a Zeppelin, directly overhead. The noise fills the whole sky. The camouflage of cloud is gone, and I cover my face in case it sees me, as it travels like a second moon, following the railway line inland. Through the slats of my fingers I let it go, and I stay like that, alone in the street, until the noise has faded to a purr.

The inn is quiet when I let myself in, the last customer, used now to the rules of Dora, having long gone home. I peer into the main bar. All is neat and orderly, and treading through the snug I pull myself up the ladder. Father is asleep, and Mother, to guard against his snores, lies with one arm over her ear.

I'm so tired that for a moment I forget, and I stop on the step of my room, and stare at the empty bed. The sheet is turned down, the pillow smooth, and the fact of it pounds into me, I'm on my own. I take off my jacket and crawl into the cold, and I'm lying there, my arms around myself, when I hear the Zeppelin turn.

The engine roar is low at first, but it gathers as it nears, and soon I can feel the airship pressing down, its body pinning me to my bed. What can it be that's called it back? Have we been careless? Is our washing out? Are the geese too white against the village green? I hold my breath. The noise is deafening – it must be directly overhead. Where are the searchlights? Where is the constable who shot Danky in the leg? And then there is a hiss like a stone falling and a thud that shakes the earth. It's not possible. They couldn't . . . And there is another explosion. Nearer this time. And as it dies away, so does the roar of the Zeppelin, moving out across the sea.

I'd get up but I'm too scared. I think of the airmen shaking each other's hands, laughing to think they ever bothered risking their lives for London when they could cut their journey short and drop their bombs on us.

'Tommy?' It is Mother in her nightdress, standing in the door. 'Tom?' and together we hurry through to the good room where Ann lies undisturbed and palely still, as sound asleep as she ever was.

'Ann,' I kneel down beside her. I take her chill hand, but Mother has run back into her own room and I can hear her, cursing and crying, as she shakes Father from his sleep.

Chapter 46

Bombs it seems are good for business. The next day as soon as the Blue Anchor opens its doors the bar is full of men.

'Ran out into the garden,' Tibbles is saying, 'couldn't remember whether to run out or stay inside.' And he looks around, nervous, as if he's still not sure.

'It came by that close,' Father brings up the drinks, 'that I put my head out of the window and I shook my stick at it.'

I sit in the corner and pretend that I have work. I use the last pages of my schoolbook to draw a picture of the airship, its bloated body and small propellered tail, the little cabin of its control room like a row of teeth.

'I'd have struck it too,' Father goes on, 'but the wife said: think of the girl, ailing in her bed. We don't want that great beast dropping its bombs on us.' He takes a gulp of his own pint. Fred Snowling stands at the bar. One of the bombs just missed his cottage. And this morning the whole village trooped out to see the crater that it made in his front garden, big enough for his wife and two small daughters to roll into from their beds.

'If I'd been there . . .' Father has started up again. And Mother looks across at me and her lip twitches in the faintest of smiles. I smile back, and when her mouth begins to quiver, she turns and she goes out to the kitchen.

Mary arrives that afternoon. The first bomb fell on Henham Hall. It crashed through the conservatory, and the men, whose nerves are thin as straw, are so shaken she can only stay away for a few hours. But all the same she uses her time well. She helps Mother wash and change Ann, combing out her hair and plaiting it. A three-plait, she uses, like the simplest of George Allard's twines, and she winds a ribbon through its fastened ends. She listens, more than once, to Father's story of the stick, which has come now within an inch of knocking the Zeppelin from the sky, and when his back is turned, she puts her arms round Mother and their shoulders shake.

'Don't go,' I hold tight to her arm.

'I must,' she says, and I follow her to where her bicycle is parked by the wall.

'I'll come when I can,' she tells me. 'Look after them for me.' She wobbles as she cycles away and it is only when she turns to wave that I see the tired shadows that have gathered on her face.

There is a new poster outside Mrs Lusher's shop.

WARNING – Daylight Air Raids

In order to provide, as far as possible, for the safety of the inhabitants, it has been decided that on information being received of the approach of Hostile Aircraft during the day, if time permits,

The Church Bells shall be 'jangled' for a short time, as a warning to any of the public who may be out of doors to at once seek safety in the nearest house, and on no account to remain in the street.

When the danger is past, one Bell will be tolled as a notice that normal conditions may be resumed.

The above warning will be in force from half an hour before sunrise to half an hour after sunset, and it is displayed to impress upon the inhabitants the necessity for strict compliance with these regulations.

As well as the promise of bells jangling through the day, at night minesweepers trawl the bay, and blackout police patrol the streets, searching for a chink of light. At Southwold, the constable climbs up to the roof of St Edmund's church tower and sits there till morning to survey the town. If he sees a light, he sends a message down and his men march round to the offending building, and the inhabitants, whether they be soldiers or civilians, are fined.

There is no constable on the roof of our church tower, but even so, Mother and I pin sheets of black paper up against the windows of the inn, and she hangs a curtain made from sacking just inside the door. It is there to seal in light, and customers too it seems, for more than once I see a man tangled up in hessian as he grapples his way out.

At night I lie in blackness and listen to the Zeppelins flying over, straining my ears for the high whine of the bombs about to fall. I'm ready to leap from my bed and drag Ann with me to the cellar. I'll prise up the trapdoor and step down those dank and mossy steps, to a path long since silted up. We'll be safe there. Ann, a sleeping princess in my arms. But the planes fly on to London and for the moment we are saved.

'Ann,' I whisper. 'Wake up, why don't you?' But she is in the good room, dreaming, white as her sheet, and it is only myself I jolt out of sleep.

There's been a burst of rain, and the ground is broken up with flowers. Bluebells, and daffodils, all come at the same time, and a sprouting of forget-me-nots. There is a cherry tree drenched with blossom leaning out over the corner of the lane, and I am tempted to reach up and snap a branch off for the grave. But I hesitate. Mother has taught me that every blossom bears the promise of fruit, and when I come to the churchyard I find that she has already filled our pot. A clump of wild raspberry, pink and green, its smell as sour as piss. I lean down to breathe it in, because there's sweetness in there too, and as I do I hear the chattering and squawking of my birds. There's a newborn William, with his beak open, head out over the nest, and beside him the next William, looking at the sky. James, his feathers downy brown, his eyes fast blinking, makes a high peeping squeak, and as I strain for Thomas I see the parents, sleek and yellow-beaked, swoop in with a haul of worms. The volume rises, a flurry of flapping wings, and soon they are away again and the chicks are left alone.

Mac has every flower to choose from – wild garlic, bluebells, narcissi and fritillaries – but when I walk past his shed I see he has three sticks of hazel in a jar. 'I could find you something?' I offer. I'm thinking I could snap off a branch of sloe, no one would miss that, there's a bush of it up by Keepers Cottage. But he doesn't seem to have heard me, and only leans closer, squinting at the yellow fluff of the lamb's-tails, and the tight green buds still waiting to unfurl.

Mrs Mac is inside. She's making a sketch across a wide brown sheet of paper. There's a woman at its centre, and on each side, with strings of flowers between them, are girls, their bodies swirled in cloaks. 'Where are the roses?' I've learnt to look for a Glasgow rose in everything she does. But Mrs Mac tells me that this is the May Queen and her flowers are those of spring. It is a sketch for a gesso panel she'd like to make, if she has the strength, and as I watch she mixes an auburn mess of paint and dipping in her brush fills in the May Queen's hair.

'But I'd need to gather the ingredients,' she is talking mostly to herself. 'Plaster of Paris, rabbit-skin glue, of course, and I'll need some string, tin inlay, and glass beads.' She carries on scattering small dots of flowers at the women's feet.

That evening, I go to Mrs Horrod. She opens the door to me and starts back fearful, but when I don't mention Ann, or Mother, and smile at her and nod, she takes a breath and lets me in. 'Could you tell me how rabbit-skin glue is made?' I ask, and it's clear from her long pause that for once she isn't sure. 'With rabbit skin, I s'pose,' she frowns. 'Boil it up until the water's thickened. Let it cool. And then boil it up again.'

Later I go over to Sogg's Fen just as Father did the night that I was born. But there's no storm now. It's clear and bright and my pockets are full of flints. I lie on a mound that hangs over the hollow, and I wait, still as I can, until the rabbits creep back into the open. They are big rabbits, large as hares, a patch of white behind their tails, so that when they hop, they flash bright as a lamp. God's trick on them, I tell myself, for when they are still, there is nothing but a shadow. All the same I pick one out. It is near. A big loping animal with fine long ears.

We had ferrets once. A pair of them in a pen out in the garden. And Father would take them when he went rabbiting and set them down the holes. But he lost one in a warren when the line got knotted on a stump, and when he sent the other after it, he lost that too. 'You should have dug them out,' Mother scolded him. And Father protested that he did try digging. Dug halfway to Australia. The ferrets were in too deep. Our ferret cage is empty now. And it's some time since we ate rabbit. But I'm sure that if I lie here still enough I can aim a flint and strike one on the head.

The grass was dry when I lay down, but the chill of the night is turning it to damp. Slowly I lift my arm. The rabbits pause.

I pause with them. And they're nibbling again. I draw my arm back, and the stone, for all that I've been practising, flies from my hand. I've got one. Stunned, if it's not dead. And while the others melt away, I take out my knife and I cut across its throat. Its eyes cloud over. White as Ann's when they roll back. And with warm blood oozing through my fingers, I run home fast across the marsh.

Can your mother skin a rabbit? It was a chant the village children sang when I was first at school with them, and I'd chant back: *Yes. Yes. Yes.* Because the chances were if you said no, you'd never taste its meat.

Mother is up, sitting by Ann's bed. I stand beside her and look down. Ann's eyes are closed. Her face pale, her hair brushed out. I've never seen her look so beautiful, and I'm reminded of the sleeping princess in Mac's pamphlet, lying in its frame of beaten silver. *Love, if thy tresses be so dark, how dark those hidden eyes must be.* I don't know how those words stayed in my head, and to shake them away, I bring the rabbit out from behind my back. 'I'll need the skin,' I say. And Mother is so surprised she screams.

'Not in here.' She pushes me from the room. But she climbs down the ladder and hangs the rabbit by its feet, and with one long cut down its belly she pulls its coat off like a glove. I leave the skin to dry out in the wind. And then I have the task of peeling away the soft layer of its fur. Mother can sell it. There's a lady at Blackshore who'll give good money for a hide, although she'll not be pleased to see that it's so thin. When it's done I stoke up the stove, and draw a pot of water from the well. I don't wait for it to boil but squeeze in the skin and leave it there to cook.

The smell is terrible. It fills the room and, firmly as I shut the door, soon the house is thick with it. Men come in for a drink, covering their mouths, and Mother shouts at me to go into the garden and leave it there to cool.

But I can't leave it. Instead I build a fire under the cover of our trees, and hoping that no wisps of smoke will float out and betray me, I set the pot above it. Slowly, very slowly, the hide softens and the water shrinks. I add a little more and keep at it. Stirring and prodding and waiting for the leather to dissolve. Boil and leave, and boil again, it is the same instructions Mrs Horrod gives for herbs. And when the fire has died, I hide my pot in the woods, and I come out the next day to start again. And there has been a change. The water is slick when I put in a finger. And I smear it against my shoe and watch while it dries. I light the fire again and leave my pot to simmer, running back and forth between my chores to stoke it up with twigs. 'That wretched smell will never go,' Mother shakes the table-cloth, and she throws open the windows and sprinkles vinegar over the floor to freshen up the room.

By late afternoon there is no water left but the skin is slimy with a mush of paste. I cut a page from my sketchbook and I fold it together and pointing the ends like an envelope I glue it closed. 'Yes,' I dance around the fire, and I don't allow myself to think how easily Ann sealed Old Mac's letters with a paste of flour.

I scrape my glue into a jar, squeezing every last drop of it from the skin, and leaving Mother's blackened, stinking pot to catch the rain when it should come, I carry it to Mac's.

I knock, I wait. But there is no one there. And so I run back through the garden, and skirt around the harbour until I reach their shed. Mac is alone with his lamb's-tails. They are thick as a flock, soft as pillows, and I must stare at them for a long while before I see the faces, smiling at each other, caterpillar folk they are, the lady in a hat.

'Where will I find Mrs Mackintosh?' I ask him, quiet, so as not to disturb, and I'm right, because he carries on, his head bent, filling each stem with grey and turquoise, black and green. 'London,' he says when I think he can't have heard.

'London! Is that not dangerous?'

'Less dangerous, they say, than staying here.' He turns then and hands me a letter. Mrs Margaret Macdonald Mackintosh.

'I'll post it for you,' I promise him, 'soon as I can get across the river.' And I slip the letter into the pocket of my shirt.

My dear Margaret.

I have steamed open the envelope myself, and taken it upstairs to Ann.

It has been beautifully warm and soft all morning, just as you like it, with a silver rain falling for a minute or two, and no Zeppelins daring to cross over and follow you to London.

I'm hoping you'll have seen the doctor by now and that he has good news for you. Whatever he says, he'll have to admit this sea air suits your heart, I haven't seen you weakened since you've been here, only with distress on your return from Glasgow after seeing your sister so reduced, and I hope, after this journey, you'll be back here at least as well as when you left. And soon.

You can offer the doctor Larkspur as payment if he'll have it. Or Petunia. Or if needs be, both. And while you are there if you could show the flower pictures to B at Bramerton Street, and tell him if he'll take some you'll have them framed. You'll do that twice as well as me, of course. But ask him first what he'll pay. I'm sorry to treat you as my London agent. But it would help, with the situation with Muthesius impossible, if I could sell something. Anything. We're getting very low. Dear Margaret, nothing is the same without you here. Do write and let me know when you'll return. There are only two things that are important to me. You first, and then my work.

MMYT

'You first,' I whisper the words to Ann. 'And then my work.'
She would have liked that. I tug her arm. 'Wake up, why don't
you.' But her breath remains even, her face closed. 'All right,'
I tell her, 'have it your way.' And I kick the door as I go
through.

Chapter 47

The Royal Sussex Cyclists have laid barbed wire along the beach. Roll after roll of it, the spikes already rusting in the spray. I scan the shoreline and think how if a man was washed in now, he'd be caught and tangled in the wire. There was an advertisement in yesterday's *Gazette*. Cyclists needed. Bicycles provided. Must have keen eyesight and be above the height of 5ft 2in. Training will be given. Comfortable billets in Colchester. Uniforms and rations. For men between the ages of 19 and 38.

How old do you have to be to pass for nineteen? I wonder, and I drag my foot along the canal path towards Southwold.

It's not so long since I was last here, but in the days after the bombs soldiers have fortified the town. There are pillboxes and gun emplacements, and between the oak trees and the water tower a new double row of wire. As I walk along the promenade I see the old colonel Danky once told me fought in the Crimea – and I wave at him and try out a salute. I want him to know we'll carry on where he left off. But he doesn't seem to see.

There's a funeral procession winding past the Grand Hotel. It's the fisherman Winner Harris, whose trawl boat was caught in the warp of a minesweeper and sunk. His family are there, clinging together, weeping, and behind them a sad cluster of fishermen, Danky among them, and Thorogood too. I take my hat off and stand and let them pass, and I think of Winner who carved boats from blocks of wood and sailed them on the yacht pond over at Paul's Fen. I see his careful hands, sure never to damage the bowsprit, nosing them round before they hit the bank, lifting them from the water to set their rudders straight. The procession moves on, and I make my way towards the post office, passing as I go whole divisions of soldiers, newly arrived to protect the town. Their horses are housed on the common, stall after stall of them, under canvas, and I imagine what George Allard will be saying to his wind-powered sail: *Any day now. Any hour. The enemy will be here to burn and murder and destroy.* And although I attempt a smile at the thought of it, the breath catches in my throat, and I promise myself I'll walk back along the beach, however hard the going, to cast an eye along our coast.

The hazel is finished and Mac has started on a spray of speedwell. Veronica, he says it is, although I've heard Mrs Horrod call it gypsyweed or bird's-eye. I sit beside him and count the leaves, watching to see where he might smuggle a bird in, knowing I'll not see it until the thing is done.

'Have you any news of Mrs Mackintosh?' I ask. I'm concerned for her weak heart, all the way in London. And the rabbit-skin glue is hardening to pellets, so that if she doesn't make use of it soon I'll have to start again.

Mac nods, but he keeps drawing. 'You'll not start something?' he asks, and so to please him I take a sheet of paper from the shed, and with a pencil I sketch as closely as I can the face of the woman in my miniature. Her oval eyes and tilted mouth, the softness of her neck. I work on a circular outline, unsure how to re-create the curve of the miniature itself, subtle as an eyeball inside its double-width surround.

It doesn't work, and I scrunch the paper up in anger. And then, ashamed, I smooth it out, and turning it over, I try again. This time I draw Ann. I sketch her asleep. Her lashes fine and pale, resting on her cheeks, her hair loose about her shoulders. I give a smile to the corners of her mouth and I enclose her in a circle. Not too bad, I tell myself. Although there's not a soul that would know it was her, and so I sprinkle her nose and cheeks with freckles and turn her into Betty.

It's easier the second time to steam open the letter, and whether or not she wants to hear it I take it up to Ann.

It's eight o'clock and I have had no letter from my Margaret and no news of her, so now I will have to wait till tomorrow morning anxiously because you said you would write.

But I must tell you the most surprising thing. I was sitting outside the 'studio' at five thirty eating my heart out with depression when our old friend T arrived. He's staying near Rendlesham and heard I was here. There's no teaching for him now, all his students are off at the front, and while they are assigning him some war work he said he was down in the dumps. He looked at my Hazel and said that's going to be a very fine thing, I assured him I was trying to make it a fine thing. After a while he said, by Jove, Mackintosh, you are a marvel, you never seem depressed. You're always cheerful and happy – I told him it was health – but I didn't tell him that I was much more depressed than he was when he arrived – nor that his deepest depression was something equivalent to my not being very well – I keep my deepest depressions to myself. He shows them all the time like a young child – and that in a way makes him an object of

*sympathy and attraction – he came in his car, a fine black
Crossley, we had a drink and he departed. But he thinks he
will come again because I am a cheerful soul. Nothing more
to tell tonight. No letter from Margaret.*
MMYT

I'm not sure what to think, so I think nothing. Instead I stand
quite still with the letter in my hand. Is there nothing that will
cheer him? Nothing I can do? And I back out of the sickroom,
my own heart heavy in my chest.

The next day there is another letter. I watch Mac while he is
writing it.

*I've been working hard, although you'll laugh when you see
what I'm painting now. And you'll see too that the desire to
eliminate green from my work has failed. You will understand, knowing as you do my insane aptitude for seeing
green and putting it down here there and everywhere the
very first thing – it complicates every colour scheme that I
am aiming at so I must get over this vicious habit. It is one of
my minor curses. Green, green, green. If I leave it off my
palette I find my hands – when my mind is searching for
some shape or form – squeezing green out of a tube – and so
it begins again. But my Veronica, although tinted with silver
and a hint of yellowish grey, is underlined with green. No
flowers for her. Although I've noticed that another variation,
growing conveniently by the back wall and untouched so far
by our ravenous rabbit friends, is bursting with a purple
flower, and I shall try that next. No other visitors. Just our
boy. Mysterious as ever. So another lonely night without
you. Did you find the words I sent? There are three of them.
And you will see them anywhere you choose to look.*

'Mysterious?' I seal the envelope back again. 'Their boy?' And I race with the letter down towards the ferry.

Beware of Female Spies

I stop only to read the posters pinned up outside the town hall.

Women are being employed by the enemy
to secure information from navy men on the
theory that they are less liable to be suspected
than male spies. Beware of inquisitive women as
well as prying men.

See Everything
Hear Everything
Say Nothing

Betty's quick form flashes up before me. Betty and her sister Meg. Inquisitive. Roaming through the back lanes of the village! Asking questions. Befriending Mrs Horrod. I distract myself by looking at the next poster.

It is far better
To face the bullets
Than to be killed
At home by a bomb

There is a painting of a Zeppelin, its body caught in a beam of light. I inspect it and compare it to the ones I've seen. Here it is nothing more than a fat yellow cigar, with no sense whatsoever of its threat or speed. And I wonder about Count Zeppelin and what would I do if I lived in a castle with enough money to experiment with engines, aluminium frames and silk? What devastating missile would I invent? A submarine. That's it. Incapable of detection, with sensors as delicate as minnows. I picture it streaking to the defence of any ship that is in trouble, scooping the grateful men into its hold. Our saviour! The whole kingdom would rise up in gratitude. And I'm sure I hear them, even now, raising a cheer for the great Count Thomas Maggs.

Mac's letter crackles in my pocket as I puff out my chest, and I remember I'm on an errand, and when it's done I must get back to help open up the inn. I hurry on, one eye tilted skywards, my ears wide open to catch the chatter of any kind of spy.

Mary is at home, and she and Mother have moved Ann into the garden. She lies on a bench softened with quilts while the sun and the breeze wash over her face. I kneel beside her and give her a small sharp pinch. 'Wake up,' I hiss, and I'm sure I see her eyelids flutter.

'Tommy,' Mother calls, 'help me with the sheets.' And when I turn to look at Mary, Mother says to me, 'Let your sister rest.'

It is the perfect drying day, bright and blustery. I frown to think of George Allard's wheel and how it must be spinning as he weaves. Too fast, I hope, and the taste of spite is bitter in my mouth. To banish it I race through my chores – stoking up the stove, sweeping the hearth, polishing the glasses, even passing a rag over Father's boots, which wait patiently at the bottom of the ladder for him to get up. Mother chops the vegetables and watches me, in silence, and we keep the back door open so that we can hear Mary, singing to Ann as they sit in the sun.

'A sailor and his true love
Was awalking one day
Through the green fields and the meadows

That was scattered with hay.
And the blackbirds and the thrushes
Sang in every green tree
And the larks, they sang melodious
At the dawning of the day.
Now the sailor and his true love went awalking next day
Said the sailor to his true love
I am bound far away
I'm bound for the Indias
Where the loud cannons roar
For to go and leave my Nancy
For she's a girl that I adore.
For to go and leave my Nancy
For to go and leave my Nancy
For she's the girl that I adore.'

Chapter 48

As well as patrolling the beach each morning, I decide I must go out last thing at night to check our village is dark.

'Where are you off to now, young man?' Mother reaches for me as I slip through the door, but I'm too fast for her, and I turn and wave, closing my eyes against the vision of her, standing in the curtained doorway of the inn, alone.

I run along Main Street and round the corner into the loop of the back lane. My heart hammers. It is dark here at the best of times, but tonight there is not a chink of light, and soon I'm swallowed by the overhanging branches at the edge of Dingle Farm. I keep going, clicking my tongue for company, until I burst out on the green, and I stop and gasp, and look up at the moon, for that is the only light that shines. More slowly I walk towards the beach. The sea is rough tonight and there is no chance of hearing guns across the water. But the houses are dark. The water protected. And everything is as it should be. I stand on the beach and tilt back my head and I count the few stars that have pierced the cloud. There are less than a dozen, although the longer I look the more I find, and I'm searching so hard that at first I don't notice the shadow of the Zeppelin, its belly only slightly blacker than the cloud. I stand quite still. It's got me by the eye. And then fear rips through me and I'm awake again. I turn. I shout. What if it drops its bombs now? Destroys our village while it sleeps. But there is no one to hear. Stumbling against pebbles, I run with the airship back across the beach, up over the dunes, following it along the street and past the church. If there was someone on the flat roof of the tower, then I could shout to them and they might, just this once, jangle their bells or, better still, aim a rifle at it, but there is no one in the churchyard, only my family of starlings, keeping watch over our grave.

I'm still running when the coastguard's lights arc through the sky. And there it is, they've caught it, floating above me, a golden finger, pointing south. I stop and stare, and then the light falls and it is gone. But when it rises again, a volley of shells come with it, missing, and falling down like sparks. The Zeppelin must be over Blythburgh now, the shells dancing below, and I keep running, wanting nothing more than to catch on to its tail. And that's when it happens. Just as I'm thinking how Count Zeppelin has made damn sure it flies too high, a shell catches against its side, and another, and soon the whole unwieldy gas-filled envelope of an airship bursts into flame. I can see the fire race across its skin, tear into the metal of its body, and even as my heart soars with pride I'm sick with pity for those men trapped inside. I stand, my hands up to my face, waiting for it to fall on Blythburgh Cathedral, but unlike a plane, the Zeppelin floats on, lighting up the countryside, sinking slowly lower, until, somewhere above the tail of the estuary, it crashes to the ground. The earth echoes with it. Louder than a bomb. And I feel the road beneath me shiver. Pheasants that have been asleep since sundown crow wildly in the woods.

I stay like that, crouched over in the road, my eyes on the horizon where the fire burns. I want to get to it. But I can't move. And then with a roar an armoured car blasts past me, and another, but they are too fast for me to flag them down.

Slowly I begin walking, passing the shadows of small animals, voles and shrews scattering across the road. My feet are heavy. My throat burns, and I think of the 670 bicycles of the Royal Sussex Cyclists and how I'd only need one. I even allow myself to yearn for our old horse Kingdom, who I sometimes see, collecting visitors from the station, and who nuzzles me with his velvet mouth when I put my hand up to his neck. I keep walking. I hum tunes to myself. And mutter verses on the weather:

> *Evening grey and morning red,*
> *Keeps the traveller in his bed.*
> *Evening red and morning grey,*
> *Sends the traveller on his way.*

I take a deep breath and start in on another:

> *If the ide before Christmas will bear a duck,*
> *You'll get nothing after – only slush and muck.*

I remind myself of George Allard's stories. Spring-heeled Jack, who refused to chant the psalms, but would insist on singing them, and ended up at the assizes, where his case was thrown out of court, and Danky's tale of two fishermen who drowned when their boat turned over on the beach. They were buried in the churchyard, just outside the ruins, when, two weeks later, a storm blew in, the water rising so high that the men were taken back out to sea where they most wanted to be.

The clouds have cleared and the stars are coming out. The night is alight with them. I pass Dead Man's Corner but I'm in too much of a hurry to imagine how the bodies of the smugglers were cut down and taken home to be buried by their mothers and their wives. Even so, once I've passed, my strength returns, and I'm free and fearless and I begin to run.

I'm nearly at Blythburgh when a boy cycles by with his father. 'Going to see the Zeppelin?' I shout after them, and the boy slows, although the Father doesn't, and I climb on, and perch on the rack above the back wheel, doing my best to make myself as light as I can. But the roads are flat, and the bike is a strong one, and we wheel along, passing others now, following the smell of burning and the red glow of the fire. The nearer we get the stronger is the smell, and shreds of blackened silk fly into our faces so that we're ducking and dodging as if from a swarm of bats. 'Mind how you go!' We pass a piece of the skeleton of the aircraft. I want to stop and gather it. But we're hurtling on towards the blaze, and we round a corner by a farmhouse, and there, in a field below, is a flaming mass of metal, the hoop of the airship half a mile high.

Our officers are here, their cars parked near. And the family from the farmhouse, the children wide-eyed, coats on over their nightclothes. I stand as close as I can. But the heat is powerful. And there's nothing we can do for the men. They're dead already. Twisted and charred. Seventeen of them. I hang my head. And wonder at their slow floating death, and whether Count Zeppelin imagined it, or whether it was only the bombs dropping he thought of, and the enemy dying below.

I stay till dawn when a crowd arrives, by foot, by bicycle, by donkey, horse and trap. There's one man pulls up in a car, a Crossley it is, and I wonder if it is Mac's friend, the teacher who came to tell him he was 'down in the dumps'. He talks at some length to the officers and a policeman who is there – he wants to know what will happen to the bodies of the airmen, and the vicar joins them, and it is decided they will have their own small corner of the churchyard. We'd want nothing less for our own men. 'Yes,' they all agree, and they mutter a prayer.

By the time I'm ready to leave, my friend with the bicycle is gone, and so I turn away along the lane and follow the shreds of blackened silk that lead back the way we came. I look out for the piece of Zeppelin on the verge, but it's been taken, and although I search the hedgerows, looking for another, every scrap and splinter has been scavenged away.

I'd like to think I saw a sign as I approached the inn, had an idea just from looking at it, that there was something changed. But my head is too full of the adventure, my hurry to tell Mother of it, my hope that Father will be sleeping, and won't steal my story with one of his own. But as soon as I open the door I know it. Steam rises from the stove and Mother is dashing back and forth, alive as she's not been these last two months. And there, by the fire, a sliver in her nightdress, her eyes open, is Ann.

'Ann!' I shout. I throw myself on her. And Mother comes shrieking across and hauls me off. 'Careful,' she says, 'the girl's too weak.' And she cuffs me, just for good measure, and tussles up my hair.

'It was the crash that roused her,' Mother beams. 'Threw her half out of her bed. And the chickens squawking and the dogs barking, and the birds.'

She sits beside Ann and places down a bowl of porridge and Ann smiles and fiddles with the spoon.

I wish now more than ever I had a piece of the Zeppelin to give her, so instead I shake myself and watch as a blackened flake of silk falls from my shoulder. I lay it before her. A shred of Zeppelin sail, and she presses the end of her finger against it and lifts it to the light. 'Thank you, Tommy,' she says and after gazing it at for some minutes she drops the disc of it into her mouth.

'No!' Mother cries, but Ann looks at her and smiles and to quieten her she takes up the spoon and dips it in the porridge.

Father, it seems, has made a pact with God, for now that Ann is strengthening he swears he'll never take another drop of drink. 'How are you, girl?' he asks, gentle, as she sits by the window, and when Ann says she feels a little better, I swear I hear him sniff away a tear.

Mac writes to his My Margaret a long letter about the shooting-down of the Zeppelin. I bring it to Ann, for, even though Mac wasn't there, it is so much better than my own telling. The brass bed shakes, the gesso almost crashes to the floor. And every rabbit in their garden scuttles for its burrow.

A week goes by before I have more news to bring to Ann, and this time, when I do, I catch her watching, eyebrows raised, as I steam open the envelope.

My dearest Margaret.
    I look up in case such tenderness will make her sad. But she nods encouragement, and I go on.
    I got off to work so early this morning that the post had not arrived, but on returning at lunchtime there was a letter waiting on the table, and Mrs Mollett so happy to tell me the news of it that she led me to the very place and stood there pointing and smiling and waiting till I opened it. I had to go into the bedroom to read it in private.
    I'm glad everything is going well in London. And that your most recent tests are clear. I'm glad too that you are sending the Larkspur and the Winter Stock to Homes and Garden; remember, any money that comes in is for you. I think that the Petunia might be more suitable for the cover of a magazine. Or maybe B has decided he wants to buy

them, framed or unframed. Did he say? I'd let each go for as little as £10 10s. But if he can't give an answer what can we do? What can any of us do?

Sorry to talk so much of business and money, when it is only the three words I want you to hear.

Chesterton says, 'Our wisdom belongs to the world – our follies to those we love.' Browning puts it better – 'We must have two faces, one to face the world with, one to show a woman when we love her.'

Do write again as soon as you receive this. You see I am very greedy for news of you – from you. Goodnight. YT.

PS Do not worry if you've not sold anything. Come home. Or write at least that you intend to soon. This house is too large without you. And my life too small.

Ann watches, glassy-eyed, while I seal it up again. I don't use the rabbit-skin glue. I keep that hidden at the back of the cupboard in my room. It is hard and dry now. White as pebbles. And I wonder, as Mac does, what is keeping her away so long.

Chapter 49

At the start of June there is to be a sale on the green at Westleton.

Present Entries Include

40 Portions of the Wrecked Zeppelin

Old Coins, What-Not, Dining-Room Chairs, Smokers' Cabinet,
Music, Pictures, Flour, Old China, Potatoes, Japanese Stick,
Tea Cosy, Jewellery, Fireguard, Wheelchair, Clothes-Horse,
Miniature, Pincushion, Tea Cloths, String of Pearls,
Stuffed Birds.

I heave up the mattress and count my money. What would my own miniatures fetch? I wonder. And I imagine exchanging them for a piece of the wreck. But instead I take a sixpence and I walk to the top of the village where after a minute or so Mr Button passes with his cart. He stops for me when I put out my arm and although it was winter when I last flagged him down and now it is almost summer, he doesn't say a word. Instead we listen to the sound of his horse's hooves, the echo as they hit against the patch of road, the dry thud as they move on to the mud of the lane. He had two horses when I first started riding with him, but since the war he manages with one, parting with the other when the recruits swept through the country. I glance at him now to see if he is sad. But how can you tell what a man like Mr Button feels when his face is covered with whiskers and his eyes are creased so small against the sun his forehead is a frown? Where does he go each morning? But I don't ask because I've heard he works at Bulcamp, out on the estuary, where the madhouse is.

'I'll end up at Bulcamp,' Mother has been known to sob when my father's drinking, and the damp, and the rats, and the never-enough money, force her down on to a stool, her head in her hands, and on those days I stand with her and stroke her back, solid as a wall, and not a bit of give in it, and I promise myself that this will never happen, and how can it when I have a small stack of coins waiting for when she's run out of luck?

The auctioneer is the same man as sells sheep over at the market square at Southwold. He scans the crowd and nods and calls, so fast I can hardly keep up. Potatoes. They are gone. Flour. Four hands are raised. But no one bids for the miniature, or even the stuffed bird, and I hold tight to the coin in my pocket and think how grand it would look at the inn, just like the eagle that sits under a glass dome in the Sailors' Reading Room. It was rescued from the Norwegian barque two years before the war, and I remember how we heard the distress calls, ringing out at midnight, and rushed down to the beach, Ann and I, with Mother hurrying after with coats.

'Gone!' The clothes-horse is sold. But all I can see are the Norwegian crew being winched to safety high above the waves.

No one wants the pincushion. And I remember the next morning, how I took the ferry at first light, and stood with the crowds of people on the pier to see the strange sight of the barque lying high and dry like some black whale.

The smokers' cabinet remains unsold. As do the dining-room chairs. But someone has raised their hand for the pearls. They are white and milky. The auctioneer holds them up. 'Going . . .' A short strand, they are, more like a choker. 'Going . . .' I crane to see. But no one else is bidding. 'Gone.' And they are sold to a man in seaman's uniform. A small man. But I only see him from behind. 'Yes!' His fists are clenched. And he leaps into the air.

They are selling off the wreck of the Zeppelin now. I put my hand up. I don't even know what for. But soon the bids are beyond me. And I put it down. The auctioneer starts with another lot. A zigzag of metal. My hand shoots up. Thruppence. Yes. He nods at me. And now my face is burning. But thruppence rises to fivepence and I daren't go on. Some other fellow gets it. I try again. My face hot as the sun. Thruppence. Thruppence halfpenny. Fourpence. There are three others against me. And as it rises I forget about the smallness of my coin and I keep nodding. Sixpence, sixpence halfpenny. A shilling. Two shillings. Three. And it is mine. A twisted piece of metal. Tall as a small tower and charred at the top. I can hardly breathe. What am I to do with it? How am I to pay? And I look about as if I might find some pricey item on my person, an ebony cane or crystal monocle that I could quickly sell.

'Tommy.' I turn. I'm squinting. All I can see is a clothes-horse, held up like a rail. 'How are you doing, lad?' It's George Allard. And I want to say, 'What's that for? Surely you can make one of those yourself?' But I say nothing. I'm too busy waiting for a policeman to clamp a hand down on my head. 'How is your sister?' he asks.

'Ann?'

'And your ma and pa?' He stands thoughtful, and my heart races. He's about to offer me my job back. He must know I need it with things as they are.

'Well done,' he says, nodding at the wreck of metal, and lifting the clothes-horse higher he turns away.

The auctioneer has promised to keep my Zeppelin portion safe until I can come back with three more shillings. I leave my sixpence with him and walk fast across the edge of the heath. It is hot today, the flowers blazing, and white butterflies flutter by my feet. The air smells sweet of elderflower, and the sheep on the low field are fattening and content. If I don't look east to where the barbed wire is coiled along the cliff, I wouldn't know there was a war. I stop and listen for guns across the water, but hard as I strain my ears I can only hear the birds chattering, and the heavy drone of a bee.

Ann is in the garden, sewing, when I get home. I go straight to the well and pull up a bucket. 'Where've you been?' she asks me. She is thin as a cat still, and pale, but her eyes have lost the cloud look they had when she first woke.

'You'll see,' I say. I take a swallow, and another, and when my stomach is swooshing with the sweet, dank water, I haul myself upstairs. It hurts to separate my coins so harshly. They should lie together as they have done, growing these past years, but there's nothing I can do now if I want to avoid prison, and I slide them into my pocket.

It's not easy walking with a piece of Zeppelin. I have to stop and rest every few hundred yards. At first I grip it in my arms, then I hang it like a bow across my back, but my hands soon tire from stretching for it, and I balance it on my head. All the while I think of the look on Ann's face when I present it to her. Her own Zeppelin. The one that brought her back to life. And I imagine Father pinning it horizontal to the beam above the fireplace so that everyone will see it as they come through to the main bar.

I rest for a while in Betty's hollow. Betty Maclellan. I hear her voice as if she's said it. And I snap up a stem of reed grass and whistle to her through it, counting the months till autumn when she will return. I lie back against the short warm grass. This is the day the world was made for. Sun. Breeze. Blue. Gold. And my body aches with the thought of sleeping. No, I tell myself, but I close my eyes, just for a moment, and when I open them again, the blue has darkened, and there is a sharp edge to the air. My Zeppelin! My heart roars as I thrash round for it. But it is there, lying by me, the zigzag of its metal brackets cool beside my arm.

I stagger up and homewards. The inn is in shadow, the sun catching on the trees of the Hoist. I push open the door. It is too early for first orders, but all the same there are voices drifting out from the main bar. I clutch my Zeppelin tight. It's taller than me, and half as thin. The sharp edges of it dent into my arms. There's a man's voice. Stuttery. And a girl – Ann it is. And she is crying. Then Father cuts through with a cheer, the door bursts open and he rushes past me and down the steps to the cellar. I don't move. There is silence from the next room. And then Mother begins speaking. Low. Soothing. A question, although I can't hear what it is. Father is up again. A glass of beer, full-strength, frothing, splashing on to the floor.

'Pa?' I need to remind him he's not drinking. But it seems the pint is not for him.

'Don't just stand there.' He has seen me. 'Come in and say hello.'

I keep hold of my Zeppelin, and I edge after him into the bar. But still I don't see who it is, with Mother and Ann crowding so tightly in around the visitor who is sitting on a chair.

'Here you go, boy.' They part for Father to hand in the beer, and that's when I see him. The man from the auction. The thin man in navy uniform who leapt into the air.

'You'll say hello to Jimmy, won't you?' Mother is all smiles. And I feel my eyes start back in my head.

'But you ... you're ...' I have no good words to describe how the *Formidable* went down. 'You're drowned.'

Ann takes hold of Jimmy Kerridge's hand. 'Jim was just telling us what happened.' And she looks at him as if he might begin again.

'You tell.' His sailor's hat is lying on the table. And now that I am facing him I see he has a deep red scar down one side of his face.

Ann sits down and, grateful, Jimmy takes a long pull of his pint.

'I couldn't,' she says. But she tries all the same. 'On the night of the sinking,' her voice is a whisper, 'Jimmy was on deck when the first torpedo hit.'

'Not that I knew what it was,' Jimmy interrupts. 'None of us did. Not at first.'

'The second torpedo caused the ship to list to starboard.' Ann's memorised each word. ' "All hands muster on the quarterdeck." That's right, is it?'

'That's it,' Jimmy nods.

'The men started queuing for the boats. But Jimmy didn't want to leave the ship. He had back pay, a gold sovereign, stowed away in his kit locker and he wasn't leaving that.'

'That's it,' Jimmy nods again. 'I wasn't going to lose that.'

'It was dark between decks and the ship was rocking.' Ann's eyes are wide. 'It took a long time to reach to the locker. Water coming in. The whole boat heaving. And when he did, it was a fight to get back on to the deck.'

'And when I did,' there is a pause, and Jimmy frowns, 'there was no one there. The lifeboats had gone. Smashed up in the water. Although I could see one, quite close, I could make out the faces of the men in her. I shouted. But they kept on with their rowing, pulling hard as they could away from the ship.'

'Jimmy was alone then.' Ann is trembling. 'And so he started praying, and then, as if in answer, there before him stood the ship's own chaplain.'

Jimmy swallows and he hangs his head. And we bend our necks with him and wait till he's recovered. 'God heard my prayers.' He rocks a little and then he looks up and smiles. 'The chaplain knew what to do for the best. "Stay on the ship," he told me. "As soon as they find we're missing, they'll be back." And he explained how the first lieutenant was his brother-in-law. He'd been chaplain at his wedding. "As soon as he discovers I'm not with them, he'll turn right around to pick us up. We'll not be forgot." I looked up at the stars. I thanked the Lord. And I promised that when I got home I'd use the sovereign to buy a present for my girl.'

A tear rolls down Ann's cheek. And that's when I see them, the same milk colour as her skin – the pearls, soft and warm against her throat. 'But no one came,' Ann says, 'and the wind got up into a storm so that soon the ship was wallowing in rough sea.'

'The starboard side was three parts underwater,' Jimmy grips her hand. 'We held on to the quarterdeck, but holding on was hard. So we waited till we dared and scrambled up to the guardrails, and from there on to the port side. But the ship turned turtle, and as it went, we pulled ourselves on to her bottom. We rested there and then, when there was nothing else for it, we struck out into the sea. The chaplain caught hold of a boom that floated by, and we attached ourselves to it best we could, and all the while air was rising from the sinking ship so that as we tried to paddle away it pulled us back. We gave up and lay still. I couldn't feel my legs. And then, just like that, the ship slipped down under the water and was gone.'

We stood quiet in the inn. Our eyes lowered.

'All our work now was to keep our heads above the water. And to keep ourselves awake. Shouting, praying, singing, waiting, cursing, hoping. Where was that blasted escort? We used worse language than that. I don't remember how long we drifted. But I heard later it was fourteen hours before we were found. And when the rescue came I thought I was dreaming. A voice was shouting, loud, quite close. And I looked up to see three fishermen looking down at me from the deck of their boat.

'They threw me a line, I remember that. But it was all the strength I had to untangle myself from the boom. They heaved me in, and gave me brandy, and I was taken away to a hospital where they stitched up my face.' Jimmy puts his hand up to the scar which is pale as he is now, a rough seam of white.

'It was later they told me about the chaplain. I have no memory of it. They say he must have been taken by the swell. I didn't know that till later. And then for a long time I didn't know anything at all.'

'He was looked after at Lyme Regis by a family called Blunt,' Ann says. 'They think it might have been the propeller that struck him on the head. He couldn't remember anything. Not where he came from. Or who he was. And there was nothing left on him but the gold sovereign.'

'Not any more.' He smiles at Ann, and she blushes fiercely and raises her fingers to her throat.

'So when did you get back?' Mother asks.

'A few days ago. But I wasn't coming by without a gift. So when I saw the sign for the sale . . .' He looks over at me then, and his face breaks into a smile.

'What the . . . ???' Father rocks back on his heels. And I step away from my piece of wreck and stare at it with the others.

'What have you got there?' Mother frowns.

'What is it anyway?' Ann looks disgusted. She has one hand on her pearls, as if she daren't let go of them, and with the other she holds tight to Jimmy Kerridge.

'I . . . it's . . .' I look at it with new eyes. A charred, scarred wreck of metal. 'It's something that is needed, I was collecting, for a friend.' I turn and I rattle it out before they can ask another question.

My arms are aching. I don't have the strength to walk another yard, but all the same I drag the Zeppelin down the street, fast as I can, until I've reached the Lea House gate. I hoist it over and climb in after it, and then, lying it across my arms, I heave it up the path.

'Hello!' I don't see her until she's opened the door, blinded as I am by metal. 'What have you got there?' Mrs Mackintosh puts out a hand.

'I . . . I . . .' I have no words to tell her. All I want to do is set it down and leave.

'What a marvellous thing!' Mac is beside her. 'Where on earth did you get it?'

'Did you find it?'

'It's the wreck. There's nothing else it could be.'

'Come in, come in.'

'Thank you,' I manage, and then, with no warning, tears are pouring from my eyes, blinding me, stopping my breath.

'It's all right.' Old Mac eases the Zeppelin from my arms, and Mrs Mac draws out a handkerchief and presses it into my hands.

'My sister, Ann . . .' now my tears are falling freely I don't want them to stop. 'I carried it from Westleton, and I thought . . . I thought she'd be . . .' I gasp for one more sob.

'Westleton? That's not so easy.' Mac lifts it and brings it to stand beside the fireplace, and we all look at it, just as we once looked at the gesso. 'But it is beautiful. I'm proud to think we shot it down.' He goes close and inspects each strut and hinge, and for a long time no one speaks as he lets the imprint of its surface show him how it is made.

'It's for you,' I swallow. I was a fool to think there was anyone else who would admire it more. Mac stays still, his back to me. 'Thank you.' He doesn't turn around.

'It's very kind,' Mrs Mac tells me. 'Thank you from us both.' And Mac keeps his face turned away from me as he stoops over the singed frame.

It's night when I leave. I look behind me and see that there's a chink of light running above the window ledge. I step back and rap on the glass.

'Hello?' Mrs Mac mouths at me.

'Tape up the window,' I tell her.

'What's that?' she asks.

'Blackout paper,' I shout. 'You need more.'

She nods, serious, and waves goodbye and as I walk away down the garden I'm followed by the flickers of the lamp as she does her best to tug down the blind.

Chapter 50

I've a letter in my hand. I'm to post it first thing in the morning, Mac says. Or before if I can manage. And in payment he gives me a penny and a new German word. *Bild.* He says it means picture. And I'm so pleased with it that Mrs Mac gives me another. *Bunt.* It is the name for colours all together. It's a word that we don't have.

The envelope is addressed to a Mr William Davidson, of Glasgow. I don't show it to Ann. It hurts me not to, but I can't bring myself to take it out until she's gone to bed. She's an engaged woman now. Father will say yes to anything. And she walks about with her head held high. 'Night then, Tommy,' she climbs the ladder, and I want to follow her and bite my teeth against the pearls to show her they're not real.

Dear William Davidson,

I wonder how you are and how this war is affecting you? It has nearly finished me off completely. I have been down here for ten months now and nothing seems to get any forwarder. I am sending you some watercolour drawings of mine and I shall be glad to know whether you would like to or can buy one or more of these. They are quite straightforward frank work and have been much thought of by the few people who have seen them. I have done some much larger work (that is, in size) but of course to buy these is a larger consideration. These I am sending you I would catalogue at £10 10s and I would be glad to let you have one or more at £7 7s each.

If you can see your way to take even one you would be doing me a great service. And if you don't want any of them please don't hesitate to return them.

With kind regards to you,
Yours sincerely
C R Mackintosh

Pressed tight inside the envelope and wrapped in fine layers of paper are three pictures. *Larkspur*, *Witch Hazel* and *Gorse*. I take a clean strip of linen and lay it down before I spread them out. I smile to see my birds amidst the larkspur, crowing and comfortable, and I find a nut-brown finch, and then another, kissing, among the stems of gorse. Soon they will be speeding by mail train to Glasgow, and as I pack them up again I consider these small pieces of our village travelling out into the world and wonder how long it will be before I set off too.

Father's not had a drink since Ann got well. And he doesn't have one now. Not even with the news that Ann and Jimmy are to marry at the end of the month. Jimmy has an official letter. Discharged. Medically unfit for naval service. He holds it out, and as we huddle round he nods and smiles but he doesn't say a word. Ann takes it from him and reads the words herself.

I shoot her a sharp look, but she doesn't meet my eye.

'They'll be giving Jimmy a certificate too,' she says proudly, 'signed by His Majesty the King.' And she hands Jimmy back his letter and he takes it, as he must have taken so many of her own, unread.

'What will you do now?' Mother asks him and he says that next week he'll be starting with the greengrocer, hauling sacks, delivering orders. Mr Steley. Opposite the pier.

'Mrs Kerridge says we must make our home with her, to be closer to Jim's work,' and she looks over at Jimmy and she bites her lip to stop her whole self smiling. 'I've put in for nursing training, so I can help out at the hospital at Henham with Mary. I can go in by bicycle. It's not far. The boys from the brigade do it – taking and carrying messages, back and forth from Southwold, as much as six times a day.'

'And what'll we do here?' Mother's voice is hollow. 'How will we manage losing you again?' And although I can see she's trying not to show it, her face creases with the pain.

'Thomas,' Father puts a hand on her arm. 'He'll be going nowhere.'

Mother turns to me. 'Thomas,' she says. And I hear the echo of those other names. William, William, James. William, James, Thomas. 'Thomas,' she says again, and she catches hold of my hand.

I watch Mac over the days that follow to see if he's a man with money. I inspect his face for a trace of £7 7s, or even of £10 10s, and when I don't find it, I scan the walls and ledges of his house to catch a glimpse of the watercolours returned. But I learn nothing. Instead I come across him, wandering through the lanes, standing on the beach, using his banned binoculars to watch the naval flying boats searching the sea for signs of enemy ships. They fly so close to the water that they have to hop over the pier at Southwold, and as they leap, Mac raises his binoculars as if he daren't lose sight of them for a moment. I say nothing. Instead I walk past the Lea House late at night, and I'm glad to see that there is a new layer of blackout paper sealing up the window. But one evening, as I'm passing, the door opens and the flare of a lamp flashes out into the dark. I spin around to see if anyone else is watching, and when I turn back, the tall black shadow of Mr Mackintosh is walking down the path towards the gate. I stand still against the bridge and hope he doesn't see me, but, the lamp snuffed out, he turns inland, and moves off in his dark cloak. I follow him. Careful not to drag my foot too heavily against the ground.

Mac cuts over the green and walks down towards the river. He stops by the ferry and peers across, and then turning, he hurries off along the path. I run from hut to hut, keeping to the shadows, Danky's with its nets tucked messily below, Shrimp's and Watson's and May's, and when he gets to Thorogood's, Mac crouches down and lights the wick of the lantern. 'Come in if you're coming,' he says, as it flickers into life, and I hobble out from my hiding place and, glad of the dark to cover my blushing, I step into the shed, pulling the door closed, hard as it will go.

Mac says nothing. He lifts a sheet of Whatman from a shelf and lays it on the table beside two stems of flowers. Anemones they are. One dark purple, upright as a tulip, the other lighter, furrier, a shade closer to blue. Without taking off his coat he begins mixing his colours. He holds them to the lamp and goes on stirring, shaking his head as he does so, and muttering, 'Stupid, selfish, stubborn . . .' the words turned around to pierce only himself.

I keep quiet. He's forgotten I am here. And still cursing, he starts on a leaf. It is the colour of seaweed, with the same forked edges and frills. 'There you are then . . .' he's talking to the anemones now, and as he works, the paint darkening and lightening from tip to stem, he begins, slowly, to calm.

'Will Mrs Mackintosh be starting her gesso of the May Queen soon?' I ask after some long time.

Mac wipes his brush and dips it into green. 'My wife can't work unless she has tranquillity,' he says. 'And that it seems I'm unable to provide. All day she's been trying and failing to make a start on a new panel. She's been asked, we both have, to enter a work for next year's Arts and Crafts Exhibition in London. She'd like to make a set of panels . . .'

'Panels?' I've still not had a chance to show her the pellets of my rabbit-skin glue.

'*The Voices of the Wood*, she wants to call it.'

'My wood? The Hoist?' And Mac looks up, amused.

'Her own wood, I expect,' he says kindly as he bends back over his work. And I see he means the wood of her imagination. That grey, green dripping world she invented with her sister, with its women, and its flowers, and the long weeping strands of their hair. 'The truth about Margaret Macdonald,' Mac says slowly, frilling the edges of a leaf, 'is that she has genius. Where I have only talent. And now through this . . . merry dance I've led her, her genius is being sapped away.'

I wait for him to darken the wine-stained stem of the first anemone but he looks so forlorn that I offer up, 'But it was you who made the Glasgow School of Art.'

'That is true,' he frowns as if he'd half forgotten. 'But Margaret was half if not three-quarters in all my architectural efforts.' He stops then and looks up. 'When I made the Willow Tea Rooms for Miss Cranston, it was my wife that determined the colour scheme. She designed the cutlery, the carpets, curtains, metalwork, lighting. She even designed the waitresses' uniforms. And arranged the flowers. You know Miss Cranston had flowers sent fresh from her house in Nitshill three times a week. And the waitresses had to look just so. Miss Cranston interviewed each one, and if she liked a girl and had thoughts of hiring her, she'd go and pay a call and meet her parents. See what kind of home she came from.'

I think of Sir Bly calling round to see where Mary had been raised, but in a village as small as ours everything is known. 'Margaret and her sister Frances came to the art school together.' Mac is bent over his brush. 'That was before we moved to the new building. By then they'd set up in a studio of their own. Poster design, leaded glass and metalwork. They put on exhibitions, caused quite a stir, especially after the editor of the *Studio* magazine paid them a visit and wrote glowingly of their talents. And lucky that he did, for there were enough others who were ready to tear apart their work. "Ghoulish," people said it was. "Hideous." One review even asked the authorities not to halt until such offences should be brought within the scope of the Further Powers.'

'Further Powers?' I ask, for he'd said it with such menace.

'A branch of the police introduced to curb drunken and unruly behaviour on the streets.' He laughs. 'And all for a poster.' There is green on his brush again and he's filling in the tips at the top of the stem of the second anemone. I watch from over his shoulder. There are no birds here. I've already searched, unless there is one hiding in the bowl of the flower. And I think of my own starlings, grown to half their size, chattering and scrapping in a gang. Who are your birds for? I want to ask him. And I wonder if, like mine, they are the ghosts of his brothers, the ones he lost and the one that ran away to sea. And that's when I see the eye, and I laugh, and my hand flies to my mouth. The eye is black, and now that I've caught it, the rest of the body is clear as day. The bird is upside down, that's all. The stalk a beak, the fluff of down – the ruff around its neck. I'm grinning so hard I'm sure he'll notice. And I know who the bird is then. It's him.

'What happened to the studio?' I ask.

'Well, they worked there for three years, before Frances married. She married my friend Bertie MacNair – as you know

– and it was not long before they had a child. That was not easy for Frances. My wife saw how she suffered. How she struggled with the belief she held that there should be no conflict between motherhood and a professional life. How it tore her apart. She loved the boy, that was the problem. So how could she neglect him for her work? How could she work and not neglect him? Well, they were in Liverpool by then. And although we missed her – we missed them both – at least now I had my Margaret to myself.

'We were married that year. And we made our own home at Mains Street. Just as we wished it. Just . . .' he looks ahead as if he can see it, 'as we'd dreamt it. News spread of it. Photographs were published. Architects from Austria, men interested in the modern – *Der Jungen*, they called themselves – there's another word for you, The Young – came to call on us, and we were invited to exhibit in Vienna. We made a Scottish Room. ' "There is a Christ-like mood in this interior." ' Mac tilts his nose in the air. ' "This chair might have belonged to St Francis of Assisi. The decorative element is not proscribed, but is worked out with a spiritual appeal." That was the art editor of the *Wiener Rundschau*. And although there were voices raised against us – "a hellish room, furniture as fetishes" ': he is Scottish again – 'it was considered a triumph. What a time we had in Vienna. Even though we were announced as Mr and Mrs Herr Macdonald, we were treated with grace and grandeur. The students even pulled us to the station in a flower-bedecked carriage.' Mac laughs and shakes his head. The light from the lantern warms his face.

'It wasn't so long after that Keppie made me a junior partner, I suppose he had to – although he kept much of the commissioned work for himself, and I was to rely on work from Miss Cranston and her tea rooms, and keep a lookout for competitions. But I could hardly complain, not with Jessie

Keppie still unmarried, while I had my own Mrs Mackintosh, and Hermann Muthesius too as a supporter – I've told you about the German, the art historian – I became godfather to his son? Muthesius began to write about my work, and it was through him that I heard about the competition for "House for an Art Lover", organised by Alexander Koch at Darmstadt. I was well enough known in Europe by then for my name to be recognised, but it was a requirement of the competition that all entries be submitted under a pseudonym. Anonymous.' He tapped his nose. 'A pen name.'

'What did you choose?'

'*Der Vogel.*'

'*Der Vogel?*'

'The bird.'

'The bird!' I want to jump. 'I knew it.' But he is still talking.

'*House for an Art Lover*. The best thing I ever did,' Mac's eyes are gleaming. 'We made it together. Mr and Mrs Herr Macdonald. Well you've seen it, you know. It was not just a house.' He's talking to himself now. 'It had our three words in it. On every wall. But the drawings arrived late, apparently, and were missing the required number of interior perspectives. And although the design met with admiration and even wonder – it was the closest I ever got to bringing an ocean liner in to land – these errors, all on my behalf, meant it could not win the competition. And now our house sits in its blue folder, on a desk in a rented room, where most likely it will remain for ever.'

'Maybe one day, when the war. . . .'

But he is not listening. 'When I'm out walking, and I look into the distance, up over the heathland and across the estuary, I think I see it, shimmering white against the sky. I even see the rose bushes, when I search with my binoculars, and the poplars, their green heads in a row. "What is it then?" I ask myself, but it's usually a cloud, or the sun squinting against me, and when I look again it isn't there.' Mac stares down at his work. For a long time he doesn't speak. Then he takes up his pencil and with sure strokes he makes a fine grey box, his initials on one side and his wife's on the other, CRM, MMM, and the date – 1915 – linking them across the top.

Chapter 51

Now, at night, after checking the Lea House and the beach, after listening for Zeppelins, and the loose chatter of anyone who may or may not be a spy, I scurry up the river path and tap on the hut door. I tap once and wait, and then I tap again and let myself in. Mac sits bent over the sprig of a flower. He looks up for a second and nods. 'Evening,' he says, although by then it is night, but I don't contradict him. I sit in the corner and I watch him work. He has a rare plant, a strawberry tree he says it is, from the garden at The Lodge, although the Latin name, he tells me, is *Arbutus*. I think of all the foreign words I know. *Vogel. Kist. Jungen. Bunt. Cutag. Rundschau. Arbutus.* And I imagine packing them up and taking them out into the world. Vienna I'll visit first. Then Rome and Florence. And when I've seen Paris I'll set sail for Australia just to feel what it's like to be so far from home.

Mrs Mac is dreaming of her *Voices of the Wood*, Mac tells me. She would have liked to make it from gesso, but the work is too taxing for her, the panels too heavy. Labourers would be needed to transfer the panels when they're done, and labourers, quite rightly, are away at war.

I take the hard white pellets of my glue to her. They are sealed in their jar like jam under gingham, although if the cloth

255

is folded back, a rancid smell escapes. 'Thank you,' she reels back from its strength. And although she is grateful, she tells me she'll be making these new panels from paint. She would make them in embroidery, she says, but it will be overlooked as women's work, most probably dismissed by the Royal Academy where the exhibition is to be held, although maybe, and she gives a mischievous smile, she will slant the strokes of her brush like stitches to give the desired effect.

'But I have nothing to offer you,' she holds the jar against herself. 'We are clean out of cake, we've not even any bread until Mrs Mollett comes.' And so, instead, she opens a pamphlet that is stacked with others on the table and shows me a photograph of a gesso panel she once made. It is titled *The Seven Princesses*, and is so large each picture only captures a small section before we have to move on to the next. '*The Seven Princesses* is a play by Maeterlinck,' she tells me, 'and is the story of a princess, one of seven sisters, who pines away for love.'

I look closely at the serene face of the princess, her cloak wrapped around her like a shroud, roses, shells and beads meshed into it. There is the prince, coming to claim her in his ship, three black swans sailing ahead of it, their necks curved down as if they know it is too late.

I stroke my fingers against the page. 'I'd like to see it.'

'Yes,' Mrs Mackintosh nods. 'It was commissioned by a very wealthy man, an Austrian – Fritz Waerndorfer, who wanted the *Princesses* for his own home, but by the time I'd finished it, and it took almost four years to make – imagine, each panel was taller and wider than a door, and there were three – Waerndorfer's fortune had already begun to dwindle. Now it is completely gone, the house sold, the contents dispersed. Waerndorfer sailed away to a new life in America. But I hear from his wife that my panels have been taken to a museum. The Österreichisches Museum für Angewandte Kunst.'

I look round fearful at so many foreign words, but Mrs Mac sets down the magazine. She goes to a desk, the desk on which the *House for an Art Lover* sits in its blue folio, and she slides open a drawer. I follow her. There are letters there, arranged in neat piles, thin envelopes heavy with stamps, and after flicking through them, she draws one out.

'This arrived not so long ago,' she tells me. And she sits on a chair and, beckoning for me to stand beside her, she frowns at the words of the letter. *Liebe Frau Macdonald Mackintosh,* I read over her shoulder, but she swallows and changing each word into English, she begins to read.

Dear Mrs Macdonald Mackintosh,
I want, very much, for you to know the fate of your panels. After much thought and anxiety that The Seven Princesses *may now be considered an acquisition by an enemy artist and possibly destroyed, the museum that holds them has taken each panel to the basement, placed them into crates and put them against a wall. Then, and in this way they will hopefully remain undetected, they have built a second wall in front of it. Please, dear Mrs Mackintosh, do not alarm yourself when you think of your masterpiece so far away from home.* The Seven Princesses, *at least, are safe.*
With affection,
Lili Waerndorfer

'So,' Mrs Mac shrugs. And then with no warning tears are streaming down her face. 'What if no one remembers? What if everyone who knows must leave Vienna, and the seven princesses remain forever sealed into their tomb?' Her shoulders shake. 'But at least,' and to my surprise I find that she is laughing, 'the colours will not fade. Not like the panels I made for my husband's houses, which sit above the fireplaces and are already mottled by candle flame, gas lamp and smoke.'

She rises then, and folding the letter back into its envelope she presses it into place in its drawer. 'She gives herself a little shake. 'Tell me, how are preparations going for the wedding?' And without waiting for an answer, she moves through to the kitchen where she pours us both a glass of water from a narrow jug. 'The thing to remember,' she takes a gulp, 'is that it is nothing more than a great lump of plaster of Paris. There are thousands, millions of people who are suffering. It is they who need our prayers.' And, as if to convince herself further, she turns to me and smiles.

Mac gives me another letter. It is addressed once again to Glasgow.

Dear William Davidson,

Since I wrote to you I find I am in a much worse plight than I imagined. If you cannot buy one of my pictures will you please lend me one pound and send it so that I can get it on Wednesday. I am very sorry to trouble you but please try to do this.

Yours sincerely

C R Mackintosh

I run with the letter to Southwold, and I don't stop until it's in the postman's hands. I run so fast, and with such urgency, that when I no longer have it, I am lost. I walk down to the beach. The tide is out and the longshore boats are pulled up against the shingle. The bathing huts have long since been shunted from the shore, and above us where the cannons once stood are coils and rolls of wire. I climb the steps towards Gun Hill, curious to see the drift of feathers and sticks caught up there, but when I reach the top I slip instead into the warm wooden cabin of the Sailors' Reading Room. I stop and breathe in the smell. The dust and polish, the mouldering covers of the magazines. I kneel down before the boats and say a prayer for every sailor out there, and when I'm finished I hear the thwack and scatter of a billiard ball hitting the cushion of the table behind the fishermen's private door. Please God, I add, let me one day be invited into that room. And I feel a beat inside me. To be invited in, I must first strike out to sea.

There is another crack, and a rumble of men's voices, and I get to my feet and press my eye against the panelled door. There are several men inside. I can make out the leg of one, an arm of another. I stand quite still and listen.

'If you're lucky enough to have one good woman and one good dog in your lifetime . . .' I smile. It is Danky and I've heard this line before. 'I had one good dog,' I mouth along with him, 'but the good woman, that was harder to find.'

There is laughter, one soft chuckle that may or may not belong to Jimmy Kerridge, and the smack of a cue against a ball, as I rest my eyes on the lush green of the billiard table.

I could stand there all day, I'm sure of it, before anyone would come out and notice me, but I'm needed at home, and so I turn away. 'What do you say, boys?' A voice is raised. A voice that I'm not sure of. 'Is there a reward in it, do you think?'

I turn back.

'I shouldn't see why not.' It's Danky again. 'Information delivered is a valuable thing.'

There are a series of thuds as balls thump against the corners.

'So who'll it be then? Who'll be the one to whisper a warning in the policeman's ear?'

Danky grunts. It'll not be him. For he'll not go near that gun-wielding constable again.

'But how can we be sure?' It is Jimmy.

'How can we be sure?' Danky sounds disgusted. 'That's what they want you to think. That's the trick they play on all of us, turn us into cowards. Meanwhile the law is turned on good patriotic fellows like ourselves.'

'I'm no coward.' I can see the scar on Jimmy's face filling up with blood. And I wonder if he'll mention the certificate of honourable discharge that is waiting, even as we speak, to be signed by the king.

'Of course you're not a coward.' The other voice is certain. A fisherman's voice it is, from further along the coast. 'Which makes you first choice for the job. Listen, son. No one's asking you to arrest anyone yourself. Just go along to the constable and tell him what you know.'

'And what do I know?' Jimmy sounds unsure.

'The man's been seen, more than once, sending out signals with his lamp. He's a foreigner, for Christ's sake. Who knows where he is really from?'

'Wandering about all times of the day and night.' Danky is gruff. 'I come across him just last week, past midnight, roaming about over the common.'

'And aren't those spyglasses of his banned? Now what are they useful for if not . . .'

'For spying?' Jimmy's voice has risen.

Carefully I step away. My face where it's been pressed against the wood is numb. I'm quiet as I unlatch the door, but once outside, I streak across the common, not stopping till I reach the bridge, not even checking on the hour before I thrust my body forward on to the rails. I'm halfway across before I think of the danger, and by then my foot is singing loud enough to drum the blood out of my ears, and I'm deaf to any other noise. Come on, I tell myself, and as I stop for breath I twist around to gauge the position of the sun. But it's a hazy day, the sunlight filtered behind white, and I've no time to waste in guessing how many minutes there are before the hour.

I'm half dead when I reach the other side, but it was quicker, I am right, and I run, my back uncurling, my foot sharp. I stumble on to the river path, and hop and drag myself along, until the huts come into view and I pause to get my breath.

Mac is sitting on his stool. He has his board before him and he's working from four bells of blossom. They are delicate, deep purple, with a small lattice of squares across each petal.

'*Fritillaria*,' he tells me as I sink down on to my crate.

'Snake's-head,' I nod. Although I've known them too as chess flower, guinea hen and leper lily, for the bells the lepers used to jangle as they walked. A gloomy plant, Mother calls them. She won't have them on the grave. But flowering now under Mac's fine brush, even she would see the beauty in them.

'Snake's-head.' Mac smiles at their shimmery skin. 'I like that.' And he taps in a white spot of light.

'Mr Mackintosh,' I try. And he stops for a moment. 'Could I . . . would it be possible, just for a short time, to borrow your binoculars?'

'The binoculars?' He's mixing up a yolky yellow. And he turns his eyes on me, as if I am the one that is suspicious. 'If you really need them. My wife is at home. She'll hand them to you.' And he begins painting in the golden centre of an open flower.

I'd like to sit there longer. But there's no time to waste. 'I'd better get them then,' I tell him, and I hurry away along the path.

Chapter 52

Ann and Jimmy are to marry in the village church, and not, as Mother feared they might, in the larger, grander church at Southwold. Mrs Kerridge is there. It seems she's the only family Jimmy's got and we sit with her in the first pew, Father, Mother, Mary and I, all staring ahead at the happy couple, so thin and pale they look like goose down. Mrs Horrod is there, weeping from the first word. And her husband, who nods off as soon as he sits down. Danky sits behind me, his leg sticking stiffly out into the aisle, and from the smell of him he's taken something strong to see him through. Mrs Lusher brings her mother, and sits her bundled in her blanket at the back, although we still hear her mumbling and wheezing through the service. George Allard is near the back too, squeezed in beside the Tilson brothers and Frank Tibbles, and even Mr Gory from Lowestoft. So glad are they to have good news, no one can stay away. And when Ann lifts her eyes and says I do, and they lean towards each other in a kiss, there is a ripple of happiness that runs through the church, as if after almost a full year of war, a small clear victory has been won.

There is a party at the inn. A barrel of beer is rolled up from the cellar, and the tables and chairs that Father and I dragged outside that morning have been covered with white cloths.

Ribbons hang from the branches of the trees, and the hollyhocks by the back door wave welcoming as men. The whole village is here now. I walk between them. One eye out for Father who I've not seen since the church, and the other for the speck of a Zeppelin coming in across the sea. But it is a clear blue day and no cloud for cover, and there is nothing in the sky but seagulls drifting and a scattering of starlings, swooping down across the field.

Fred Tilson has brought his fiddle. He strikes up a tune. And his brother starts in on a song.

'*In the merry month of June, when all the flowers were in bloom . . .*'

People clap their hands. Ann and Jimmy dance. And then Mother, through her tears, protesting, is swept into the arms of the landlord of the Bell and swished across the grass. It's then that I see Father, his eyes shiny, his mouth grinning, as he leans into a crowd of men. 'Pa.' I go to him. There may still be time to help him save his promise. But as I near he puts out his hand and, gripping me by the shirtfront, he holds me off.

'So has it not been done?' It's Danky. Red in the face. Redder than Father.

'Truth is,' Father slurs, 'there's no reward.'

'No reward!' Danky spits. 'No reward but honour, and the safety of our land!'

A new song starts. Louder than before. Tibbles squeezes an accordion and the dancing starts again. 'If Jimmy said he'd do it . . .' Father swerves round. 'Well, I'll do it myself if no one else will. Although I'm fond of the old fellow.'

'Report him?' Gory asks.

'Give him a fright.'

Mary is dancing now. With a soldier billeted at the rectory. And there's Kett, the widower, leaning against the well shaft, talking to Mrs Lusher who has a dazed look on her face.

'Leave it with me.' Father lets go of my jacket. And as he reels away I see he has an empty glass looking to be filled.

'Dance with me, won't you, Tommy.' It is Ellen from the blacksmith's, grown taller than me, her lips painted a cheery pink. I need to look for Mac. But she takes hold of my arm and slides me inside the music, twisting and turning till her hair is falling in loose strands from under her hat, and I'm laughing with the speed and heat of her, as I hop from foot to foot. After, we sit together and she asks if I still play coppen ball up in the churchyard, and I blush and say I don't. I'm sure I never did. 'Ermentruda,' she whispers and I laugh, but all I can see is the short grey grave at the far end by the gate.

'Make way.' It is Father again, his voice behind me. Louder. 'I've important business to attend to.' And grandly flinging out his arm, he smacks Mr Horrod in the face.

'Ahh,' Mr Horrod shouts. It may be the first sound I've ever heard him utter. 'I'll saw your bleeding ear off.'

Father rounds on him, he's so surprised. 'I see no fear, nor care for no man.' His eyes are wild, his fists up.

'We should take a walk one of these evenings,' Ellen is saying, 'with the weather so fine.' But I've turned away. I must find Mac.

Mac was invited, I'm sure of it. I can see him nodding over the bell of his snake's-head, saying he'd be glad to come. And even though I'd know if he was here, I spring up and rush around the garden, hoping to catch sight of the red flame of his wife's hair.

'Let's have another dance.' Ellen has caught me. And the music starts and I'm swallowed up in it. Lost in the heat of her arms.

Betty Maclellan, I think to myself as we stagger into the woods. And I see the upturned smile of Betty's Highland mouth, even as Ellen hovers for a kiss. But once I've kissed her, all else is forgotten. A spark shoots through me and I'm clutching at her, pulling her against me, so desperate am I to feel the softness of her body against mine.

'Tommy, Tom!' Ellen is wriggling out from under me. I don't even remember how we came to be on the ground. 'Calm yourself, there's not such a hurry.'

I lie still and stare up through the trees. The blue has gone out of the sky, the light behind it low. The music is still playing. And below the fiddle I think I hear the sound of Mother sobbing, for tonight Ann will be sleeping under another woman's roof. 'Come on,' I say to Ellen who is picking leaves out of her hair. And I take her hand and I lead her back to the party.

The crowd has thinned. But Mrs Horrod is still there, standing with Mother, their arms entwined. Mr Horrod is asleep on the chair by the back door. And Ann and Jimmy are dancing, their feet slow, their faces close.

'Where's Father?' I look about me. But Mother takes my hand and tells me to put out the fire. There must be no sign of it by the time it is dark.

I push the cover from the well and peer down. No one knows how deep our well is. It was dug when the Blue Anchor was first built. Two hundred years ago. Or more. I look round for George Allard, he will know. Maybe give me the exact date. But George Allard has gone too.

I let the bucket fall and listen to its drop. And when it's full and tugging at the well shaft, I heave it back up and drag it over to the fire. The fire hisses like a nest of snakes. Thick grey smoke streams into the air, but when I throw another bucket over it, it stutters, and turns to coils of white.

'I'll be seeing you then,' Ellen's hair is tucked neat inside her hat again, and with a quick kiss against my cheek, she runs out into the lane.

A pony waits in harness in the street, its tail plaited with ribbon, its mane decorated with flowers. Jimmy goes to hand Ann up, but Mother catches hold of her. 'Promise you'll call in on me before too long,' and only when Ann swears to it will she let her go.

'Where's Father?' I try again. But Mother is too busy with her tears to do anything more than wave at the departing trap.

The music has stopped. Fred Tilson is wrapping up his fiddle. And Tibbles has squeezed shut his accordion and fastened it with a latch. I hear Mrs Horrod from inside the kitchen clattering over the washing up while her husband sleeps by the back door.

I pick the bucket up and tip the last of the water over my face. And then because I like the drop and splash of it, I throw it down the well again, so there will be water for tomorrow.

The Lea House is dark as I come down the lane. Since the party ended I've been restless to do my rounds, but till now Mother wouldn't let me go. Not even with Mrs Horrod there. But the bar's closed up now. And Mother is asleep. Dreaming, I hope, of the flowers in the horse's mane, and not of Father who is still not home.

I stop by the gate. But no lantern flickers at the open door, no figure looms along the path, so I walk down towards the beach, trudge up through the dunes, and as I come over the top I'm stopped by light pouring off the sea. I duck down. Fearful. A submarine is the first thought I have, after an army, swarming in with torches, but as I crawl forward I see the light is coming from itself, moving, darting, skipping across the tops of the waves. I creep closer. It's as if a shoal of jellyfish have broken into pearls. And the pearls themselves have turned to oil. Phosphorescence. That's what it is. And eager to catch hold of it I step into the sea. Ice water cuts into my legs, trickles through the laces of my boots. But not just water, silvery-blue caterpillars of light. I laugh and wade out further. It's on my arms now, clinging to my fingers. My heart is high, I'm so fearful it will go. 'No,' I whisper as the light scatters, and I dip my head under so that the sparks can dance across my face. The waves are gentle, the sand is soft below my knees, and I flip on to my back and for a moment I am floating. But then my body buckles and I swallow water and there's nothing below, nothing on either side, but black. A wave lifts me, tips me forward, and just as it is about to drag me back, there's sand again and I am safe. I scramble out on to the beach and breathe. Already the dancing lights are fading, moving off along the coast. I'd like to wade in, grasp one last flicker, but I stand, and with my clothes still dripping and my feet squelching in my boots, I make my usual inspection of the beach.

I'm on the shingle by the ferry when I hear their voices. Shouting and hollering ahead of me in the dark. My first thought is there may be another battle, like the one that took place all those years before on the green. But as I hurry up the street towards the Bell, I see there is no fight. Instead the men from both inns are standing, swaying, their arms around each other, their voices loud with nothing more than drink.

'You're a good man, Maggs,' it is Danky, 'for all that you're a drunk.'

A roar of laughter rises, and Father interjects. 'A drunken man will get sober. But a fool will never get wise.' And he keels forward, laughing so hard I fear he may never straighten up.

'Happy as a dog with two tails.' George Allard of all people! And I stick to the shadow of the hedge and watch them straggle down the hill.

> 'It was a cold and stormy night
> The snow lay on the ground.'

Danky's voice floats on the night air.

> 'A sailor boy stood on the quay
> His ship was outward bound.
> His sweetheart standing by his side,
> Shed many a silent tear
> And as he pressed her to his breast
> He whispered in her ear.
> Farewell, farewell.'

The others all join in, and under cover of the chorus I trot after them.

> 'Farewell, my own true love,
> This parting gives me pain
> I'll be your own true guiding star when I return again.'

They're at the river, and they're bending to untie the knots that tether Danky's boat.

> 'My thoughts shall be of you, of you, when I return again.'

I creep forward. The tide is high, and Father, swaying, stands not a foot from the river's edge. 'Are we ready to depart?' George Allard swings his arm, and Danky holds the rope tight, waiting for them to get in.

'Father?' Alarm pushes me forward. 'What are you doing on the water?'

The boat rocks as Gory steps into it and laughs.

'What am I doing?' Father gives me his old offended look. 'My duty, that's what.' And his head jerks as if for a fraction of a second he's fallen asleep.

'Father, if you're going out on the water, let me come too.'

He pauses for a moment then he seizes hold of my collar. 'You,' he draws me close, 'you'll be staying here. That's how I planned it. That's how it will be. You'll stay here on dry land, where you'll be safe.' He pushes me away, and turning, he lunges down into the boat.

'But where are you going?' I need to know.

'Where d'you think?' he looks at the far shore. 'Now get on home. This is men's business and I'll not have you dragged into it.'

Danky unloops the rope and flings it down, and taking hold of the oars he leans back to make the first stroke.

'The spyglasses,' I call after them. 'You have nothing to fear. They're for looking at flowers. I've seen him do it. I know.'

Danky's voice drifts back towards me. '*Farewell, my love, remember me . . .*'

And I hear Father muttering, 'Flowers. I should say so. The boy has nothing but cloth between his ears.'

The laughter of the other men ripples out over the water.

There's no one in Thorogood's shed, so I race back down the lane towards Lea House. It is dark as before. But all the same I rush up through the garden and I thunder at the door. 'Mr Mackintosh? Mrs Mackintosh, do you hear me?' And when there is no answer I walk round the side of the house and bang on the window. 'Hello!' I call. But it seems there's no one here.

I stumble home and climb into my bed, and certain as I am I'll never sleep, soon I'm dreaming of Betty, winding me tight into her shawl, and then later, once I've woken and kicked the sheet from round me, I'm sure I hear the tall lady emptying her barrel. It's the early hours and dawn is creeping in, but there's the rumble of apples, pouring through my window, and then later still, the sigh of Allard's wheel, wheezing as it catches the wind, the creak of the pulley as the twine is spun. A fox is screaming. Or is it a peacock escaped from Blyfield House? And then it is morning, for all I can hear are the wood pigeons burbling, the sound as round as pebbles, so soothing I drift back to sleep.

It is late when I wake and Mother is sitting at the table. 'Morning,' I say. The stove is out. The chickens are still in. I heave the water bucket in from the garden, and unbolt the hutch. The hens come out aggrieved, their feathers ruffling, the cock high-stepping, eyes darting left and right.

'Will you have breakfast?' I ask Mother. She lifts her head and gives me a weak smile. I make tea, careful not to watch the pot, feeding the stove with sticks left out for last night's fire. 'Did Father not come home?' I ask, and she says nothing while I pour leaves into the teapot and picture him, passed out with Danky, sleeping off the night's adventures on the common.

I stay with Mother for as long as I can. 'Ann's only across the river,' I say. 'And Mary will be back to visit soon.' I kiss the top of her head where the parting has pulled her hair to white. And when her back is turned, I run.

The door to Thorogood's hut is still closed. But it's not locked and when I push it, I find Mr Mac inside sitting in a fog of pipe smoke. By the look of him he's been here half the night. He is still working on the snake's-head fritillary. Sketching with the fine tip of a pencil, a fretwork of squares against the side of the initialled box.

'She's back in Glasgow,' he tells me, before I can say anything. 'Her sister's in trouble again.' And he shakes his head.

'MacNair?' I guess.

'Aye.' Mac's soaked his paper in a wash of green. 'He's no money, that's the problem. Although, too often there seems to be enough for him to have a drink.' He paints in the fine stems of the grasses that make up the leaves.

My breathing slows. I've run the length of the harbour to give him my news, but what do I have to tell him? That there are people in the village who don't know where he's from? That whisper he's a foreigner? That consider it their duty to go and tell the police?

He knocks out his pipe. There's nothing to say. And I take up a sheet of paper and I sketch the stray ears of corn that edge the lane and the thicker, darker reed grass that brought Betty to me when I whistled.

'Are you not thinking of visiting Glasgow yourself?' I ask then, hopeful.

'They don't want *me*,' Mac laughs. 'I'm hardly better than MacNair to them. Now that my business is sunk. No. There's no one in Glasgow hankering for my return.' And he stares down at his work. The stems of his leaves lean sharply one way and another. The heaviest bell head droops. 'You know when John Keppie said goodbye to me, I'd just completed drawings for a training college?'

I didn't know.

'Jordanhill. I'd worked long hours at it, sitting up some nights so late that the cleaners found me in the morning, sleeping beneath the desk.' He pauses and packs his pipe with long trails of tobacco. 'It was on one of those mornings that John Keppie called me into his office. "We have standards to uphold," he told me. He didn't like the empty bottle of whisky lying beside me on the floor. And I wanted to say: "And who has set those standards? Who?" Whisky or not, the drawings for Jordanhill were good. I knew they were. But what did

Keppie say when I presented them? "Where are the hand basins? You've left no room for a hot and a cold tap." '

Mac's staring at me, but it's not to me that he's talking. ' "I've made places for poets," I told him, "and now I'm being reprimanded for misplacing the toilet facilities." But Keppie came closer. He was pale. Business was falling off, he told me, the city was struggling, and his job was to please the client. "While mine", I shouted, I could feel the whole office listening at the door, "is to make them gasp in wonder." That was when he asked me to go. And I was glad to. How much longer could we continue anyway, with the shadow of Jessie hovering, unhappily, between us?'

I stare at my boots. I'm wretched for him. That anyone should ever ask Mac to go.

'It was not long after,' his pipe is out again, 'that I set up on my own. I put out my script. C R Mackintosh. FRIBA. Yes. I'd become a Fellow of the Royal Institute of British Architects. I sent out letters. *I assure you of my best professional attention* . . . All I needed was a commission. And I waited. And waited. But nothing happened. Not a thing.' He sighs. 'I had all day long to think about my woes then. The fight it had been to get the art school finished. Three years of work. Every day. Most of the night too. I had time to think about my father, dying just as I was to start the second stage, and how furiously I'd worked, completing it on time. And within its budget. As I'd promised. At least this time the architects were named as Honeyman, Keppie and Mackintosh. Although that year in *Who's Who* the Glasgow School of Art was described as having been designed by John Keppie, with *assistance* from C R Mackintosh.' Mac laughs. A bitter, worn-out laugh. He's forgotten about the snake's-head. He's forgotten about me.

'There was praise. Of a kind.' I look up, hopeful. ' "This is not the plain building we commissioned," the governors accepted, "but it is at least a place that makes one think." But that was not the worst thing that was said. People asked why the authorities had allowed a house of correction to be built on such a site in the centre of the city. That's how it looked to them. And others recommended that I should be horsewhipped for showing my bare arse to the face of Glasgow.'

Blood flushes to my face. But Mac is pale and fierce.

'There was a party, thanks to my dear friend Newbery. He even wrote a symbolic masque and got the students to perform it.

> '*Fall! Good St Mungo's blessings on this school,*
> *its work make prosper and its fame let spread.*'

Mac laughs. This verse has cheered him. 'And when the masque was finished, and the speeches done, the curtain that divided the two parts of the building was thrown aside and the art school became one.' Mac sits back, exhausted. He looks down at the *fritillaria* and frowns.

'The thing is, I'd not stopped working for three years. And now all I wanted was to go on. To do bigger, better things. But all that came along was a commission for a dwelling house at Auchinibert. With the owners interfering with their small ideas, and Keppie too, and soon I was in the doghouse for letting the lunch hour at the nearby inn last into the afternoon. I knew what I was doing. Drink or no drink. All the same Keppie picked me up on small errors. "Small errors can be corrected . . ." I told him.' But the fight has gone out of him, then, and now, and Mac drifts off.

'So there I was, in my own office, waiting. Some said I should go to Europe, others suggested America. But I wanted to work in Glasgow. I wanted to work *for* Glasgow. Miss Cranston still needed me. You know her vision for the tea rooms was to make a place where no drink would be taken? Somewhere enticing. To save the city from itself. She'd seen too much suffering. Too many wages drunk on Friday night. Too many children hungry. Now instead, men would flock to the tea rooms to refresh themselves with non-alcoholic beverages! Well, as you can imagine, there was only so much work she had for me. A commission for a hairdressing salon came in.' Mac hangs his head. There is green on his cheek. And he sets down his brush. 'And it was then I heard that Honeyman and Keppie had won the contract for Jordanhill, despite the missing hand basins. And the taps. Despite the fact I'd not be there to oversee it. That news laid me low, I'll not deny it. I was sitting there, head in hands, when my old friend Mr Walter Blackie came in. I'd built Hill House for him. One of my first commissions. He was a man who had faith in me. And when he asked after my health, I told him how desolate I was. The Jordanhill place would be built without my superintendence, be built by others who might not understand what I had intended in my plans. I told him how hard I found it to have so little work. To receive no general recognition. And you know what Blackie said to me?' Mac puffs on his pipe and stares out through the window. ' "You were born too late, that's all it is. Some centuries too late. Your place was among the fifteenth-century lot with Leonardo and the others." That's what he told me, and wretched as I was I did feel a little cheered. Although how that helped I wasn't sure. With us living off my wife's inheritance. And that already running low.'

I want to ask who Leonardo is. But I stay quiet.

'Then I came down with pneumonia, and Margaret closed the office. She put the house into her name. For safekeeping. I'm not proud to say it. But I was in no condition to take care of such things. Nor had I a mind to. She brought me here. It's a good place. And I'm grateful. I'm back to my beginnings. Painting flowers, just as I once did in my father's garden, my mother waiting for me at home.' He smiles and turns back to his work. 'I'm thinking we might stay. Settle here. Yes.' And I see that in the centre of the first flower is a golden bird, not screaming as I'd first thought with its open mouth, but calling out in song.

Chapter 53

Mother needs my help to open up the inn, and soon I'm running to the cellar, fetching pints of ale and stout for those that need to soothe the pain of last night's drinking. I'm coming up when I kick against the hinge of the trapdoor, and dribbling beer, I kneel and listen for a moment, wondering if he's down there. Father. For he's still not home.

'On the run, is he?' There is much laughter from the men that straggle in. And I promise myself that later I will take the cart up to the common and, if needs be, find him passed out there, and load him on.

I give him till evening before going out. It's been a warm day, and the sun slants bright and low across the grass. Our field is thick with dandelions, and the brambles in the hedgerow sizzle with the sound of bees. There is a clearing on the common, scorched to sand, scarred with the hooves of horses brought up here for drills. I stand in the centre of it. 'Father?' I shout, and hearing nothing, I run around the edge of it, from one dense patch of scrub and bracken to the next, sure each one must be the shoulder of his coat, the weave of his cap, an old log, scorched with weather, the length of him, asleep.

I try old Snowling's cottage next. Look into the outhouse, scour the woodshed, even peer into the crater in the garden where the Zeppelin dropped its bomb. Finding no sign of him, I follow the path along the estuary to where Danky lives. I stand by his door. The sun is sinking, the moon has risen pale over the sea. *Father, where are you?* A streak of fear cuts through me. And I knock.

'Yes?' Danky steps away from me, as he never used to do. But when I tell him about Father he comes close. 'I've not seen the man since we parted, in the early hours it was. Not sure of the time. But it was late. I knows that because I saw your old boy Mac, striding by with his pipe alight, swinging his arms as if he'd not a trouble in the world. Someone should have mentioned that to the constable. Or maybe they did.' And shaking his head, he moves back into his house.

The moon is filling up with light as I walk towards the harbour. 'Pa?' I try. 'Father?' Even, 'William?' But there is nothing. I pass two soldiers coming from the Bell, and I search their faces, but there is no news there. I stand by the ferry and look out. Where would he have gone? I'm looking in the wrong places, that must be it, and I turn away and traipse across the green and down along Lea Lane, glancing into ditches, poking a stick I've found into the marsh. 'Father?' I try again, but I'm stopped short by the figure of a policeman standing by the Lea House gate. My first thought is to go to him. But he's so still, it chills me, his eyes towards the sea.

Where's Mac? I wonder then. And I think how I never found the right words to warn him. 'I'm sorry, so sorry,' I mutter, and before the policeman turns and catches me, I crouch down among the sedge and hold my breath.

The moon is silver now, the air still light. And there is no wind to ripple through the reeds which are as dry and dusty as thatch. I hold my hand against my face to stop from sneezing and I wonder how long I'll have to wait. I try and move, my foot is rammed against a ditch, my body twisted, but when I look up again there is our own old Mac, striding down the lane. He has a frond of honeysuckle hanging from his pocket – I catch a draught of it as he goes by – and his stick is tapping on the path. 'Mr Mac,' I hiss to him, but he is gone.

'Evening?' I hear the question in his voice, and the policeman dips his head as he addresses him. They talk, in tones that I do not catch, and then they turn together and unclasp the gate.

I slip from my hiding place and I run after them. The rabbits have already vanished, and I have the shadows and the hillocks to myself. The door is open. A shaft of light falls through, and hoping to block it with my body, I stand up on the step. There must have been other men, policemen, waiting inside, for now I hear a rabble of raised voices, Mac's the loudest, the fiercest, his accent thickening in anger so that I strain to understand. I inch my way inside, pulling the door closed after me. The men have walked into the living room, taking their lamp with them, and so I limp through the dimness of the hall and make a place for myself against the door jamb. There are three policemen, four, including the constable that shot Danky in the leg, and they are leafing through Mac's books, his magazines. One man has the blue folio, and he points to the words on the front. *Deen Wettbewerb für ein Herrschaftliches Wohnhaus eines Kunst-Freundes.* I squint as I read it for him. And then another puts his hands into the open desk drawer and brings out the Mackintoshes' letters. 'These correspondents,' he has a sneering voice, 'seem to be entirely foreign. Turin. Berlin. Budapest. Do you not have any acquaintances from our own shores?'

'*Meine Liebe Frau und Herr . . .*' The constable reads, and Mac strikes out at him. He no longer has his stick, but the policemen aren't expecting it and they scatter, the letters flying out over the floor. 'These are my private belongings,' Mac shouts. 'They concern my business, my work. These men are my colleagues. Architects and artists. They may be from an enemy nation but just last year they were all our friends.'

'Vienna, Frankfurt, Rotterdam.' The first policeman is still sneering as he lifts letters from the floor. 'And finally, a missive from within the British Isles.' He frowns as he reads it. 'I have found your three words, hidden as they are . . .' His eyebrows rise. 'Thank you. I hope that in this letter you'll find mine.'

Mac lunges at him, but the men are ready for him this time, and they hold him tightly by the arms. 'I ask you to leave these things alone,' he is spitting. 'These letters are private and are not for your eyes.'

The constable stands in front of him. 'Mr Charles Rennie Mackintosh.' He is as straight and stiff as a toy. 'We are arresting you on suspicion of espionage on behalf of the enemy. Anything you say will be taken in evidence against you.'

And when Mac's protests have spluttered to a stop, 'Men,' the constable says, 'let's take him away.'

I follow, as far as I can, but once on the green they force him into the back seat of a car, and drive out of the village. I stand and watch him go. Imagine him, restless fellow that he is, shut up in the cells below the courthouse. And I hope that he has, secreted about his body, a sheet of paper and a pencil.

The moon is bright now. It lights my path to the Blue Anchor. I don't want to go home, but there's nowhere else for me. I push open the back door, hoping to creep through unnoticed, but Mother is sitting alone in the main bar. 'I always thought it was your father losing business,' she says. 'But it seems when he's not here, no one comes at all.'

I sit with her.

'He's not a bad man,' she says. She reaches for my hand. 'Just scared of what can happen to a man. And frightened most particularly for you.'

'For me?'

'That's why he did it.' She looks down at my foot.

'Did what?' I feel my hand go cold in hers.

'If there's ever another war,' she's hurting me, she's pressing my fingers so tight, 'this boy will not be asked to fight, will not be taken halfway across the world to be beaten and mistreated. That's what he promised me. That's what he promised himself.'

'What other war?' I ask. 'Father never fought in any war.'

'He did,' she says, 'he made me swear I'd never say. It scarred him. The Boer War. Not that I knew him before. But I could see it in his face. The first day he turned and smiled at me. I saw that he'd been hurt.'

I look down at my foot. The ankle twisted to the side. He did that to me. And I cover my mouth for fear I'll be sick.

'What about the others?' I see their bird selves hopping bold across the grave, chatting and scrapping as they fight over a worm.

'No,' Mother shakes her head. 'Not them. He never harmed a single one. But when we got you, and it was clear from the start that you were strong, he said he couldn't bear to ever let you go.'

You'll be staying here. His fearful face comes back to me as he forces himself aboard Danky's boat. And I turn away, for through my sickness there's pity stabbing at me, to think he had a plan.

I write the telegram that night. And send it to the last address in my head. To Mr William Davidson of Glasgow. *Tell Mrs M Mackintosh to come. Urgent. CRM arrested.*

I take it to Mrs Lusher at first light, and wait while she sends it through. 'Anything else?' she asks. 'I have some aniseed. Awdacious good.' But I'm on my way out.

I let the chickens free and throw the bucket down the well. It lands with a thud and fails to fill. I pull it up and try again. 'What's with it?' I peer down. I see nothing but a pale glint of sky. 'Mother,' I shout, 'the well's dried up, or something's stopping it.' I run up to my room, and crawling under the bed beside the chamberpot I find Mac's spyglasses and bring them down.

I put them to my eyes and stare down into blackness. There's nothing. Black made blacker. And then I see the curve of a shadow. The moon, reflected. Although there is no moon. I adjust the glasses. And lean in further. And something shifts into the frame. The pale arc of a face.

'Ma!' I shout. I'm doubled over. 'Ma.' And I lurch into the house.

I must have fainted. Or lost hold of time. For when I can think again Mrs Horrod is beside me, and she has a bottle of something sharp under my nose. Mother is at the stove, her hair tied tight into its bun, her pinny on, and she is humming.

'There are men on their way,' Mrs Horrod tells me, 'with a pulley and a dray. They'll not be long.'

I stand up and look around me. 'Was there no fight then?' I ask. 'No battle on the green?' And I lift my left shoulder, wincing as I ease it down, just as Father has done all the years of my life.

Mother nods. She knows what I mean. 'Not on the green, no,' she says. 'Not there. Or if there was, your father wasn't in it.'

Mrs Horrod stands before me. She's as small as I am, or maybe I've grown, and she looks straight into my eyes. 'He must have fallen,' her voice is even. 'It's not the first time someone's been unlucky. And it'll not be the last.'

'He always was afraid of water,' I tell her. Although till now I'd only thought of the sea. And I think of Grace, the last publican's daughter, and how she climbed into the water butt and held herself under till she drowned. My stomach heaves. I turn away, and all I can hear is the sighing and the creaking of the well shaft, the noise of apples tumbling through my dream. 'I thought it was a ghost,' I say. 'The night of the wedding.' And that's when I seize the tablecloth, with its small stitched flowers, and I take the spade and I dig a hole and I throw it in.

Mother doesn't come outside to see her husband brought up. Buck is there with his dray, a horse as quiet and surly as himself, and George Allard with a pulley, stronger than the one we have. He has a length of rope coiled over his shoulder. 'This is the twine you spun for me,' he says, 'the day you walked out backwards through the gate.' He runs his fingers over the gold twist and I remember Betty flicking it as she walked by.

They need someone small, they say, to be lowered down, to attach the rope. They don't say to the body. And they look towards me, although their eyes lose hope when they reach mine.

A seagull hovers, its large body hanging, waiting for my answer.

'I'll do it.' It's my punishment for so often wishing him dead. And with a shriek the seagull soars away.

I shiver although the day is hot. 'Go easy, mind.' George Allard ties the rope around my waist. And when it is done, he weaves it through the pulley and wraps it round himself. Buck stands by. Waiting. A second rope attached to the yoke of his horse.

I step in backwards, bracing my boots against the soft brick of the rim. I feel it soften as I give it my full weight, a red dust drifting down. 'We've got you,' Mr Allard is gentle, but I wedge myself in against the tunnel all the same, and let them lower me, step by step into the dark, the other, heavier rope twining down beside me.

How deep is it? I think of the scrap of sky I saw, reflected, when I last looked down. But I don't look now.

The brick is damp, and smells of the underside of stones, and soon there is a green slime, growing, which creeps against my back. 'Ahh,' I cry out. The echo of my voice rises above me. 'Keep steady,' Allard calls in answer. 'We've got you. We've got you, we've got you.' And I drop lower.

The sides are too slippery to cling to now, and I let myself hang. There's nothing else to be done. Down, down, I'm lowered into the dark, and just when I'm used to it, my eyes sorting through every shade of grey, my ears awash with the silence at the centre of the earth, one foot splashes against water and I scream. My arms flail, and half sunk, I shout for them to stop.

Even without looking I feel him beside me. A great weight, bobbing in the water. But the rope twists and I'm spun around so that my eyes look into his. They're white, turned up to the light, and his face is swollen, scragged with stubble, as if his hair may still be growing. I fumble for the strand of the second rope, and when I have its end I stretch my arms around his chest and fasten it tight. I tie it in a slipknot – the first knot Danky showed me – and for a moment I lie pressed against his cold, broad chest, too tired to move. 'William James Thomas Maggs,' I whisper. And then I turn away and I give two yanks to let them know we're ready to come up.

I'm lying where I fell, the rope still round me, a hen pecking fretfully, when they bring him up. But I hear the dray's hooves scrapping with the effort of that last long heave, and then the thud of the body as it flops on to the ground. 'I'm sorry,' I say, although he'll never hear me, and I wonder what is keeping Mother in the house. I close my eyes again. I need to clean myself, is all I can think, need to wash away the dark smell of the well, and with no water in the house, I stand up, and without a nod to anyone, I walk down to the sea.

The tide is out. The beach is silver, and there's not a breath of wind. I lie myself down in the shallows and let the cold sea run over my arms and legs. I sink further, slide down a sandy drift and, tilting back my head, I feel the water close over my face. I hold my breath and wonder at it, this underwater world. They say it is the easiest way to die. Like sleeping. But then I take a gasp and salt water cuts into my lungs.

When I've stopped coughing I crawl from one inlet to the next, following the minnows drifting against sand banks. Water flows through my hair, cleaning it, sifting through my clothes, between my toes. I look back. I can see my boots, so neat, against the shore, the tide lapping at the leather, and I turn back into the sunshine, and there are the two seals from the ferry, their black noses, whiskery, staring at me. 'Hello,' I say. And at the sound of my voice they duck down out of sight. I duck down after them. The sand dips away too. And just as I lose ground, I wash up against another island and I'm safe again. I imagine it was an island like this that grounded the Norwegian barque two years before the war, and I remember marvelling at the boys who had the courage to swim out to her and back again with boxes of ship's biscuits in their arms. I keep paddling. I have the courage now. And then with no warning the sea bed drops away, and before I can stand, the current has taken me and I'm flailing in the open sea. I look up and there's the lighthouse, sparkling in the distance, and the white light of the sun bounces off the waves and stings my eyes. I strain to find my footing. The island is gone. Although I know it must be there, below the surface, and I fight and kick for all I'm worth to turn myself around. A wave picks me up and pushes me towards it, and then I'm dragged into the swell, and swept back out to sea. For a moment I am floating, look at me, I want to shout. To Father who made so sure I'd never leave. To Mother who turned my face to land.

But I'm not floating for long. I'm under the water, tumbling through the roots of a wave, and I think of Mother and the day the gypsies robbed us of our clover. Every summer they'd come into the county. Small, fierce men, with hands like leather, and girls whose hair hung the length of their backs. One night they hired the big room at the inn. They ordered food and drink and Ann, Mary and Mother were busy in the kitchen rolling out pastry for a dozen pies. The music was loud. I stood in the doorway and watched as the men began to dance, and then the women. They danced till nearly midnight, clapping and taking their turns while one played the accordion and another a tin whistle. 'Away with you,' Father said when he saw me tucked in behind the door, but there was no reason in going up to bed while that music spiralled through the floor-boards. Even Mother was jigging while she served the food, and Father was caught up in the crowd, drinking with the men, hot-faced, laughing.

Then they were gone. Into their caravans and off into the night, with their dogs trailing, and men whistling and children sleeping in their wooden bunks. Father began to clear the tables, unsteady on his feet, and Mother went out to check the hens which I'd forgotten to shut in. 'Lord!' I heard her shout. But it wasn't the hens that had been taken. I could see that from her face. 'The clover's gone,' she said. 'The clover in the field behind the inn is cut and stolen!' And she was so stunned she had to sit down on a stool. They'd brought sacks, the gypsies, and must have crept out while the music was so loud, and we were all standing at the door, listening and watching while the women danced. But Mother wasn't having it. She rose up and brushed herself down and called Ann out from the kitchen where she was scrubbing pans. 'We'll go after them,' she said, and ignoring Father who was stammering and muttering that nothing was his fault, they put Kingdom in the chaise. 'Let me come along,' I ran after, and although Mother pushed me away, I grabbed hold of the harness and pulled myself up.

Mother was a good horsewoman, and soon we were trotting towards Blythburgh. But Blythburgh was asleep. Not a sound, not even the ticking of the church clock, and without a word we went on to Westleton. There was a field at Westleton where horses grazed and although there were signs that they had been there, they weren't there now. Mother left the chaise under a tree and jumped down to wake the constable and while we waited for him to rouse I looked up through the grainy darkness, into the branches above, and imagined I saw an owl look back at me, its orange eyes winking. I took Ann's arm and pointed and she raised her face, and together as if our eyes were twice as strong I saw the branches weaving up and round the trunk, the patterns of the bark, the leaves flitting like copper in the dark. I could live out here, I thought, right through the balmy summer, sleeping through the waning of the moon, and when Mother came back with the constable, all buttoned into his wool uniform, I was that surprised to see him, I'd forgotten why we were there.

From Westleton we drove to Culvers Green and that's when we heard their dogs, and saw the caravans of their camp. I could feel my mother shivering as I leant against her back, but when she jumped down and raised her voice I found she'd shaken off her fear. 'Come on out,' she shouted to the dark shapes of the vans, 'and give us what is ours.' And the constable pushed out his chest and tried to think of anything to add.

We didn't have the sacks of clover when we set off again, but a handful of coins that Mother gave to Ann to tie into her sleeve. We drove more slowly on the way home, to spare the horse, and to dodge the black shapes of the bats as they flitted overhead. We could smell the sea too, out here, with no distractions, long before we reached the village, and the night was so gentle and so sweet with summer I forgot to even look for the ghost at Dead Man's Corner or think of how a man was burned there in a blaze of flames. They say his shadow lingers, not that I've ever seen it, but if you go too close you can sense a kind of lurking. Something dark that wants to pull you in. But that night we ambled past, full of rejoicing, and I pressed my knees against Mother's back, so that I could feel her strength. I feel it now as I lose sight of land, my lame foot acting as a paddle, and I wonder why a live body will sink, as I know mine will, and a dead one will float up to the surface. I remember Runnicles telling us that it wasn't just to make the body easier to find, it was gases that rise up in a person and push them to the surface. Although of course there are always some that are never found. I'm not frightened any more. Not of anything. And as my mouth fills with water, I see events unfurling, not as they are meant to do, from the start, but away into the future. I see Old Mac's My Margaret jump down from the train and storm into the police station, and I watch her find him there, standing before a magistrate and the captain of a Royal Navy vessel, anchored off the pier. They were thinking of taking him to Lowestoft for further questioning, but Mrs Mackintosh with her flaming hair, and her smart

English voice, puts an end to any such idea. 'Yes,' she says, grand as can be. 'I do know about the letters. I'm a German speaker myself. I can translate them for you if that would be of help.'

I cling fast to a piece of floating timber, and I watch as Mac is handed into her care. I see her face, the courage that she shows, as they go together into the chaos of their home, and begin to sort through the letters and the books, the precious blue folio, its leaves scattered across the floor. *Zimmer, Dekorative, Musik, Vogel.* I can read anything now. And it takes her most of the night, as Mac sits stunned on a chair, to put things to rights.

'Toshie?' she comes to him when she is done. 'My dear?' she strokes his greying hair. 'We'll go away from here, you'll see, we'll find somewhere else. Somewhere safe where you can work.' But Old Mac doesn't move. He doesn't speak. And so with a soft kiss, My Margaret arranges the piles of magazines so that their edges run in a straight line.

It's harder to watch Mother, lying, her face to the wall, while Mrs Horrod tends to her. And Ann and Jimmy Kerridge, having only been gone a matter of days, returning to take up their places as the new licensees of the Blue Anchor. So instead I follow Mac as he goes up before the magistrates again. I see their old heads bent together, and hear how eager they are to condemn him as a spy. But they are prevented from doing so by an acquaintance of My Margaret, a woman with a title, who impresses upon them the extent of Mr Mackintosh's patriotism, and how, unwittingly, they are holding one of the most influential architects in Europe. 'A man to be honoured,' she says. 'One of our own of whom we should be proud. Of whom, one day, we will be.'

The magistrates are suitably impressed. They put their heads together again. Surely the fact that no spyglasses were found in his possession counts for something? And maybe it does, for they dismiss the case. Although with one condition. That Mr Charles Rennie Mackintosh remove himself from East Anglia, and never again enter the counties of Essex, Suffolk or Norfolk.

I'm halfway to Holland, my foot still flapping, thinking of Betty and what she'd say if she knew that I could swim, when the Royal Navy catches sight of me. They think they've spied a slip of cargo, or one of the seals drifted off course, but when they haul in their ropes they find that it's a boy. They try pouring spirits down my throat but I spit and kick for all I'm worth, so they leave me on deck, the water dribbling out of me. A sea creature after all. But I keep watching. Even after I'm fit enough to be put to work. Even after three months of sleeping in a hammock when the ship tilting to the side is all that I know. And I'm still watching when Mr Mac defies his ban and comes back into the county. It's the end of the summer and he arrives by train and walks across the common. He takes my old room with the outshot window. There is no other available, for Ann and Jimmy have the good room now. And I see him stumble up the ladder, late at night, and slump into the bed. He's been drinking, half pints of beer, chased down by whisky, and he's run from the Blue Anchor to the Bell, just as he used to do. But he's up in the morning, standing outside the inn with his watercolours and his board, when Betty comes by, and he stoops to listen to her, as she whispers in his ear. 'We don't know,' he tells her. 'The boy always did have a yearning to see the world. So for all we know he's out there.' He tells her to wait. And he goes back up the ladder. And when he comes down he has something for her. It is wrapped in cloth. 'Keep it safe for him,' he says. And Betty presses her lips together. She doesn't cry. Not then. Although later, back in Vic's old room, which will forever be called Vic's, even though they know now he's never coming back, when she unwraps the gift and sees it is the picture of my boat – the *Thomas* – she kisses it. And one salty tear runs down her freckled cheek. She places it in her trunk. *Kist*, I remember. And she sits beside it and she says a prayer, and then she takes up the *cutag*, and she runs down the street, past the Blue Anchor, towards the ferry.

Father was right. The war is no place for a boy. With a bad foot or not. But I only know that once I'm in it, with the boat I'm on sunk, and the captain lost when it went down. I'm not ready for home, though. I'm sixteen, nearly, not that anyone is asking. And if they notice that I'm limping, there are so many who are worse. I'm sent out on to the battlefields of France, and at night while I lie and listen to the flares, I'm sure I feel the wings of my starlings, soft against my face. Is it them, keeping me alive? For shells are bursting all around, and braver, stronger, luckier men than me are struck down where they stand. But even through the noise and filth and panic, I keep watching out for Mac. I see him in London. A place I've never been. Scratching out a living. Working on designs for houses, studios, theatres, none of which are built. And when the war is over, they don't go back to Glasgow, no, he and Mrs Mac they move to France. It's cheaper there, and the bright sea air of Port-Vendres is perfect for My Margaret's heart. The light is good too. And Mac works outside, with his watercolours and his board, challenging himself to avoid green, although it is the colour he loves most. 'Art is the flower,' he once said. 'Life is the green leaf.' And he smiles when he remembers his old friend Fra Newbery showing him a letter from a colleague. 'Hang it, Newbery, this man ought to be an artist.' For now that's what he is. Although there are precious few that know it.

I don't go home either. It's my chance to see the world, and I roam from land to land, marvelling at the skies and seas of it, making small pictures of boats to buy myself a meal. I don't need much to survive, for there's no one but myself, although I'm glad to know Mac has his My Margaret to look out for him. She is in charge of finances, and she makes sure they have enough each month after board and lodging, and the tip they give the young boy who works at their hotel, for her husband to have paint. She's stopped working herself. She doesn't have the heart for it. Not since news came of her sister's death. And with it the story that MacNair, in a frenzy of grief, destroyed much of his wife's work. When they write letters, which they sometimes do, to offer up a picture, to offer it again at a reduced rate, they write close across the page, so they can afford the postage, and when Mac takes a drink, it is the wine that is given with dinner, and he is careful to drink no more than half the bottle.

I'm in Australia when I next hear news. As far across the world as it is possible to get. I've worked on boats that have taken me to Newfoundland, South Africa, Japan. And wherever I am I look down into the swell of water, and I think of the browns and greens and silver of the sea where I was born. It's in Australia that I see it. A small square of black amongst the print of the paper I am reading. *10th December, 1928. The architect Charles Rennie Mackintosh has died.* I close my eyes and I think of how his wife cared for him. Always making sure there was enough money set aside so he could have his tobacco. For Mac's pipe was not something that he could ever give up. Even after a blister bit into his tongue, burning him, and a bulge formed on his nose, forcing him back to England, where, in a small nursing home, he endured his treatment, paid for by an admiring friend. But the treatment was brutal, and hopeless too, and soon, without ever once having returned to Glasgow, he died. Even before My Margaret, with her weakened heart. Who, I see now, must wait five years to join him.

I did not have to wait so long before Mother found the money that I left her. Ann's baby was due, and Mary was coming back to stay, and Mother went into my old room to turn the bed. 'What's this?' she says to herself, and she unwraps the packet of coins, and the miniatures that are with them, and she stares into their faraway faces, although the only face she sees is mine, and when she has looked as long as she is able, she holds them hard, just as she once held me, against her heart.

I've spun once or even twice around the world, and I'm not so restless as I used to be, when Mac's fame rises. His work sells at auction, as does his wife's, for hundreds of thousands of pounds, and almost a full century after it was finished the Glasgow School of Art is voted Britain's Best Building and men and women from as far away as China stream through its doors.

And then, in the basement of the Vienna Arts and Crafts Museum, a false wall is discovered, and hidden there in crates, they find My Margaret's *Seven Princesses*. The gesso colours are not sepia, as has long been thought, but kept from the light for all those years, they are as bright as day. The experts use this knowledge when they re-create the panels that make up the *Life of the Rose* for the interior of the *House for an Art Lover*, which has been built on the edge of Bellahouston Park in Glasgow. It takes seven years to build and for the people who do it, it is a labour of love. 'Would you like to see it?' my granddaughter asks on the day that it is finished, 'or do you want to wait until your hundredth birthday, which is, after all, only five years off?' I tell her I've waited long enough, and I'd better not wait a moment longer, and so together with Betty – for the girl is named after her grandmother – we travel down from the Highlands, slow as you like, in her small car.

And there it is: just as Mac dreamt it, a great ocean liner brought in to land, and when I take hold of my courage, and step through from the dark interior of the hall into the white light of the music room, I see the three words written there, on every wall.

Acknowledgements

I'd like to thank Richard Scott, who, many years ago now, whispered the story of Mackintosh in Suffolk into my ear. Sarah Lawrence for providing me with a silent and inspiring place to work while I was in the village. Bill Ungless for handing over some invaluable books. Richard Reeves for the brilliant research work that startled me into an entire re-write. Barry Tolfree for his generous help and the uncovering of two wonderful memoirs: one, unpublished, by Cyril Steley, and the other, *People at War 1914–18*, edited by Michael Moynihan, which contains the experiences of Ernest Read Cooper, solicitor and Town Clerk of Southwold. Also for introducing me to Ronnie Waters, now in his 90s, whose research inspired the local history website southwoldandson.co.uk

Of the many books I read, these were the most helpful: *Can Your Mother Skin a Rabbit?* by Bert Allard; *ABC of Boat Bits* by James Dodds; *Ferryknoll* by Carol Christie; *Colourful Characters of East Anglia* by H. Mills West; *Remembering Charles Rennie Mackintosh* by Alistair Moffat; *Glasgow Girls*, edited by Jude Burkhauser; *The Chronycle: The Letters of Charles Rennie Mackintosh to Margaret Macdonald Mackintosh, 1927*, published by the Hunterian Art Gallery; *Charles Rennie Mackintosh* by Alan Crawford; *The Quest for*

Charles Rennie Mackintosh by John Cairney; and *Charles Rennie Mackintosh: Art is the Flower* by Pamela Robertson. I am indebted to Pamela Robertson for meeting me on one of my trips to Glasgow, for her invaluable help with facts and information, and for her close reading of the manuscript.

Thanks also to my agent Clare Conville for her enthusiasm and insightful notes, and to my editor Alexandra Pringle for her gentle guidance and her passion. To Harry Ritchie – Scottish accent coach extraordinaire – Kitty Aldridge for her continuous support, Manuela Stoica for her patience and loyalty, and David Morrissey who makes so much possible. But above all thank you to the village – for making me feel at home, right from the start.

I would also like to add my own heartfelt appreciation of the Scottish Fire and Rescue Service for the skill, courage and determination they showed in overcoming the blaze that raged through the Glasgow School of Art just as this book was going to press.

A NOTE ON THE AUTHOR

Esther Freud trained as an actress before writing her first novel *Hideous Kinky*, published in 1992. *Hideous Kinky* was shortlisted for the John Llewellyn Rhys Prize and made into a film starring Kate Winslet. In 1993 Esther was named a Granta Best of Young British Novelist. She has since written seven other novels, including *The Sea House*, *Love Falls* and *Lucky Break*. She also writes stories, articles and travel pieces for newspapers and magazines, and teaches creative writing at the Faber Academy. Esther lives in London and Suffolk.

@estherfreudrite
www.estherfreud.co.uk

A NOTE ON THE TYPE

The text of this book is set in Linotype Sabon, named after the type founder, Jacques Sabon. It was designed by Jan Tschichold and jointly developed by Linotype, Monotype and Stempel, in response to a need for a typeface to be available in identical form for mechanical hot metal composition and hand composition using foundry type.

Tschichold based his design for Sabon roman on a font engraved by Garamond, and Sabon italic on a font by Granjon. It was first used in 1966 and has proved an enduring modern classic.